Patricia Hall is the pseudonym of Maureen O'Connor, whose career as a journalist has included working for *The Yorkshire Post*, *The Guardian* and *The Observer*. Since becoming a freelance writer she has turned her talents to crime fiction, and this new novel follows the success of *The Poison Pool*, *The Coldness of Killers*, *Death by Election* and *Dying Fall*.

Born in Yorkshire, she now lives in Oxford.

In the Bleak Midwinter

PATRICIA HALL

WARNER BOOKS

A *Warner* Book

First published in Great Britain in 1995
by Little, Brown and Company

This edition published by Warner Books in 1997

A CIP catalogue record for this book
is available from the British Library.

ISBN 0 7515 1712 7

Typeset by Palimpsest Book Production Limited,
Polmont, Stirlingshire
Printed and bound in Great Britain by
Clays Ltd, St Ives plc

Warner Books
A Division of
Little, Brown and Company (UK)
Brettenham House
Lancaster Place
London WC2E 7EN

In the Bleak Midwinter

ONE

'THERE'S ALWAYS SOME CLEVER BEGGAR thinks he can get away with murder,' said Amos Atherton, his voice sharp with the self-justification of the almost-fooled. 'We'll make it look like an accident, they think. Well, I tell you, lad, it's not so bloody easy.'

Chief Inspector Michael Thackeray gave the telephone receiver a wry smile.

'Tell me, Amos,' he said, his voice as controlled as the pathologist's was excited.

'I've got a lass here, supposed to be a road traffic victim,' Atherton said. 'Can you come over straight away?'

Thackeray looked around the deserted CID room which he had been about to leave and sighed. Another dinner date cancelled, another round of apologies proffered and accepted, perhaps with a little less readiness this time. Next time he was invited to talk to the new recruits, he thought, he might warn them that chastity was a good qualification for the job.

'Give me ten minutes,' he said.

It actually took him rather less to walk through the quiet midwinter evening calm of Bradfield town centre, his breath hanging in clouds in the bitter air, the street lights, each with a shimmering halo of frost, casting dark pits of shadow amongst the cornices and alcoves of the Victorian town hall.

Entering the hospital by a side door, where a security guard casually nodded him in, he made his way down the dimly lit corridors of the infirmary basement to the morgue, where the screaming white lights made him screw up his eyes in pain as

1

he took in the familiar post-mortem scene of Amos Atherton, like some portly frog in green, and an assistant bent over the marble body of a young woman.

Thackeray had paused before leaving police headquarters only to ascertain from the uniformed branch which traffic accident victim had just been committed to Atherton's surprisingly tender care, and to glance through the spare prose of the fatal accident report. Linda Wright had been found dead in her own car partly submerged in a lonely reservoir on a moorland road above the town. By rights, the car should have sunk in thirty feet of freezing black water, with little chance of being found for months. By chance, its front wheels had wedged on an imperfection in the concrete embankment and its boot had been spotted by a passing motorist who had raised the alarm probably within a few hours of the vehicle's leaving the winding and icy road. It had been treated as an accident by the emergency services, the body retrieved and delivered to the hospital, no questions asked.

Atherton merely nodded at Thackeray's arrival, intent on the removal of internal organs from the body which had been dissected with perfect precision from breastbone to pubis. He worked with a delicacy belied by his enormous bulk, belly bulging beneath his green gown, pale blue eyes bright above his mask. With a grunt of satisfaction he straightened up and placed Linda Wright's lungs in a dish his assistant held out for him.

'She drowned,' he said. 'See the froth she's churned up. Just what you'd expect in a body recovered from a submerged car. Just what we were expected to expect.'

'But ...' Thackeray prompted, knowing and trusting Atherton well enough to be sure that if he was not satisfied by the obvious there would be very good reason for it.

'Look here,' Atherton said, lifting the young woman's long blonde hair, damp and tangled but drying to a still stunning gold sheen under the blazing lights. She had been a very beautiful girl, Thackeray thought, seized, as he always was, by the sense of waste which a premature death engendered. Linda had been twenty-four years old.

The pathologist touched the pale neck with a gentle gloved finger and Thackeray could see the faintest of blue marks just beneath each ear.

'There are bruises there, and there . . .' He ran a finger under the chin and rested it in the soft hollow of the neck below the windpipe. 'And here,' he said. 'She drowned all right, but someone had his hands around her neck before she died. Not hard enough to kill her, but hard enough to knock her out, perhaps hard enough for him to think he'd killed her.'

'She couldn't have been bruised as the car went over the edge?' Thackeray asked, though he knew the answer. If Linda Wright had been knocked unconscious in a skidding car she might have hit her head, a seat-belt might have scored her shoulder, but nothing mechanical could have made those three faint symmetrical marks on her neck, the marks of thumbs and fingers just perceptibly indelible in death.

Amos Atherton gave Thackeray the glance of contempt which they both knew the question deserved.

'She was alive when she went under,' Atherton said. 'Lived long enough for her lungs to fill, which doesn't always happen if the water's freezing cold. Often the shock is enough.'

'Anything else unusual?'

'Nowt I've spotted with the naked eye. I was told it was a routine traffic accident, but now I know it's not I'll get all the usual tests completed. She's not a virgin and she's not pregnant, by the way. And she'd not had sex recently, as far as I can see, though the water's not much help there. It's washed her pretty thoroughly, left a lot of mud and not much else. A written report in the morning, any road.'

Thackeray sighed heavily. It was not just the scouring powers of the reservoir water in which Linda Wright had died which would cause problems, he thought. A murder which was not immediately recognised as a murder was, in his limited experience, a pain in the neck. The scene of the crime would have been churned up by the rescue services, the car would have been carelessly consigned to the police pound, or perhaps even towed to some convenient civilian garage, and both would now be at the mercy of the sleety rain which had been slanting over the town all evening. The hunt for Linda Wright's killer, he thought, could not have got off to a more inauspicious and tardy start, even without the car sinking to the full depth of the reservoir, which was no doubt what her murderer had intended.

Laura Ackroyd, with whom Thackeray had hoped to have dinner, had also had a bad day. As she whiled away yet another hour that evening impatiently waiting for the policeman to arrive she consoled herself that, with her back against the wall, she at least knew how to accept defeat gracefully.

Late that morning, she had crossed her slim legs, brushed a strand of unruly copper hair out of her eyes and given the two men facing her across her boss's desk a sedate half-smile as she surrendered.

'All right,' she had said. 'I'll go. But not for too long. Two months?'

She had flashed a glance at her immediate superior, editor of the *Bradfield Gazette*, Ted Grant, who was hunched morosely on a hard chair slightly to the side of his own black leather executive throne which had been commandeered by his companion. Laura knew that the time she spent away from the *Gazette* could not be long enough for Ted, but it was the other man, lean, tanned and fashionably elegant in his Italian suit, but with the mien of a hungry shark eyeing a careless swimmer's leg, who answered, as she knew he would.

David Ross had come to Bradfield from the company's London headquarters with a single objective and neither Grant, who had clout, nor Laura, who had none, would deflect him one millimetre from his task.

'Three months. Minimum,' Ross said. 'And I want regular reports, direct to me in London.'

Laura picked up the dismembered copy of the *Arnedale Observer* which lay strewn across the desk between them. The weekly *Observer* was owned by the same company as the daily *Gazette* but there the similarity between them ended.

While Ted Grant's tabloid headlines screamed every evening at the inhabitants of urban Bradfield, the *Observer's* clung to the style and tone of another age. The Temperance League warned inhabitants to beware of alcohol as the festive season approached while local vicars still sought support for their continuing campaign against women priests, all amongst the quaintly old-fashioned classified advertisements. These were not discreetly hidden on inside pages but spread right across the front in the nineteenth-century style. Inside, local worthies basked in a deference which had long vanished like moorland mist in other parts of the county.

'It's not the politics which bother you?' she said, flicking a hand over the *Observer*'s weekly column from Arnedale's MP.

'They vote for the swine,' Ross said, with a shrug. 'I told you. It's not that. It's this new radical rag and its innuendoes about Reg Fairchild. The competition's bad enough, but we can fight that off. We'll put the *Observer*'s price down if we have to and squeeze him out. I don't need Rupert Murdoch to show me how to kebab the opposition. But that'll take time, and it'll be a damn sight harder if Reg is implicated in some scandal. Mud sticks in these tinpot towns. That does the circulation no good at all.'

It was not the morality of the situation that bugged Ross, Laura thought wryly, but its effect on his bottom line.

Laura glanced again at her glowering boss and smiled sweetly, brushing another wayward strand of hair from her face. She could feel Ross's eyes on her, assessing and, she guessed, approving, and she deliberately uncrossed her legs and arranged them more demurely beneath the short skirt of her deep green suit.

She did not mind admiration but felt no desire to have Ross on the end of her phone line, or anywhere else, that evening. There were plenty of women, she knew, who would open their legs for promotion, but she did not want him thinking she was one of them.

'And not a word to that copper you're so friendly with, either,' Ted growled. 'We don't want the police poking their noses into company business when they're not wanted. Now what about a bite of lunch at the Clarendon, David?' he went on, turning to his colleague and tacitly dismissing Laura from the conversation. 'They do a nice bit of roast beef from the bone dinner-time . . .' Ross winced slightly and his response was curt.

'Thanks, but no thanks. I've booked myself an hour at the gym at my hotel, then I'm due in Arnedale to see Reg Fairchild and fill him in on his new assistant editor.' He patted a flat stomach under his dazzling white shirt complacently and cast a disparaging glance at Ted's corpulent frame slumped awkwardly on his unaccustomed hard chair. The cold blue eyes said all that needed to be said and Ted scowled and looked away, turning a faint purple colour which augured ill for his health and that of anyone else who crossed him for the rest of the day. When David Ross had swept into the *Gazette* office that morning he brought fear and loathing with him, Laura thought, and not even Ted Grant was immune.

Dismissed, Laura had walked slowly out of Ted's office and into a newsroom silenced by her arrival, every eye on her slow progress back to her desk.

'It's all right,' she said to Jane Archer, the young trainee who had wept on her shoulder more times than she could remember now, and who was approaching with a distraught expression on her pale girlish face. She spoke loudly enough for the whole room to hear. 'I'm not the latest redundancy. I'm just being seconded for a couple of months to Arnedale to help old Reg Fairchild out of a hole.'

'Oh, shit,' Laura said under her breath to her reflection in the blank grey computer screen in front of her as she sat down again at her desk. A pale and serious oval face looked back at her, the usually bright eyes clouded, the stunning red-gold hair reduced to dirty brown, the likeness a fair reflection of her mood.

It was not that she did not relish the idea of a change. Ted Grant's irascible moods increasingly frustrated her: more responsibility on a smaller paper might be an enjoyable challenge, she thought. And if Reg Fairchild, a legend for his unswerving devotion to old-fashioned values as much as for editorial longevity, had taken to lining his own pocket she had no objection to exposing his hypocrisy or worse.

There was more crime in plush offices than on the streets

6

of impoverished council estates, she had once self-righteously told Chief Inspector Michael Thackeray, hearing her grandmother's fierce fundamentalist socialism in her voice, but Michael had merely smiled his slow smile and said that she might be right, though it was difficult to prove. If the half-veiled suggestions being made in Arnedale's upstart new free paper were true, Laura thought, this might be an occasion where proof was forthcoming.

It was Michael Thackeray's reaction to her enforced move which troubled her most. Thackeray, with whom Laura sustained an ambivalent relationship too close to be called friendship and too precarious to be called an affair, would be the one to object fiercely to a move to the place where he had grown up and which he had made clear he detested.

Telling Thackeray she was going to Arnedale filled her with more foreboding than Ted Grant and David Ross could ever generate between them although both men, both bullies in their own way, would have been astonished to hear it. She had flashed Ted a malicious smile as he passed by on his way to lunch alone.

'It's not a bloody holiday you're going on,' he snarled.

'I'll send you a postcard anyway,' she said kindly. 'Glad you're not here? That do?'

In the end she put it off, as she knew she would. Thackeray had arrived late and tired, preoccupied, he said, with a murder which had been identified too late for comfort, with a major investigation to start early the next day and every chance that most of the useful evidence had been washed away in the icy waters of the Scarsdale reservoir.

'Are you going to tell me what's wrong?' he asked quietly at last. He was leaning on his elbow in bed beside Laura, smoking what she categorised mischievously as his post-coital cigarette. He was a big man, broad and muscular, with the physique of the rugby forward he had once enthusiastically been, but it was his eyes, an oddly discordant blue beneath unruly dark hair, not his body, which held Laura's attention now. Passion spent, he had rolled away from her, lighted his cigarette and adopted an expression of watchful caution which she had half hoped she had banished for good.

She sat up against the pillows and pulled the duvet up to her chin, shivering slightly. She was naked, her hair falling in a copper cloud around her flushed face. It was midnight and Thackeray had arrived hungry, though not for the supper she had prepared him, and they had found themselves in bed together before she had summoned up the courage to tell him what she knew he would not want to hear. She pushed her irrepressible hair away from her eyes, leaned across and kissed him gently on the cheek.

'I don't seem to be able to fool you any more.'

There had been times when old loyalties and professional caution had led her to be economical in what she told the policeman.

'I hope you wouldn't try,' he said seriously.

She sighed, unsure of what he really wanted of her apart from the energetic coupling they had just enjoyed. Of the sexual chemistry between them there had never been much doubt but she did not know, and she suspected he would not even ask himself, where the journey they had embarked upon would take them.

The present problem, though, was more practical and she was aware of Ted Grant's warning, not to involve Thackeray in the company's affairs, echoing in her mind. She would be away in Arnedale a couple of months, she told him, a temporary arrangement, and she would get back to Bradfield as often as she could. She did not mention the company's suspicions about Reg Fairchild.

'Christ,' Thackeray said, swinging himself out of bed abruptly and standing with his back to Laura, gazing out of the window at the dark garden behind the flats and the faint orange glow of the town in the valley below. He knew that he could not even begin to explain the turmoil she had thrown him into and felt old despairs close in on him like a fog.

'Couldn't you have turned it down?' he asked.

'And put my job on the line? You know there's more unemployed hacks out there than there are unsolved burglaries.'

'He'd have sacked you?' There was disbelief in Thackeray's voice.

'David Ross would sack his own grandmother,' she said. 'You wait until the police have been privatised. You'll see what it's like in the real world.'

Thackeray stared silently out of the window saying nothing more and Laura wrapped her arms round her knees and buried her face in the soft sweet-smelling quilt.

'Is Arnedale as bad as that?' Her voice was muffled and almost in spite of himself Thackeray turned back to her and put his arm around her naked shoulders.

'I never go near the place,' he said. 'Not if I can help it. Sometimes I have nightmares about it . . .'

'It was all a long time ago,' she said tentatively.

'It might as well be yesterday.' He spoke with such chilly finality that she did not dare pursue it further.

'So don't come to Arnedale. It's only twenty miles or so. I'll come back at weekends, during the week too if I can. It's not too far to commute.'

'Fine,' he said, but she knew from the strain in his voice and the tension with which he held her, crushing her shoulders, that it was not fine at all.

'Come back to bed,' she said. 'I'll make us some coffee.' But he wouldn't. He got dressed in the half-light from the bedside lamp. The early start he needed in the morning, he claimed, meant that he had to be at his own place to meet his sergeant at seven. Laura did not believe him. He stood for a moment at the bedroom door in his trench-coat, running a hand through his hair, spiky against the lighted living-room, his eyes in shadow, an almost menacing figure, and Laura felt that she did not know him at all.

'I'll call you,' he said and as the front door of the flat slammed she lay back on the pillows and wondered where, if anywhere, she and Michael Thackeray were going.

It was the sort of night when the hamlet of High Clough could have done with a dose of Christian charity. It was bitterly cold on the high Pennine moors, with a keen wind from the east, when the vicar of Arnedale edged his battered estate car up the tortuous lane to conduct the annual carol service in mid-December.

It was too bloody early for the Christmas service, the locals agreed grumpily over their pints of Tetley's in the Quarryman, but better early than not at all. When all was said and done, they had reluctantly accepted the fact that even on Christmas Day those who wanted a proper service had to travel down the steep hill into the town for the privilege.

Except on the fourth Sunday of the month, the day the parish qualified by right for the attentions of its shepherd, their own squat stone church, with its tiny turret and single exposed bell which swung and sang eerily to itself as the wind whistled down from the rolling moors which enfolded it, remained locked and empty. The parishioners were too few now to attract more than token support from a diocese interminably strapped for cash.

But charity was not what Faith Lawrence earned that evening. Some hundred souls, Anglicans, Methodists, a handful of the Yorkshire Moravians, and perhaps a majority who professed nothing much at all but liked a rousing carol at the appropriate season, had gathered in the church.

Almost the whole village was there, Faith thought, glancing round. Except for Joe Thackeray, of course, who was a Roman Catholic of the old school, with an invalid wife. He occasionally drove his mud-stained truck down to Arnedale for Mass and tolerated no ecumenism from the likes of St Hugh's or the Moravian chapel further down the valley.

The tiny church seemed crowded, although there could not have been more than sixty adults there, every one of whom knew the rest. It was bone-chillingly cold, a cold which seemed to seep out of the ancient stone walls and finger every inch of uncovered flesh, totally untouched by the wheezing electric heater which the vicar had positioned optimistically in front of the altar. But the sturdy folk of the high Pennines were not to be deterred by a snap of winter weather. They pulled their scarves up, kept their gloves on and stamped their feet discreetly in time to the music.

It was not until the second hymn, a ragged rendering of 'It Came Upon a Midnight Clear', for which the ancient harmonium seemed even more out of tune than usual, that a faint ripple of disturbance swept over the congregation. Heads surreptitiously turned, eyes slid covertly from hymn-sheets and children unashamedly stared at the newcomers who had slipped in the door behind them.

It was another family, the father a tall young man, with dark hair tied back in a long pony-tail, and his partner, smaller, fairer, with a jumble of tiny beaded plaits escaping from the collar of her duffle coat. The children were silent and wide-eyed in the strange environment, but were unmistakably their father's, both with his dark eyes and almost black hair, pink-cheeked from the wind, bundled up in an assortment of scarves and jumpers and leggings and wellington boots like two small Russian peasants dressed for the worst the steppes could hurl at them.

The little group scrambled into the empty rear pew and the man leaned behind, smiling faintly at nothing in particular, to take up a couple of the service sheets, which lay on a shelf beside the neatly stacked prayer- and hymn-books. As he did so an audible murmur of unchristian discontent swirled like a tide of dirty water around the rest of the congregation and the glorious song of old almost drained away.

Firmly the vicar commenced the next verse in a clear baritone and gradually his flock acquiesced, turning back to him sullen-faced to take up the carol again. Only one man, broad, ginger-haired and ruddy-complexioned, remained half-turned in his pew with a look of glowering discontent on his face. Faith Lawrence glanced at him and then behind, offering the faintest smile of sympathy to the newcomers before dropping her head to her hymn-sheet again. Even that small gesture of support did not go unnoticed.

The service had almost run its course before the family at the back drew attention to itself again, this time because the younger child had become bored and restless and when told by her mother, with an anxious look, to be quiet, had broken into a piercing wail of protest. Disturbed, the congregation resorted to angry stares again, an audible muttering from the ginger-haired man breaking into the churchwarden's reading of the final lesson at the lectern.

With a heavy sigh, Faith, who was sitting at the end of a pew several rows from the back of the church, got up and swept up the aisle, her boot heels thumping on the worn quarry tiles, silver hair swinging, picking up the irritable child as she went.

'I'll take her outside for a bit,' she said firmly to its startled parents. 'Come on Melody my love, you can't make all that noise in here.'

By the time the service ended and the congregation began to straggle out to shake the vicar's hand in the church doorway, the whole family had gone, slipping out as 'Hark the Herald Angels' disturbed the insect life in the rafters which had become unused to such fervour. Faith herself was huddled in her thick coat, a scarf over her hair, sheltering from the wind in the porch as she waited for her own husband and son to emerge.

She was a striking woman, not slim but tall and assured, strands of silver-grey hair escaping from the dark, enveloping scarf which gave her the look of some Victorian heroine standing on a windswept moor, deep-set eyes faintly amused at the unfriendly glances she was getting from some of the congregation as they passed.

'What d'you want to do that for,' asked the surly red-headed man who shouldered his way out between frailer members of the parish to meet Faith face-to-face in the porch. 'Bloody gyppos!'

Faith shrugged. The last thing she wanted was a public row with Ray Harding in front of the whole village. She slipped sideways round the truculent farmer and shook the vicar's hand warmly. There was a hint of amusement in the cleric's eyes as he took in her determined face, middle-aged and innocent of make-up but not unattractive as the wind put colour into her cheeks and a sparkle into her clear grey eyes.

'Well done,' the vicar murmured, the wind whipping his words away and making it impossible for others to overhear.

Faith shrugged. It had been an act of kindness she would soon forget. Others evidently would not.

'Happy Christmas,' the vicar added.

'Yes, maybe,' Faith said without much conviction as she saw

her husband, Gerry, and son, Tim, making their way towards her through the crush. Greying and with a skin the colour and texture of worn leather, his gait curiously stiff-legged, Gerry Lawrence appeared some years older than his wife. The tall, ungainly youth in jeans and anorak who slouched behind him partly hid his unhealthy pallor beneath a mop of fair hair which almost covered his eyes and straggled down his collar. Faith smiled faintly at the two of them and gave the vicar the tiniest of despairing shrugs.

'If we can keep the demons at bay,' she said, in that same confidential murmur before she turned away to join her family. 'What chance a low-alcohol Christmas?'

TWO

'BOYFRIENDS, GUV,' SERGEANT KEVIN MOWER said with brutal certainty. 'A stunning looker like that has boyfriends, lots of them.'

Michael Thackeray looked at his sergeant impassively for a moment as they sat in their car outside a nondescript semi-detached house in one of the less prosperous suburbs of Bradfield. It was not the first time that he had felt that Mower's avowed passion for the opposite sex might have taken him too far.

'You met her, you say?' he said, wondering if Mower's appreciation of Linda Wright's attractions had breached the acceptable bounds of the relationship between an investigating officer and an interviewee. If he had got too close to the woman whose body now lay neatly sewn up, labelled and refrigerated in the hospital morgue he could play no useful part in the murder investigation which had just begun.

'I told you, she worked for Cheetham and Moore, guv,' Mower said, letting his impatience show, never a good idea, he knew, with Thackeray. 'She was at the show house up on that new estate beyond Southwaite. I thought it was worth checking out the mortgage situation up there as a lot of Cheetham and Moore's eggs must be in that particular basket right now. If there were dodgy mortgages on offer, that would be as good a place as any to find them.'

Mower had been investigating a series of mortgage frauds, whose only common thread was the fact that the house buyers under suspicion were all clients of the estate agents Cheetham and Moore.

'But Linda Wright didn't come up with anything useful?'

Thackeray persisted, with an ambiguity which Mower suspected was deliberate.

'Zilch,' he said. 'All promise and no performance, guv.'
He grinned, returning ambiguity for ambiguity. 'If she knew
anything about double and triple mortgages she wasn't giving
anything away.'

Mower remembered the day he had driven up to the
new housing estate which, in spite of the recession, was
attracting Bradfield's better-off young couples with its stone
cottage-style bays and gables and dormer windows. He had
been wearing slim Replay jeans and a loose-ribbed Stone
Island sweater under his leather jacket, smart and fashionable
enough to impress whatever talent the agents had positioned
in their expensively furnished show house with its pale
carpets, swagged curtains and four-poster bed, a snip for
some young executive when it was eventually sold with the
contents thrown in. He had been met by a natural blonde who
had been Miss Bradfield Real Estate 1992, and was clearly not
likely to let anyone, least of all a not-unattractive young police
sergeant, forget it. Even so his suggestion of a drink later that
day had been rejected out of hand.

'You didn't see her again?' Thackeray asked sharply.

'No chance,' Mower said. 'There was a calculator behind
those blue eyes and I got the distinct feeling I didn't add up
to enough.'

Several weeks and a non-accidental death later, Mower had
been slightly surprised to learn that Linda Wright, at the age
of twenty-four and earning a generous enough salary from
Cheetham and Moore, still lived with her parents in the
semi-detached house on the tattier edge of Bradfield. The
suburban streets here gave way first to a raggle-taggle of
allotments, deserted by even the most committed grower of
fruit and veg at this time of the year, and then to scrubby
fields, broken by dark millstone grit walls, harbouring a few
huddled cattle seeking shelter from the chilly wind.

It was a miracle someone had not got their hands on
these semi-derelict acres and filled them with starter homes
at knock-down prices for Cheetham and Moore to flog,
Mower thought as he and Thackeray surveyed the drab

landscape beyond the wintry suburban gardens. They shared an unspoken reluctance to face the parents who already knew their daughter was dead but whose grief would now be immeasurably compounded by the revelation that she had been murdered.

Mower had a keen memory of Linda's carefully made-up prettiness, which had been marred only by a tiny frown of anxiety at first as he pressed her to tell him everything she knew about the mortgage deals he was interested in. But she had denied all knowledge of irregularities and he had been unable to shift her bland air of injured innocence when he pressed her as far as he had dared. He could not have explained to Thackeray or any other senior officer why he had not believed her. But it was a fact.

'So let's get on with it,' Thackeray said quietly. They got out of the car and Mower lifted the brass horseshoe knocker and let it fall. There was no car on the cracked concrete driveway leading to a wooden garage door in urgent need of a coat of paint and the house could easily have been empty. But the door was flung open almost before he had dropped the knocker and he found himself confronted by a plump, middle-aged woman with greying hair who, in spite of what time had achieved in the way of fading her looks, still had the same soft prettiness as her daughter had had. But it was a prettiness under extreme stress. Her eyes were red-rimmed, the skin which must once have been pink and white was grey with tiredness, and her hair straggled into her eyes, uncombed.

Her face fell as she confronted Mower.

'Oh God, I thought it was the undertaker,' she said. 'Dad's having a nap at last and I thought I could deal with all that before he wakes up.'

'Mrs Wright?' Thackeray asked and when she nodded he took her arm gently and led her back into the house.

'I'm sorry,' he said. 'I have some more bad news for you.'

'More?' Mrs Wright asked sharply. 'How can there be more? Our Linda's been killed . . .' Her hand went to her mouth convulsively and she took hold of the two men's arms and pulled them roughly into the front-room.

16

'Come in here,' she said. 'It's Dad. He's got heart trouble, you know, so we're always very careful. No shocks. No anxiety . . .' Her voice trailed away vaguely for a moment before she focused on Thackeray again.

Abruptly she sat down in one of the chintzy armchairs, her face rigid with pain.

'Tell me,' she whispered. She listened in silence as Thackeray explained how Linda had died and that for the moment at least her funeral would have to be postponed.

'It'll finish Dad off,' she said at length, after she had absorbed the news. 'It'll kill him. He thought the world of Linda.'

'We'll need to talk to him,' Thackeray said. 'But not today, if you think it will be too much. But if you can fill in some details for us?'

'I knew summat was wrong when she didn't come home,' Mrs Wright hissed. 'I didn't tell Dad. I just said she wanted to sleep in yesterday morning. But I knew summat was wrong. It wasn't like our Linda, not like her at all. She's usually such a considerate girl.'

'You don't know where she was going?' Thackeray asked. 'Who she was going to see?'

'She didn't say,' Mrs Wright said. 'That's what I'm telling you. She went off in her car about eight, hadn't had any tea, said she was going to eat later. I just assumed she was going to see the latest boyfriend, Jimmy he's called, Jimmy Townsend. I don't know him that well. She's a very popular girl is our Linda. There's always someone new. You lose track a bit. When I went in with a cup of tea the next morning about nine she wasn't there. The bed hadn't been slept in . . .'

Piece by piece they teased out a picture of a fun-loving girl, seldom at home in the evenings, who had had a string of boyfriends but never, according to her mother, one 'special one'.

'She was waiting for the real thing, she said,' Mrs Wright said, a tear creeping down her pale cheek. 'She'd have been better off settling for summat less, wouldn't she? There was more than one wanted to marry her. Nice boys. Good boys. But she was always looking for a little bit more.'

17

She gave them a list of names, was vague about addresses and descriptions, occasionally knew the colour or the make of a car which had collected Linda and returned her later.

Quietly the three of them made their way up to Linda's bedroom and equally quietly went through her cupboards and drawers. Thackeray took possession of Linda's diary, her address book and her financial documents and decided to leave a now distraught Mrs Wright in peace.

'How am I going to tell her dad?' she asked again as she saw them out. 'How can I tell him someone killed our little girl?'

As they got into the car Thackeray took a deep breath and Mower looked at him curiously.

'Poor cow,' he said.

'So what did you find in her wardrobe?' Thackeray asked quickly. He had watched the sergeant go through Linda Wright's clothes with more than a passing interest.

'Oh, I think she'd found her special boyfriend, guv,' Mower said with satisfaction. 'Her wardrobe was full of designer gear. And that jewellery in the dressing-table drawer wasn't any old Ratner's crap. Some of it was solid gold.'

In an office piled high with legal files, from a desk of which you could see little but more papers piled on papers, David Mendelson sighed heavily. From the other side of the room, Chief Inspector Michael Thackeray glowered and Sergeant Kevin Mower gazed studiously at his Italian buckskin slip-ons.

'There's nothing I can do, Chief Inspector,' Mendelson said. 'You have a strong case against the four you've charged, a good chance of convictions, but unless at least one of them will incriminate the agents you can't move against them. There's absolutely not enough to sustain a charge of conspiracy to defraud. It could be coincidence. Unlikely, maybe, but possible, and no serious evidence to the contrary. I'm sorry.'

'Four separate individuals conning building societies, all buying properties through the same agents, and there's no connection?' Mower said suddenly, not hiding the fury in his dark eyes. 'I don't believe it.'

'I'm sure you're right not to,' Mendelson said, taking in the fashionably dressed young detective with a glance that was not entirely friendly. His encounters as a Crown prosecutor with Mower had been brief but had left an indelible feeling that this was a man whose eye was on his own future rather than the interests of anything so abstract as justice. Mower had, he was aware, done most of the work on a case of fairly obvious mortgage fraud. That they would gain four easy convictions he had no doubt. That they could prove the involvement of one of the area's major firms of estate agents he remained totally unconvinced, in spite of Mower's pleas to be allowed to arrest and charge the local manager.

'You have no corroboration,' he said quietly to Mower, concealing his dislike beneath a professionally neutral concern.

'Right, that's it then,' Thackeray said, silencing Mower's next protestation with a chilly look. 'We'll keep an eye on it, David. If they're involved they may slip up next time.'

'Sure,' Mendelson said. 'If they are involved, it may be much bigger than we've been able to prove so far: a few Asians snapping up terraced houses down Aysgarth Lane and taking out triple mortgages on them is small beer. If you're looking for a link it's more likely to be an Asian middleman than anyone else, but they're unlikely to break ranks to tell you that. If it's anything more than that it's certainly worth keeping an eye on. But Cheetham and Moore are a big firm, long-established, branches all over the county. You'll need to have a cast-iron case. Sydney Cheetham knows everyone worth knowing up to and including the chief constable.'

'And Barry Moore's an arrogant bully. I remember him in Arnedale,' Thackeray said with unexpected force. The two younger men, much of an age but as different in appearance as town mouse and country mouse, the one fashionably smooth and the other almost scruffily rumpled, tie loose, shirt sleeves rolled up, looked at him in surprise.

'Moore still works mainly up there, doesn't he?' Mendelson asked. 'Cheetham runs the Bradfield operation.'

Thackeray nodded.

'So I understand,' he said quickly, evidently anxious to cover up his uncharacteristic outburst. Mendelson looked at Thackeray curiously for a moment before assenting to his mute plea to turn the conversation away from an area which clearly threatened him embarrassment.

'And now you have this murder on your plate?' Mendelson said.

'An employee of Cheetham and Moore,' Mower broke in explosively.

'You think there's a connection?' Mendelson pointedly addressed his question to Thackeray. The chief inspector shrugged.

'Nothing we've turned up so far suggests that,' he said. 'But I suppose anything is possible.'

He looks tired, David Mendelson thought as he closed the files the police officers had brought him and handed them back across the desk. In fact, he thought, Michael looks as if he has not slept for a week. He glanced at his watch.

'Have you finished for the day, Michael? Do you fancy a drink?' It was clear from his tone that he was excluding Mower from his invitation and the sergeant took the point impassively, the good-looking, intelligent face giving nothing away.

'I'll take the files back, guv,' he offered. 'Sort out the office. I'll call you if there's anything needs your attention.' Thackeray hesitated, running a hand through dark hair that was showing a strand of grey at the temples but which never looked entirely under control. He was suddenly seized with a tidal wave of weariness which threatened to overwhelm the frosty façade with which he normally faced the world. He handed the files to Mower.

'Thanks,' he said. 'Let me know if they've tracked down the boyfriend.' Linda Wright's latest conquest, Jimmy Townsend, had not been at work at Cheetham and Moore's that day. Nor had he been seen at his flat in a Victorian house close to the town centre, facts which persuaded the police that they needed to speak to him even more urgently than they had anticipated.

Thackeray and Mendelson watched in silence as the sergeant shrugged himself into his dark blue overcoat and made his exit.

'He has expensive tastes, that one. Is he straight?' David Mendelson asked after the footfalls had faded away down the long corridor and they had heard the lift doors close behind him. Thackeray permitted himself a grim smile.

'He'd better be, or he'll find himself back in London on a one-way ticket,' he said. 'No, I think he's straight enough. He's like me, single, no family – or none that we know of. He just spends all his money on clothes. A London boy through and through, slick, smart and just possibly too ambitious for his own good, and Jack the lad with the women, I'm told. But I trust him.'

'As far as you trust anyone,' David said shrewdly.

'That far, anyway,' Thackeray conceded.

'You look as though life's getting you down. This reorganisation must be adding to the pressure. Have you decided whether to go for superintendent?'

'And spend the rest of my career sitting at a desk?' Thackeray asked bleakly. It was no secret that the proposed reorganisation of the police force, winding its way through Parliament, was causing anxiety to middle-ranking officers whose jobs could be phased out. 'I don't know, David. I just don't know.'

'Shall we skip the drink? Come home with me for supper. Vicky'll be pleased to see you. Take pot luck?'

Thackeray hesitated. David Mendelson, a lawyer who had spurned the family firm in favour of the Crown Prosecution Service out of some unfashionable sense of public duty, was one of the few friends he had made in Bradfield since he had arrived in the town almost a year before. But in his present mood he was not sure that David's home, warm, comfortable, welcoming and full of children, was not too cruel a reminder of what his own bleak bachelor flat would never provide.

'Vicky's got enough on her plate with the new baby to want unexpected visitors.'

'Rubbish,' David said. 'Visitors are exactly what she craves after a day on her own with the brood. She needs some adult company, some conversation . . .'

Thackeray sighed and gave in.

'If you're sure,' he said.

And Vicky was indeed apparently delighted to see Thackeray when the two men arrived half an hour later. She greeted them both in the hall, flushed from cooking, with two young sons at her heels and a smile of unalloyed joy on her face as she kissed David warmly on the lips and pecked Michael Thackeray on the cheek as they took off their coats.

'I hear on the local radio there's been a murder,' she said, taking in Thackeray's fatigue. 'Bad, is it?'

'Not good,' he said briefly. 'A young woman.' He did not elaborate, not wanting to mar her contentment. 'I may have to leave if anything fresh develops.'

'It's only pasta,' she said easily. 'Naomi Laura has been an absolute little sod this afternoon. She's been wailing non-stop. I've never had all this trouble before. It must be feminine perversity.' The Mendelsons had been delighted when a baby daughter followed their sons, Nathan and Daniel.

'Like mother, like daughter,' David mocked gently.

'Like her namesake, more like,' Vicky said, giving Thackeray a sweet and patently insincere smile. 'I was never perverse.'

Thackeray did not rise to the bait, turning away to admire the two dark, curly-headed boys who had run off into the sitting-room to resume an elaborate game of cars. His face was impassive as he watched them play, but he could not conceal the sadness in his eyes.

'Do you want me to put them to bed?' David asked Vicky. 'They're late. And I've got work to do later.'

'They begged to be allowed to stay up till you came in,' Vicky said guiltily. 'They're so excited about tomorrow.'

'Tomorrow?' Thackeray asked, unsure whether he should know about a birthday imminent.

'Chanukah – a sort of Jewish Christmas,' David explained. 'The festival of lights. They'll be having presents.'

'So they get Christmas early?'

'They get Christmas as well,' Vicky said, laughing. She watched indulgently as David joined his sons on the floor, three dark heads bent together over the game, but she was not unaware of the look on Thackeray's face.

'Come and help me lay the table in the kitchen,' she said,

taking him by the arm. 'More often than not we eat slumped in front of the box but tonight I'll make an exception and put a table-cloth on.'

She moved easily ahead of him into the spacious kitchen with its big pine table still littered with the remnants of the boys' supper. She was entirely at home here, Thackeray thought, queen of all she surveyed and radiant with contentment though she had lost none of the sharp intelligence that had taken her through university with Laura Ackroyd. Thackeray was filled with a bitter misery for what he had lost. He should never have accepted David's invitation, he thought. He would not make the same mistake again.

Vicky was busy at the hob, where a pan of steaming water awaited its burden of pasta and an almost equally large pan of aromatic sauce bubbled and sent tiny deep orange-red splashes into the air and onto the surrounding work-top. Vicky glanced at Thackeray quizzically and handed him a hard, rank-smelling chunk of Parmesan and a grater.

'A bowl of that adds authenticity,' she said. He nodded and began to grate obediently.

'You don't mind Italian? It's my great stand-by because it's quick.' She eased the stiff spaghetti into the water slowly without snapping it.

'Italian's fine,' he said, grating steadily.

'And are you going to keep this up all night or are you going to tell me how you and Laura are?' she challenged at last, turning to face him.

'Ah,' Thackeray said and let the silence deepen as Vicky took glasses, wine and mineral water from cupboards and fridge, pouring Chianti for herself and water with ice and lemon for him. He stood looking at the bubbles dashing themselves to death against the ice, his face as glacial, and she thought she had lost him. Then suddenly he gave her his rare smile and nodded as if in agreement with some thought she had not even expressed.

'I suppose she told you I was being a bastard about her new job?' he said.

'She gave me the merest hint.'

'I hate Arnedale,' he said. 'It has too many bad memories

23

for me. But I will go and see her. I had a call from my father today and he wants me to go up there soon anyway. He wants to sell the farm. It's all getting too much for him. I will make the effort, I promise.'

'I don't want Laura hurt,' Vicky said, suddenly fierce and embarrassed by her own vehemence, looking down at her wine, cheeks flushed and eyes very bright.

'I know,' Thackeray said, almost inaudibly, unable to reassure her as he knew she wanted to be reassured about the happiness of her best friend, and hating himself for it. The moment was overtaken by Daniel and Nathan, who rushed in to say goodnight before being chivvied upstairs by their father. They did not mention Laura again that evening.

THREE

THE THICK PILE CARPET AT Cheetham and Moore's main town centre office in Bradfield gave an impression of opulence which was belied by the silent telephones and the largely deserted desks. The brightly-lit display windows facing the busy street of Christmas shoppers might be full of tempting houses on offer but the lack of business within was more than a pre-Christmas lull, of that Michael Thackeray was convinced, as he and Mower were ushered into the sanctum of the manager. A tall, slim young man in a white shirt of dazzling brightness rose from his pale oak desk to greet them with a welcoming handshake, a fulsome smile and cold eyes.

'Stephen Stokes, Chief Inspector,' he said affably enough. 'I'm sorry to have to meet you in these circumstances. I've heard a lot about your successes since you came to Bradfield. How may I be of help?'

Thackeray gave Stokes an appraising look, taking in the fashionably lightweight suit, the silk tie in tasteful pinks and blues, and the nicotine-stained fingers which trembled slightly as he withdrew the hand which Thackeray had ignored.

'You seem to have lost two of your staff, Mr Stokes,' Thackeray said. 'Linda Wright I know you know about. But I'm also interested in talking to Jimmy Townsend and my sergeant here tells me you don't know where he is. Is that right?'

'A dreadful shock, Linda's death,' Stokes said. 'A dreadful shock for all of us. Such a lovely girl . . . lively, intelligent, everything going for her . . .'

'And Jimmy Townsend?' Thackeray's voice was still light, but there was an edge to it that he knew Stokes had recognised from the momentary, faint look of panic which flashed across his face.

'Jimmy,' Stokes said, licking his lips. 'He had holiday booked for Christmas, a long break, from Thursday. I had no objection. We're always quiet at this time of the year in the property business, you know.' He glanced through the glass of his office door at the half-deserted sales floor outside, his fingers drumming on the polished surface of his desk. A man at the end of his tether, Thackeray thought, and wondered if it was simply the property market which had reduced him to this state.

'And you don't have any idea where he was going for this holiday? Tenerife? The Seychelles? Butlin's holiday camp?'

'He never said,' Stokes said quickly. 'Your people have talked to all my staff. No one seems to know. Of course, he probably told Linda . . .'

'But Linda is not in any position to tell us,' Thackeray said, that slight edge of menace in his voice still as he recalled Amos Atherton's clinical description of how he deduced that Linda Wright had died, probably semi-conscious and still strapped into her seat in her sinking car.

'How long had that been going on?' Mower asked from the far side of the room where he had draped himself elegantly against a radiator, watching the proceedings with dark, impassive eyes. 'You knew about Jimmy and Linda, of course?'

'I knew they'd been seeing each other, but they didn't give the impression that it was anything serious,' Stokes said. 'Just a casual work thing, as far as I was aware. I don't keep tabs on my staff after hours, Inspector Thackeray. Why should I?'

'I'm told Linda had a succession of boyfriends,' Thackeray said. 'Did she go out with anyone else connected with the firm that you know of?'

Stokes shook his head vehemently at that and lit a cigarette without offering the packet to either of the other men.

'Not that I'm aware of,' he said through the smoke. 'As I say . . .'

26

'You don't keep tabs on them after hours,' Mower came back brusquely. 'Were you happy with Linda and Jimmy as employees, Mr Stokes? Giving satisfaction, were they? Linda up at the show house, and Jimmy . . . doing what?'

'Linda was a marvellous little sales girl,' Stokes said enthusiastically. 'We never thought that estate would sell the way it did, in the prevailing circumstances. Marvellous girl, marvellous. Could sell fridges to the Eskimos with her personality.'

'And Jimmy?' Thackeray repeated.

'Jimmy was a negotiator here in the office. As good as anyone, given the recession. I had no complaints.'

'Responsible for arranging mortgages, was he?' Mower asked sharply.

'All our negotiators will offer mortgage advice,' Stokes said. 'It's normal practice.'

'But not double, or triple mortgages, I hope?' Mower put in. Stokes drew hard on his cigarette and stubbed it out in the cut-crystal ashtray on his desk.

'I'm not sure I like your drift,' he said. 'No one here has been involved in anything illegal. Not to my knowledge. I've been over that ground before with you, Sergeant Mower.' He flashed Mower a glance of real dislike.

'Would you know, Mr Stokes, if Jimmy Townsend had been engaged in a little freelance mortgage work on the side?' Thackeray asked.

'Perhaps not,' he admitted.

'And if you found out?'

'I'd sack him, of course. Mr Cheetham and Mr Moore would expect nothing less.'

'Mr Cheetham and Mr Moore? Your bosses?'

'Mr Moore is only indirectly my boss,' Stokes said. 'He's concerned mainly with the Arndale end of the business. Barry Moore is the second Mr Moore. His father was the original partner. Mr Cheetham lives in Bradfield, has an office here, but he only comes in a day or so a week. He's getting on, you know. He's in his seventies. He leaves the day-to-day running of the office to me.'

Thackeray nodded as if this were all information quite new

27

to him, although he guessed that he knew the Moores, father and son, rather better than Stephen Stokes did.

Stokes glanced at his watch anxiously.

'I don't feel as though I've been much help to you, Inspector, but I have an important site meeting with a client in ten minutes. Is there anything else I can tell you?'

'I'll need all the background information you've got on Linda and on Jimmy Townsend,' Thackeray said. 'Anything on your files, the names of everyone who has worked with them . . .'

Stokes pressed a button on the intercom on his desk and repeated Thackeray's request to his secretary.

'No problem there,' he said. 'And anything else I can do to help, please let me know. A terrible loss, is Linda.'

'Thank you,' Thackeray said. 'And we'll certainly let you know when we want to see you again, Mr Stokes. Don't worry about that.'

'He's up to his eyes in something, guv,' Mower said as they walked quickly back through sleety rain and Christmas crowds to police headquarters.

'Yes, but what?' Thackeray said. 'That's what we need to find out.'

Laura looked critically at herself in the mirror. Businesslike, but not too severe, had been her theme as she had rooted through her wardrobe for the most suitable outfit in which to make her first impression on the *Arnedale Observer*. It was seven-thirty on a cold, dark Monday morning and Laura's lack of enthusiasm for the project David Ross had handed her had only deepened over the intervening weekend.

Here at home in Bradfield she had found herself obsessed by the problem of Thackeray, who had reverted to morose taciturnity for two days, cancelling a date at the last minute because of pressure of work, he said. In spite of the murder inquiry, Laura had not entirely believed him. His attitude was ridiculous, she had yelled at him in the end, driven to distraction by his refusal to discuss her departure. But he had just shrugged, fending off her verbal assault with an apparent indifference which added fuel to the conflagration. They had

28

parted the previous night by telephone, a call of long silences on his part and more than one gibe about Catholic guilt on hers which she now wished unsaid.

'It won't do,' she said enigmatically, screwing up her face at her reflection. Her hair fell down in copper strands across the black wool of her sweater, framing her oval face like a slightly shredded halo.

Irritably she gave up on power-dressing, pushed a bundle of clothes into the suitcase on her bed and snapped the catches shut firmly. She had been offered accommodation 'above the shop' in Arnedale for the evenings when she would be working too late or starting too early to make the trip back to Bradfield feasible. She tossed boots and a skiing jacket onto the back seat of her car and resolved to make the most of the country life.

The drive to Arnedale in the grey early morning light took longer than she had anticipated. Commuter traffic was pouring down the main road towards Bradfield and Milford. Mist still shrouded the hills on either side of the valley, billowing across the road occasionally like smoke, so that oncoming cars loomed up unexpectedly out of the murk like animals with pale yellow eyes and steaming breath.

It was well after nine when she parked her car in the wide main street of Arnedale in one of the spaces which later in the week would be taken up by market stalls. Arnedale was a prosperous little town, strategically placed at the confluence of the Maze and a couple of its tributaries which ended their tumble down from the high fells to join a broad, meandering and altogether more dignified stream between the town and its surrounding water-meadows.

Laura stood by the car for a moment glancing at the mainly eighteenth-century façades of the pubs and shops which lined Broad Street. A watery sun had penetrated the mist, casting a mellow light over the gold stone roofs and pastel colour-washed walls and generously proportioned windows, and she gave a half-smile of pleasure, her low spirits lifting almost in spite of herself. She would enjoy her time here if it killed her, she thought. It was not a life sentence, after all.

29

It might soon begin to seem like one, though, she concluded glumly an hour or so later as she followed the tall, stooping figure of Reg Fairchild back out of the *Observer* office and into Peggy's coffee shop next door. Behind the steamed-up windows the dark oak tables were already busily filled with shoppers taking a mid-morning break, but the waitress in traditional black with white apron smiled cheerily at Reg and waved him to a small corner table for two with a reserved sign on it.

'Coffee for two?' she asked. 'And will the young lady take a tea-cake?'

Fairchild gave Laura no chance to opt for anything else from the gargantuan array of cakes and sticky buns behind the counter. He merely grunted and waved her into one of the two windsor chairs with chintz cushions. Laura watched him not too surreptitiously as he settled in. He was a gangling figure, old-fashioned in his brown tweed suit and fawn knitted pullover with Fair Isle trim over a resolutely country check shirt, almost a caricature, she thought, of the country editor, with his longish grey hair falling over his forehead and the stained briar pipe which he took out of his pocket and laid on the table.

The face above the scrawny neck and prominent Adam's apple was of a different order though, showing its years admittedly, in a maze of fine lines around the eyes, but without the ruddy glow of the outdoor man. It was an aesthete's face, long and fine-boned, the skin the colour of parchment, the eyes an unusually dark grey, only the mouth almost incongruously full-lipped and hinting at a more sensual side to his nature.

Almost against her better judgement, Laura felt herself warming to Reg Fairchild in spite of what had just happened in the office. It had been a welcome more cold than chilly and augured an uncomfortable stay in Arnedale if she did not establish herself firmly as a force to be reckoned with, and quickly.

'I must have been taking my morning coffee here for nigh on forty years,' Fairchild said suddenly, the faintest hint of a challenge in the well-modulated voice from which

Laura guessed he had never tried to eradicate the local accent.

'Have you been editor that long?'

'I started here as a copy boy when I was sixteen, just out o't'grammar school. I've been here ever since apart from National Service and a couple of years on the *Evening Post* in Leeds.' The hint of a smile that could almost have been a grimace was enough to indicate that the big city experience had not been a happy one.

'All socialistic hot air and pretentious piano festivals down there,' he said. 'Arnedale was another world then. They held the cattle market out there in Broad Street, you know? Still driving the sheep down from the fells on foot, some of them were . . . Auctioned the beasts just outside the Bull Inn there.' He waved at the misted-up window from which a panorama of the bustling high street stretched in both directions.

'They didn't build the new cattle mart until 'sixty-four, after old Frank Moore died. Of course his son wanted to move on, expand, the way young men do. Changed the whole nature of the place, that did, in ways we couldn't have foreseen. That and widening the valley road. That was so narrow in the old days it kept the city beggars out for years, afraid of bending their smart cars. After that they all came running – redevelopers, boutique owners and tarters-up of old cottages, the green wellie brigade . . .'

'You should write a local history when you retire,' Laura said.

'Is that what all this is about?' the editor snapped. 'What happens when I retire? I'm only sixty-two, damn it. They might have the decency to let me out the door before they send smart youngsters like you up the road to undo my life's work.'

'I'm here to help out,' Laura said mildly. 'To do whatever you want me to do while Greg is away.' The excuse for her presence was the sudden illness of Greg Winters, Fairchild's deputy, who had collapsed with a heart attack several weeks before.

'So the great white chief from London said when he honoured us with his presence t'other day,' Fairchild said sceptically. 'But there's always more to what David Ross does than meets the eye. I've no doubt you've been given another agenda. Modernise the *Observer*? Is that it? Get the ads off the front page at last and bring the beggars into the twentieth century?'

Laura shook her head, but Fairchild was not to be mollified.

'So what if I tell you that the customers like the ads on page one?' he went on, the veins on his forehead standing out as he became more emotional.

Laura toyed with the hot toasted tea-cake running with butter which the waitress had plonked somewhat grumpily in front of her, as if she had picked up from Fairchild's demeanour that his guest was not there exactly at his invitation, and was ready to do what she could to defend one of her favourites.

'My grandmother used to take me to Peggy's in Bradfield for these when I was a little girl,' she said. She paused to let him assess that credential.

'I don't think Ross has the faintest idea of what Arnedale is like,' she went on. 'All he cares about is his profit. What's bugging him is this free sheet, *Inside Info*, isn't it? If you can fight that off, and keep your circulation up I don't think he gives a damn whether you put your ads on the front page, the back page or on a flag flying from the office roof.'

Fairchild grunted sceptically at that and poured himself a second cup of coffee.

'The free sheet is just a fly-by-night rag. Here today and gone tomorrow. The lad running it's some off-comer, some Scotsman. What does he know about the Dales?'

Laura smiled, satisfied to have turned the conversation away from the perceived threat that she presented to another external and very real one. She had copies of the fly-by-night rag in her suitcase and knew just how insidious Fergal Mackenzie, the despised Scotsman, could be.

'You're very confident,' she said. 'What about the rest of the staff? I get the impression that Jonathon isn't too keen to see me here,' It had not taken her long to work out that Jonathon West, the third senior journalist on the paper, and the only other one who mattered on a paper staffed mainly by young trainees, was young, sharp and determinedly going places. Fairchild laughed mirthlessly.

'I caught him drinking to Greg Winters' health after he had his heart attack – and I don't mean to his good health either. He'll go far, that lad, and the farther the better as far as I'm concerned. I only took him on because his father's on the county council and his uncle's Lord Radcliffe.' He saw Laura wince at that and smiled grimly.

'These things still count for summat up here,' he said. 'This isn't Bradfield. Land and the old way of life still mean something. Change comes slowly and there's a lot of resistance to it. Our biggest stories just now are plans for new quarries up on the moors and the state of the hill farms. By the end of this winter a lot of the little men will have been driven out of business if they can't sort out the subsidies on sheep. Come on, girl, drink up and I'll give you a guided tour and a bite of lunch. It's only Monday, after all. We don't go to press till Thursday afternoon.'

FOUR

THE LORRY HAD TAKEN ON its load of stone at first light. It should not have been on the top moorland edge of Ray Harding's holding so early, but the driver had wanted an early finish that night so that he could do some Christmas shopping with his wife. So he ground up the steep hill to High Clough in a thick dawn mist to where Harding had been busy for weeks dismantling one of the limestone walls which snaked across the rough ground and up the steep slopes to the point where a pretence of good grazing land could no longer be sustained.

So it was that the heavily loaded truck bounced back across the rough terrain to the dilapidated field gate, and started out down the steep winding road, between more walls of the same light grey-white stone, just as the handful of older children who lived in the village straggled to the school-bus stop outside St Hugh's.

It was a sharp frosty morning after a bitter night. Mist clung to the fields as the road dropped into more sheltered hollows so that the sheep which had been brought close to the village to over-winter loomed unexpectedly out of the swirling wraiths with droplets of water sparkling in their fleeces, almost indiscernible until startled, when they recoiled into invisibility with a protesting bleat.

At the bus stop seven or eight children in bright anoraks jostled and shoved, excited by the fact that this was the last week of term and the bite in the air promised snow and holidays. The bus which would take them to the secondary school in Arnedale was late and it was gone half-past eight by the time they heard it grinding up the hill towards the village.

Ponderously the single-decker swung backwards into the turning space by the churchyard gate. The children gathered in a group on the higher ground next to the wooden seat – a present to the village from the churchwardens of 1974 – where they waited each morning, watching the driver crane his neck to make sure that he did not go a foot too far and demolish the lychgate.

There was a moment when the narrow road was completely blocked by the front end of the coach. It was at this point that the driver of the builders' lorry swung round the bend too quickly and found he had nowhere to go. He slammed on his brakes, skidded on the frosty road and hit the coach broadside on, catching the horrified children in his helpless slide.

The rending crash of the collision was followed by an instant of total silence before the screams of the surviving youngsters began. Faith Lawrence had been irritably stuffing dirty washing into her machine when she became aware of a piercing sound which grabbed her stomach in primeval panic. Instinctively she looked around for her son before telling herself sharply that Tim was, as usual at this time in the morning, deeply asleep, tightly wrapped in his duvet in the fug of the dark den upstairs where he spent most of his time.

Dropping her washing, Faith opened the back door of the old stone farmhouse just up the hill from the church and looked down the village street. With a conscious effort of self-control she took in the scene by the lychgate and turned back into the house to call for police and ambulance before grabbing a bundle of coats from behind the door and rushing to see what she could do to help.

By the time Laura Ackroyd and Jonathon West arrived at High Clough the worst was over. Laura had walked into the office just as the message came through that there had been a serious accident in the moorland village. West had already put on his Barbour and boots and was on his way out of the newsroom.

'I'll come with you,' Laura said, reading the message which hinted at several deaths.

'You'll need boots,' West said, without much enthusiasm. His face was unreadable, eyes cold.

'They're in the car,' Laura said shortly, following the tall young man down the stairs and back out into Broad Street. One of the first things Ted Grant had advised, on her arrival at the *Gazette* in short skirt and high heels, was to get herself a pair of boots for the mucky jobs like accidents and pit disasters. Although the latter were now receding into industrial history, Laura conceded that the advice had been sound.

'We'll go in mine. You can navigate for me,' she said, as West hesitated for no more than a second beside his own soft-top, mutiny in the blue eyes, before turning to Laura's Beetle with a shrug and a toss of fair hair. You fancy yourself a bit too much, my lad, Laura thought, and she did not just mean professionally.

There were always men who undressed you on first acquaintance and she had seen the frank appraisal in West's eyes as soon as she had walked through the office door for the first time. The *Arnedale Observer* might sell on its old world charm, but West was clearly a young man still wedded to the thrusting eighties and his appraisal had been quickly replaced by deep suspicion. If Laura was perceived as a threat to Jonathon West's career, as she had no doubt she was, she had equally little doubt that he might try to neutralise that threat in the oldest way known to man and woman. If she was to survive as Jonathon's boss, she would need to impress him fast and indelibly with something other than her figure.

They drove out of Arnedale and up the valley road in uncompanionable silence, West confining himself to monosyllabic instructions when she was required to turn off the main road and begin the steep, twisting climb up to High Clough. As they passed the village sign, the road took a dip and turned sharply across a humpbacked stone bridge spanning a tumbling stream before it commenced the last steep hundred yards to the church and the huddle of houses beyond. A uniformed policeman waved them to a stop in a muddy lay-by on the lower side of the bridge, from where it was possible to see the flashing lights of ambulances and police cars and a scene of some confusion a little higher up the hill.

The constable nodded affably enough to West as he wound down the window, evidently recognising him.

'You'll not get any farther,' he said. 'It's bloody murder up theer.'

'Fatalities?' West asked and the policeman nodded dourly.

'One little lass,' he said. 'Maybe more. They're still trying to get the lorry driver out.' As they watched, one ambulance made its way cautiously down the hill towards them, turning on its siren as soon as it had passed.

'Why don't you get the official details and I'll see if I can find some eyewitnesses,' Laura suggested, although not in a tone which allowed West much scope to dispute her allocation of responsibilities or her right to allocate them at all. Start as you mean to go on, she told herself grimly as he gave her another old-fashioned look. Give this one an inch and he'll grab a handful.

After picking her way gingerly around the edges of the wreckage of what had been the school bus and the lorry, surrounded by the paraphernalia of rescuers who were still busy dismantling the cab which had almost disappeared into the interior of the coach, Laura found herself pointed in the direction of the low stone house to one side of the church and slightly higher up the hill – Faith Lawrence's place, her informant said. Beyond a narrow strip of garden, brown and dank in its winter plumage, what was clearly the kitchen door of the solid old house stood open and she could hear the murmur of voices.

She stood on the threshold for a moment to take stock before she went inside. She was not unused to the aftermath of violence. There was no future as a reporter for the squeamish, she had also been told early on by Ted Grant after she had come back sobbing from covering some local tragedy. She had never wept again, in his hearing at least, saving her tears on occasion for her pillow as she often bore witness, too closely for comfort, to the worst life could throw at the innocent and unassuming.

Something of the emotion, she hoped, went into her writing but she never felt that it did much more than skim the surface of the reality of the worst she had seen. And even now, ten years on, she knew that she had not developed the hard shell that many reporters did, and she was already torn between sorrow and anger as she stepped over the threshold into the Lawrences' kitchen.

Faith Lawrence was standing by the Aga pouring a kettle of boiling water into a teapot and merely nodded and raised an interrogative eyebrow at Laura as she introduced herself. Three other women were sitting around the huge pine table with two dishevelled children in school uniform. Two much younger children were playing in a subdued fashion on the floor near the Aga and a thin youth wrapped in a luridly patterned red and black duvet stood in the doorway which obviously led to the rest of the house, blue eyes staring from a pale and slightly haggard face under an uncombed thatch of straggly blond hair. For a moment no one spoke.

'We'll be wanting to write something about the accident,' Laura said at last. 'I wanted to talk to anyone who saw what happened.'

The girl of about fourteen who was sitting at the table began to sob quietly at that and one of the women put a protective arm around her and glared at Laura.

'Can't you see they're in shock,' she said. 'They can't tell you owt, it all happened so fast.'

'He should swing for this, the driver of that bloody wagon,' another put in furiously. 'They come down that hill like bats out of hell, some of 'em do. It were an accident waiting to happen.'

Faith Lawrence had said nothing, busying herself pouring tea into the collection of mugs on the table, evidently in control. She was a tall women, middle-aged but with a certain elegance to her movements, and silver-grey hair sweeping around a face of delicate intelligence in a style which must have been fashionable in her teenage years. She was wearing black trousers under a flowing smock-like top, but if she was playing the earth mother, Laura thought, she was not quite pulling it off.

You might confide in Faith Lawrence, she thought, but she suspected that you would be more likely to get asperity than comfort in response. Her grey eyes were concerned enough as she busied herself with the little group at the table, but the look she gave Laura was sharp and cool.

'Suzy and Dan were waiting for the school bus with the other children,' she said crisply. 'The bus had started to reverse – it does that every day – and the lorry came round too fast and skidded. Would you like a cup of tea?'

Laura nodded and sat at the table with the other women and gradually she teased out the names and ages of the little group of youngsters who had been cheerfully waiting on the hill. Four had been taken to hospital including the child who had gone under the lorry and been pulled free of the wreckage dead. Two more had made their own way home.

'Can I see the other children,' she asked, 'if they were not hurt at all?' She was surprised at the sudden uneasy silence which fell at that.

'They're gyppos,' the boy called Dan muttered at last. 'They've gone back up to t'camp.' Laura looked at Faith Lawrence for guidance and got the faintest shrug of the shoulders in return.

Laura turned her attention to Tim Lawrence who had also sat down at the table and was spooning muesli up hungrily, still wrapped in his quilt.

'Shouldn't you have been with them?' she asked, guessing he was about sixteen or seventeen. The boy looked at her blankly and did not reply.

'Tim's left school,' Faith said in a tone which did not encourage any further questions. There was another awkward silence, soon interrupted by an ambulanceman and Jonathon West.

'I can take these two down to casualty now if you're ready,' the uniformed ambulanceman said. 'They'd best have a check-up after that little lot.' He looked grimly at the group round the table. 'Which are the mothers?' he asked. Two of the women identified themselves and the whole group was hustled away. West stood for a moment in the low doorway, one hand on the frame, taking in the scene.

'I'll go down to the hospital with them,' he said. 'Follow it up from there. Okay?' He did not give Laura a chance to demur before turning on his heel and following the ambulanceman. Laura gave a little moue of annoyance but could hardly object to West's plan, only the tone of its announcement. She knew that Faith had noticed the moment of tension before she was distracted by her remaining neighbour, who gathered up the other two children and made her way out.

Faith slammed down the top of the Aga and joined Laura and her son at the table. She looked drained now and Laura noticed for the first time that her smock was smeared with dirt and oil and her left hand was roughly bandaged. Faith caught her glance and shrugged.

'I was the first one there,' she said. 'It was like a battle-field.'

'It was one of Ray Harding's lorries,' the boy said suddenly, his voice harsh as if it had not long broken, although Laura suspected that the roughness came as much from suppressed emotion as anything else.

'Ray Harding?' she prompted.

'He has the farm at the very top of the hill, East Rigg,' Faith said. 'The poorest land, I suppose. It's marginal farming at the best of times and just now they're all pretty desperate, I think. Anyway, he's been earning a bit extra on the side by selling off the stone from some of the old walls and barns. There's been a lot of fuss about it locally – because it'll alter the landscape around here, you know the sort of thing, but there doesn't seem to be much anyone can do to stop him. It's his land, and his stone . . .'

Laura thought of the wild, rolling hills which stretched away for miles to the north, defined by the long snaking walls of rough limestone which divided each strip of bright green pasture and defined the edge of the usable land from the rough moors beyond. The fields were dotted with stone barns which had traditionally provided shelter for livestock but which now, more often than not, stood derelict and abandoned, and evidently worth more to cash-hungry farmers than the flocks they had sheltered.

Faith looked weary and defeated by what had happened that morning, but the boy seethed at her side. He glared at Faith and then at Laura.

'They're letting them get away with it,' he said. 'This is supposed to be a national park, but quarrying's been allowed right up the dale . . .' He looked embarrassed at having been provoked into saying so much. He wrapped his quilt more tightly around himself and got up to go.

'You're new at the *Observer*?' Faith asked, after the kitchen door had slammed shut behind him. 'I met your editor, Reg Fairchild. We've been doing some campaigning up here. There's a rumour that Ray Harding's planning to reopen the old quarry at the top end of his holding. It's not been worked for years, but there's demand again for the limestone for road building. It would be a disaster for the village. There'd be heavy lorries like that coming up and down the hill all day long, shaking the place to bits. There'd be bound to be more accidents . . .'

'Have you lived here long?' Laura asked, intrigued by the subdued passion in Faith's voice which echoed her son's concern though without the stridency, but puzzled by the lack of any trace of the local accent. Faith shook her head and smiled faintly.

'Not long,' she said. 'I've lived most of my life in the south, though my family came from this area originally. I inherited this house from an aunt. When my husband retired eighteen months ago we decided to come and live here.' Laura was not sure, but thought she detected the slightest hesitation as Faith mentioned her husband's retirement.

'So what's happened today is exactly what you've been campaigning against?' she asked, scenting a story beyond the immediate tragedy.

'Exactly,' Faith said. 'You've only to look at the village to see how it would be devastated by heavy traffic, quite apart from the risk of an accident. It's what we all feared, and now we've been proved right.' She looked down at her hands, and rubbed ineffectually at one of the oil stains. 'I should get cleaned up,' she said vaguely.

'Just tell me a little more about the village campaign,' Laura said. 'Or is it all in the cuttings? The *Observer* has covered it before, has it?' Faith Lawrence gave her an oddly quizzical look at that.

'You must be new,' she said. 'Your Mr Fairchild isn't enthusiastic about this sort of campaign. We must have written dozens of letters. But we don't get far. The *Observer*'s line is that the area needs all the development it can get and the environment can go hang.'

'In a national park?'

'In a national park. Have you not seen the quarries up Wharfedale? That's what we're afraid of here. We're getting much more support from the new free paper than we are from your lot,' Faith said a touch bitterly and Laura pricked up her ears again.

'Are you now,' she said. 'That would be the Scotsman, Fergal Mac-something?'

'Mackenzie. He came up a week or so ago to talk about a feature he was planning,' Faith said. 'I did hope when I heard someone new was coming to the *Observer* that we might get a more sympathetic hearing there too.'

'I'm only standing in for Greg Winters,' Laura equivocated.

'Yes, I heard he'd been taken ill,' Faith said. 'I can't say I'm sorry. At least old Reg Fairchild says no courteously. Winters imagines he's working on the *Globe* with the manners to match. He wrote the most disgraceful series on the travellers a few months back. Almost racist, I thought it was: scroungers, layabouts, bringing vermin and disease, all the old clichés.'

'Travellers?' Laura said, feeling stupid and realising that she knew far too little about the area she was supposed to be reporting on.

'There's been a travellers' camp in the old quarry since the autumn. Most of the locals hate it. Would run them out of the village by force if they dared. Harding is one of the most vicious, though it's his land and I believe they got his permission to be there originally. I suspect

42

the plan to reopen the quarry is partly a ploy to get the caravans out.'

'This isn't quite the good life you'd hoped for, then? Not exactly awash with peace and tranquillity?' Laura said, glancing round the stone-flagged kitchen with its hanging bunches of herbs and dried flowers and its plain pine furnishings. Faith laughed slightly mirthlessly.

'You got it, as they say in LA,' she said. She picked up her mug of tea with a hand that Laura noticed was shaking slightly and she did not think it was entirely the accident which had reduced her to this state of nervous tension. The feeling of unease was confirmed as the door to the rest of the house crashed open behind them again and a man Laura had never seen before came in.

'Where's he gone then, that boy?' the newcomer asked. He was a stocky figure, evidently older than Faith, dressed scruffily although not inexpensively, his sports shirt and casual trousers having seen much better days. But it was his face which held the attention: flushed a ruddy purple, the eyes rheumy and screwed up against the light, the lips and chin unsteady.

'This is my husband Gerry,' Faith said in a carefully neutral voice.

'Where's that blasted boy gone?' Gerry Lawrence repeated, ignoring Laura completely. 'I just saw him go out.'

'I really don't know,' Faith said.

'Up with those bloody gypsies again,' Gerry said, steadying himself with infinite care against the heavy pine table. 'Spends all his time up with those bloody gypsies. Should be at work. That's what I say. If he won't go to school and study he should be at work. I was at work when I was his age. None of this nancying around, playing records, up till all hours . . .'

Obviously finding an upright posture difficult to maintain Lawrence sat down suddenly, sprawling across the table so close to Laura that she instinctively recoiled. There was no mistaking the whisky on his breath.

Without embarrassment Faith stood up and ushered Laura to the door, her face impassive, the grey eyes blank.

'If there is anything else I can tell you give me a call,' she said. 'And if you could write something about the anti-quarrying campaign, we would be very grateful. It would be a pity to let your Scottish rival get one jump ahead, wouldn't it?'

Outside Laura stood for a moment on the stone-flagged garden path and took a deep breath of cold winter air. The sun had broken through now and dispersed the mist and from Faith Lawrence's garden the vast panorama of the valley lay spread out below.

Looking up the main street, the village houses with their stone-slab roofs lay low, almost cowering under the lee of the high moors as if for shelter. Beyond the last of the fields, dotted with sheep and a random scattering of limestone boulders, like the last traces of melting snow, the high hills swept in a rolling ocean away to the north and on the far horizon the massive grey bulk of Ingleborough could just be seen against the hazy sky.

Laura could imagine why Faith Lawrence had been tempted to come to live here. If she remembered it from her childhood it must have seemed like a haven after a life in the frenetic, traffic-choked south, a haven which she might have hoped would soothe the evident tensions of her family life.

But the cluster of emergency vehicles still scarred the timeless village street and she guessed that Faith's personal search for peace and quiet had been a pretty fruitless one. Her husband's retirement, she had called it. Some retirement.

As the last of the ambulances began to move slowly away, blue lights flashing, Laura guessed that the lorry driver had been extricated from his mangled cab, more probably dead than alive. With a sigh she walked wearily back down the hill to her car.

Curiosity made her turn over the narrow stone bridge to edge past the wreckage and up the hill towards the top of the village, past the church and the Lawrences' house and past the Quarryman pub, almost indistinguishable from the rest of the cottages apart from its swinging sign and a few tables and benches standing on damp concrete to one side of the firmly closed bar door. A terrace of cottages beyond that and the village proper ended, although she could see a couple more low dwellings higher up, farmhouses, she guessed, tucked into a fold of the hillside for shelter against the high winds and blizzards which would sweep across the moors and fells in the coming months.

The road narrowed near the brow and she slowed down as she saw a figure trudging up the hill ahead of her. She recognised the boy, Tim Lawrence, wearing jeans and a camouflage jacket with its collar turned up. She pulled up beside him.

'Do you want a lift?' she asked. The boy hesitated and then slid into the passenger seat beside her.

'Can I get back to the main Arnedale road if I go on over the top?' Laura asked, by way of filling the silence. It was obvious that Tim was not in a mood to communicate much, as he slumped in his seat, his chin buried in his chest.

'It's a dead end,' he muttered eventually. 'Goes up as far as the quarry and then just peters out into a track. You can get over in a four-wheel drive, but not in this thing.' He gestured contemptuously around the interior of the Beetle.

'I'll turn back at the top then,' Laura conceded. 'Is that all right for you?' The boy grunted in response and Laura thought that was all she was going to get out of him when suddenly, as they approached what looked from a distance like a massive gash in the hillside, he gave her an anguished glance and the words began to tumble out, like the bursting of a dam.

'I could kill them,' he said. 'All of them. I hate them. It's like that poem – you know? "They fuck you up, your mum and dad"? What was his name?'

'Larkin,' Laura said gently. 'Did you do him at school?'

'A bit. I would have done more, in the sixth form, if I'd stayed at school. But I had to leave, didn't I, when Dad lost his job. There was no money for the fees, was there? So that was my A levels down the drain as well as the house and everything else.'

'Boarding school?' she hazarded, aware of the slightly

45

clipped southern accent, the pale blond good looks, marred by dark circles under the boy's eyes and what threatened to become a permanently sulky droop to the lips. He nodded dumbly, as if he dared not say more for fear of what he might reveal.

'I went to boarding school in Surrey,' Laura said. 'I hated it. All those rules and regulations . . .'

'Mine wasn't like that,' Tim said quickly. 'It wasn't one of your awful regimented public schools. It was mixed, and we did lots of creative things. Drama and art, and I was in a rock group . . .' He hesitated again before going on. 'There was this girl . . .' he said and Laura nodded. He did not need to say any more.

'All that was before you came to live here?'

'I never wanted to come up here. I didn't want to go to some crummy comprehensive school where they think Larkin is some sort of bird. I went for a bit to finish my GCSEs and I hated it. They made fun of my accent, everything. Yorkshire yobbos.'

'Arnedale Grammar? I know someone who went there and got a place at Oxford. Are you sure you're being fair?'

'What's fair?' the boy said. 'Dad losing his job and all his money at Lloyd's wasn't fair, was it? It's not fair to Mum to have him boozing the way he does, is it? Caro living in Devon and me being stuck up here isn't fair, is it? Nothing's fair!'

Laura had reached the point where the gravelled road ended in a cattle grid and continued, as the boy had warned, only as a rough, rutted track, deep in mud at this time of the year. She swung the car round so that they were facing down the hill again and stopped, looking quizzically at her young passenger.

'But you like the country?' she said, recalling his fury at the possible despoliation of the valley.

'A bit like France,' he said sullenly. 'It'd be smashing without the Frogs. This place would be marvellous without pigheaded, ignorant oafs like Ray Harding. They'll wreck the environment, the ecology, everything. Rob says there are EC laws against this sort of thing.'

'Rob?'

'You can drop me here,' the boy said, and Laura noticed that to one side of the main track there was a break in the dry-stone wall which appeared to lead into the quarry which scarred the hillside with its jagged cliff-face. Just visible from the road were the tops of a multicoloured and dilapidated collection of caravans and converted buses parked in the deep basin of the quarry bottom. Washing flapped on makeshift clothes-lines between the vehicles and, opening the window, she could hear dogs barking and the laughter of children playing.

'Rob lives up here,' he said. 'With the travellers. Old Harding wants them out. He hates them.'

There was an awful lot of hate and unhappiness swirling around High Clough, Laura thought. Too much perhaps for one small community to bear. She watched the boy as he made his way down the track. About half-way he met a tall, thin, black-haired man in a tartan jacket making his way upwards and they stopped to talk for a moment, the dark head and the blond close in a moment of curious intimacy which faintly embarrassed Laura.

As he reached the top of the steep hill, leaving Tim to continue his way down, the stranger gave Laura a half-smile and came round to the open driver's window.

'I hear you're Press,' he said. 'Another rant about the feckless, lawless scrounging travellers, is it?'

'Not at all,' Laura said sharply. 'I came up to cover the accident.'

'Ah, yes, I heard about that,' the man said. 'A couple of our kids were a bit bruised, but thankfully nothing worse. They shouldn't let lorries down a narrow lane like this. It's asking for trouble.'

Laura hesitated for a moment, taking in the thin, weather-beaten face, the dark hair tied back in a pony-tail, the deep-set brown eyes with laughter lines which creased attractively as he tried out his faintly mocking smile again.

'So are we one of the "let's protect the alternative life-style" brigade, then?' he asked. 'That won't go down too well round here.' It was not an uneducated voice, and not a local accent, and it aroused Laura's curiosity.

47

'You must be Rob,' she said. 'Tim Lawrence told me about you. Would you like a ride down the hill?'

'If you want to make yourself deeply unpopular with the locals,' he said with a grin, and when she nodded, opened the passenger door quickly and got in.

'Rob Tyler,' he said by way of introduction. 'Just off to scrounge my Giro. Didn't your mother tell you not to give lifts to strange men?'

'My mother told me not to do lots of things,' Laura said feelingly. 'I didn't take much notice when she was around and I certainly don't now she's not. You don't look as though you took much notice of your mother's good advice either.'

He grinned disarmingly, but did not rise to her bait and they fell into an edgy silence. Laura felt herself being observed closely as she drove slowly back down the narrow lane to the village.

'Is that Harding's farm?' she asked as they passed one of the two isolated homesteads on the very top edge of the village. Tyler shook his head.

'No, his is the one higher up, at the back of the quarry. That's Joe Thackeray's place. He's not such a bad old stick. Has a wife in a wheelchair, poor sod. We get no trouble from him.'

Laura digested that bit of information in silence, very unwilling indeed to reveal more than a passing interest in the Thackeray family, though she took a careful look at the low stone farmhouse and the surrounding small fields thick with over-wintering sheep. Carefully she drove on, again negotiating the wreckage of the school bus and the lorry still parked outside the church waiting for the crane which would be needed to take them away.

'Christ, what a mess,' her passenger said feelingly as they drove past. 'Thank God mine aren't old enough to go to school.'

'You have children?'

'Two,' he said shortly. 'Gypsy brats, they call them up here, although as a matter of fact I'm not a gypsy, in spite of appearances. I just had a Spanish mother. But it suits me to let them think I am sometimes. It's harder to move gypsies on

48

than mere travellers. Gypsies did have a few rights. Though not for much longer, if some people get their way.'

Laura glanced at her passenger curiously, feeling her own prejudices shift slightly.

'How come you're travelling then?' she asked.

'No job, no home, originally,' he said dismissively. 'Then in the end you get hooked on the open-air life, the independence. It would be hard to settle back in a house now. It's been ten years.'

They were approaching the main valley road and as she pulled up to wait for a gap in the stream of traffic making its way towards Arnedale, Tyler opened the car door and gave her a smile which verged on the genuinely warm.

'This will do me nicely, thanks,' he said, getting out. 'See you.' He turned up the coat of his lumber-jacket and set off briskly in the opposite direction, without looking back.

FIVE

'IF THIS IS THE YORKSHIRE Dales, I think I'll stick to Marbella,' Mower grumbled as he followed the chief inspector to the edge of the reservoir. 'People actually come on holiday here, do they, guv?' He shivered. 'The bastard chose the right spot, though, didn't he? You could organise a massacre up here and no one would notice a bloody thing.'

The Scarsdale reservoir, created by a squat stone dam thrown across the valley, lay like a sheet of beaten pewter, ruffled by the icy wind, between the dun-coloured slopes of the high Pennines. Michael Thackeray pulled up the collar of his waterproof jacket and walked slowly back to the edge of the narrow road, where the gravel thrown up on the outside of the bend was still scarred and rutted by the pressure of tyres and feet. Too many tyres and feet, Thackeray thought, for any useful evidence to be left, though he had had the area thoroughly searched as a precaution.

Just one set of wheel-tracks veered from the carriageway, over the low kerb and across the stretch of dead, rustling moorland grass which was all that lay between the road and the water. It would be a lonely enough spot in high summer when a few walkers and birdwatchers might be expected to frequent the banks of the man-made lake where neither fishing nor boating was permitted, Thackeray thought. Now, in midwinter, with the slopes made puddled and boggy by winter rain and early snow, it was as desolate as death.

'On a cold, wet night like that you'd be lucky to meet anything up here,' Thackeray said. 'Since they built the M62 motorway there's not much traffic on these hill roads even in summer. In winter they can be blocked by snow for days.'

He glanced back down the valley towards Bradfield, which lay fifteen miles east and more than a thousand feet below.

'That must be the nearest farm,' he said, nodding towards a cluster of low stone buildings some distance from the road and more than a mile away. 'I don't suppose they heard anything but we'd better go through the motions.'

They went back to the car and Mower drove slowly back down the winding unfenced road where a few hardy sheep huddled against the sparse shelter of gorse and dead bracken. He turned cautiously down a rutted track into a muddy farmyard. The sergeant looked around in distaste and glanced at his Italian shoes.

'You get a drier class of dirt in Streatham,' he said.

'Yes, well, you know the answer to that,' said Thackeray unsympathetically, swinging a pair of sensible brogues into the sticky black muck. But he needed to do little more than straighten up before they were met by a ruddy-faced, broad-shouldered man of about thirty-five, well wrapped up in a duffle jacket and tweed cap.

'Doug Wetherby,' he said by way of greeting. 'You must be t'police. Come about that lass that drowned? It were on t'local radio. I guessed you'd be up.'

'Did you see or hear anything unusual that night, Mr Wetherby?' Thackeray asked.

'You'd have been lucky to hear owt. There were a gale blowing down from t'tops. And normally I wouldn't have seen owt either. I'd not have been about that late on. We've a small babby, and we don't keep late hours any road wi't'beasts to fettle early. But that night I took my wife into Bradfield wi't'bairn to stay wi'her mother. She's bin poorly and needed someone to sleep in.'

'What time did you come back?' Thackeray said, his mind swinging into gear in an instant at the prospect of hard information.

'About ten, I reckon. I didn't look at t'clock when I got in but I put telly on and t'news were still on.'

'And you'd seen something on the road?'

'Aye. I thought it were a bit odd, like. There were a big car parked on t'straight stretch just beyond our gate. Just side-lights on, else I'd not have seen him at all. I thought it must be lovers looking for somewhere quiet. We get that a bit in t'summer, but not often at this time o't'year. But as far as I could see there were only one person in t'car. Just the driver.'

'A man or a woman? Could you tell?' Thackeray asked.

'Oh, it were a bloke, I think. I weren't taking that much notice, but I'm sure it were a bloke.'

'Could you see the make of car?'

But this time Wetherby shook his head.

'I were turning into t'gateway so I had my eyes on t'road. It's a tight turn. It were a big low job of some sort, a dark colour – mebbe a Rover, or a Jag, summat classy. But I couldn't swear to owt. But weren't she driving a Metro, t'lass who died? It weren't one o'them. That's definite.'

'I've got lads checking the travel agents to see if he really did book a holiday,' Chief Inspector Thackeray said. 'I've asked the Manchester police to check out his mother's address. She moved over there when the father died, apparently, to live with her sister. But so far we've had no joy. Not a single sighting. Not a single suggestion from anyone as to where he might have gone.'

'And she was meeting him that night?' Superintendent Jack Longley asked.

'So her mother says, though I reckon her mother doesn't know the half of what her precious Linda was up to,' Thackeray said.

'What mother ever does?' Longley came back with a world-weary look. His normally jovial features were creased with an anxiety Thackeray did not quite understand.

'Have you got your search warrant?' he asked.

'We're going to have a look at his flat this afternoon,' Thackeray said.

'Good. That might give you a few leads to where he's gone. He has to be your prime suspect, this lad. It can't be coincidence that he goes missing the night the girl dies. You need to start thinking about when you need to ask the Press to publish a picture, registration number of his car, the rest of it. Sooner rather than later, I'd say, if you're going to catch up with him.'

Longley looked down at his cluttered desk for a moment, drumming his fingers, and then gave himself a slight shake, as if coming to a decision.

'I've already been getting some pressure on this one, Michael,' he said, a faint flush of embarrassment suffusing his fleshy neck, his eyes avoiding Thackeray's. 'Old Sydney Cheetham reckons his firm was already being harassed over your mortgage investigation, and now this. That's down to young Kevin Mower, I suppose. Persistent beggar, isn't he?'

'Not unreasonably persistent,' Thackeray said sharply. Not for the first time he sensed steel shutters rattling down defensively around Bradfield's élite as his enquiries edged, even tangentially, close to them. 'You don't want to believe everything you hear at the Lodge or in the bar at the Clarendon.'

'I listen, lad, that's all,' Longley said, his anger under control, but barely. 'I do nowt but listen. And if Mower has grounds for his questions you should know by now I'll back him, right up to bloody Buckingham Palace if necessary. But Cheetham'll not be best pleased to be involved in another police investigation, especially if it turns out just to be some lovers' quarrel gone awry, no connection with the business at all. Just bear it in mind, is all I'm saying. A quick result'd go down well all round.'

Thackeray straightened up from his favourite perch against Longley's window-sill, stretching his burly, rugby-player's frame somewhat wearily.

'Perhaps you'd like it gift-wrapped for Christmas?' he said, not concealing his uneasiness.

'Well, I dare say we'd all like a decent holiday,' Longley said, reverting to the slightly avuncular tone under which he generally concealed a sharp brain and an iron will. Thackeray said no more, but he was not fooled, and knew that Longley knew he was not fooled.

They took Jimmy Townsend's home apart that afternoon. Detective Sergeant Mower watched the search team which had descended on Townsend's surprisingly spacious ground-floor flat for a moment. Estate agents must still be doing all right, he concluded, looking around the expensively furnished living-room with its state-of-the-art hi-fi and TV and video and fingering the suits which hung neatly in the double wardrobe in the bedroom. There was no sign, he thought, that Townsend had intended to leave the flat for good. There was no way he would have left his Armani suit and his CD collection behind.

Stifling the niggle of envy which assailed him, he settled down to go through the contents of a small bureau in the hall which was evidently where Townsend filed the more tedious details of his life. And that faint twinge of jealousy soon evaporated. However efficient Townsend might be in the office, and Mower had had his doubts about his boss's testimonial to the missing negotiator's skills, his private life, he very quickly concluded, was a mess and getting messier.

Unpaid bills, bank statements, credit card accounts and personal letters were stuffed into the bureau in random heaps, some documents still in their envelopes, some crumpled as if they had been opened and screwed up in anger, before being smoothed out again and stuffed out of sight.

Mower read and sorted and classified what he read with a sense of déjà vu, whistling occasionally under his breath at the size of the figures he uncovered. When put into date order the documents told an inexorable tale of climbing debt and diminishing income as half a dozen credit card limits were reached and the bank account slipped month by month deeper into the red. It was a slope Mower had slithered down himself once, though not as quickly or as comprehensively as Jimmy Townsend. He knew very well how hard it was to claw a way back up, juggling a minimum payment here and a placatory letter to the bank manager there. Just as Mower knew when he arrested many a villain that as a south London teenager his own life could have corkscrewed in the same direction once, he now felt a moment of sympathy for the young man with evidently expensive tastes he could not conceivably support much longer.

After half an hour or so he rang Chief Inspector Thackeray

to give him the registration number of Townsend's car. He had just pulled the log book for the white Ford Escort convertible out from beneath a heap of garage bills.

'How would he be paid as a negotiator, guv?' Mower asked.

'A basic salary and commission, I would guess,' Thackeray said. Mower glanced again at the receipts column of the bank statements.

'Yeah, that figures,' he said. 'The only trouble is the commission payments seem to have been withering away.'

'And he had no other income?'

'Oh, yes, he had some other income. Though there's no indication where it was coming from. He's been putting large sums of cash into his account at irregular intervals for the last couple of years.'

'How large?' Thackeray asked.

'Thousands,' Mower said.

'His cut from the mortgage deals, you think?'

'I wouldn't be at all surprised,' Mower said with some satisfaction.

'I'm sorry, Michael, really I am, but I just have to go to this "do",' Laura said. At the other end of the phone the silence deepened.

'It's work,' she said as quietly as her growing fury would allow. 'You know about work?' The sarcasm was more than justified, she told herself. Their increasingly distant relationship, emotionally as well as geographically, had been far more burdened by his erratic hours than hers.

'Right,' Chief Inspector Michael Thackeray said, and put the phone down.

'Shit,' Laura snapped at the ancient typewriter on which she was trying to compose her contribution to the High Clough accident story. After the high tech equipment she was used to at the *Gazette*, the keyboard felt arthritic and out of tune with her brain.

'Having problems?' Jonathon West asked solicitously, appearing silently at her side. He did not quite put a hand on her shoulder but Laura was aware of his oppressive closeness, and the elusive scent of his expensive aftershave, and knew that she was being deliberately harassed just the same.

'Just finding it hard to shift back fifty years in time,' she answered sweetly, determined not to move a millimetre in her chair. 'I'm surprised Reg doesn't arrive by Tardis. He looks a bit like Doctor Who.'

'Temper, temper,' Jonathon said, and Laura could see from his reflection in the window in front of her that he looked pleased. 'I take it you're going to this Christmas "do" at the Chamber of Commerce tonight? There's not much to be said for it apart from the rate at which the booze flows, but perhaps we could go on somewhere for a bite afterwards?'

'No thanks,' Laura said coldly. 'I'm going back to Bradfield afterwards.' It was not what she had planned, in fact what she had just refused to do, but West's advances reminded her just how much she wanted to see Michael Thackeray. She would swallow her pride and try to catch him later, she thought, wondering what sort of a fool she was.

'Don't get done for drunk driving, darling,' West advised, turning away, unaware that she could see his petulant expression of discontent reflected in the window.

At six Laura left the office and took a narrow flight of stairs to the top of the building where a couple of rooms Reg Fairchild dignified with the title The Flat had been put at her disposal. Their main purpose was to house snow-bound journalists during the winter when roads to the outlying villages sometimes became impassable and they could not get home. What was effectively a bedsitting-room, with a small kitchen and bathroom off, was furnished with what looked like the cast-offs of several previous generations of *Observer* staff: to call it Spartan would be an insult to the ancient Greeks, Laura thought irritably as she took a black dress from the whitewood cupboard which served as a wardrobe and held it up against herself critically.

She felt little enthusiasm for the 'do' Reg had insisted she attend this evening. It was a good chance to get to know everybody who was anybody in the town, he had said, and definitely not to be missed if she was to be use or ornament about the place for the next few months. The pained tone of voice indicated pretty clearly that he expected her to be neither.

Privately, she had to admit that if she were to make any progress with the more sensitive assignment David Ross had insisted she undertake while she was in Arnedale, a chance to mingle with the great and the good of the locality, and hopefully the not-so-good, was vital. She had spent some time that afternoon, after she had completed her report on the High Clough accident, flicking through recent copies of the *Observer* trying to get a feel for her new paper.

It was true enough, as Faith Lawrence had said, that Reg's weekly editorials gave little encouragement to the local Green campaigners. The *Observer* had backed the bypass around Arnedale and the widening of the Lancashire road; it had positively promoted the development of the new industrial estate on the edge of the town; it had welcomed almost anything that might boost the income of local farmers, like the introduction of more quarrying and tourism into previously tranquil areas of the national park.

Letters came in daily strongly challenging these views, as Laura had seen for herself as she had cast a curious eye over the mail, but they seldom appeared in print. And Laura knew that a whole world of opposition, reflected in Fergal Mackenzie's free sheet, which gave most of its space to protests and petitions and campaigns, got scant mention in the senior paper.

It could be, she thought, that Reg Fairchild was genuinely reconciled to the times, that he accepted that rural England had to change to survive. Or it could be, as the mysterious Fergal Mackenzie consistently implied, that his links with those making a fast buck out of change were stronger than they had any right to be. But if that were the case, Laura had found no evidence for it yet.

With an exasperated shake of her head, Laura slipped into her black dress and added a gold chain and ear-rings, and fastened her unruly cloud of red hair up severely. She looked at herself critically in the cracked bathroom mirror and smiled with some satisfaction at what she saw.

Her expectations were not disappointed when she arrived

at the Dales Gateway Hotel half an hour later with Reg Fairchild and Jonathon West. She was not the only woman there. But as she took off her coat and sized up the competition she was pleased to see that she was younger than the handful of others by more than a decade, lighter by several stone and, in a simple well-cut dress that she had brought back from Lisbon, out-classed them all.

Reg Fairchild was immediately welcomed into the throng of middle-aged men who, to judge by the heat they were giving off, had already been imbibing for some little time. He looked slightly out of place, like a skinny black crow amongst sleek, plump pigeons but obviously a welcome guest for all that. West stayed with Laura by the door for a moment, apparently taking stock with a slightly supercilious air.

'Shopkeepers, most of them, estate agents, *garagistes*, and the bigger farmers,' he said in a low voice. 'Not worth wasting your time on, most of them. The chap Reg is talking to is an interesting character, though: Dr John Priestley.' He indicated a corpulent man in a tweed suit, the waistcoat of which strained to constrain his enormous belly. 'Our local coroner. Master of hounds in his spare time. I feel sorry for the horse. Sometime chairman of the local Tory Party. If you want a channel to the local MP, he's your man.'

Laura said nothing, though she thought privately that the *Observer*'s channels to the local MP were far too wide already, and a point of contact with the local opposition might be more useful. She would not find it here, though, she was quite sure.

West took a glass of Scotch from a tray being handed round by a waitress and continued his survey of the crowded and jovial scene. There was much interest in a table at the far end of the room which was piled high with festive food. Laura took a gin and tonic and sipped it thoughtfully, aware that she was attracting not very surreptitious admiration from some of the men present, and glances of the deepest suspicion from members of her own sex.

'You don't get the smaller farmers at a do like this then?' she said. 'The High Clough people, for instance?' West shook his head dismissively.

'They're on their beam ends in those tiny villages. There's no money in sheep on that scale. You ask Barry Moore over there. He's the Moore of Cheetham and Moore, the auctioneers and estate agents. One of our biggest advertisers, of course. I should think he handles more bankruptcy sales than anything else these days amongst those small chaps. Well on the way to being a millionaire himself, they say. It's an ill wind, of course.'

Obviously aware of being discussed, Moore caught Laura's eyes across the room, and after a moment's frank appraisal, began to move in their direction. West made the introductions.

'I saw you at work when Reg took me down to see the cattle mart,' Laura said, sizing up the man she had only previously seen bundled up in a heavy sheepskin coat and brown trilby as he dispatched cattle and sheep at astonishing speed from the auction pens to the waiting lorries and trucks at his firm's market on the outskirts of the town.

He had looked at home there amongst the press of tweed-capped and muddy-booted farmers who stood impassively around the ring, a cloud of steamy breath and pipe smoke hanging over their heads, as they silently sized up the beasts on offer and made their bids with the faintest nod of a head or twitch of a finger. Here he looked more out of place, the face a touch too weather-beaten, the hands too gnarled, to complement his expensive suit and Liberty silk tie, and the heavy gold rings. If Barry Moore had made a bob or two, as the local expression was, it must have come late. He had not been born to it.

'You're not here for long, I hear,' Moore said, his welcoming smile not extending as far as his rather cold blue eyes, sunken beneath beetling sandy-grey brows.

'Just a temporary appointment to help out,' Laura said easily, giving the auctioneer one of her most seraphic smiles.

'And how temporary is that?' Moore persisted, evidently impressed by the smile, but not that impressed.

'Until Greg Winters recovers,' Jonathon West answered for her, and she was sure that she did not imagine the note of reassurance in his voice.

'Ah, yes, how is old Greg? A nasty business that,' Moore asked solicitously.

'He's to rest for two months at least,' West said, and again Laura thought she caught an unexpected nuance in the voice, the faint hope that the period of rest might be indefinitely extended.

'Aye, well, his replacement is certainly a lot more decorative than he is,' Moore offered jovially, undeterred by, or perhaps oblivious of, the significance of Laura's ironically raised eyebrow.

'The property business isn't on its uppers in Arnedale, then?' Laura asked, more aggressively than she intended.

'Up and down, my dear, up and down,' Moore conceded. 'But it's not sunk as far here as it has down south. They've had some real problems there, bankruptcies, redundancies, all that.' He patted her hand in a way which should have been fatherly but was not. Laura looked around for rescue and found none. Jonathon West had sidled away to join another conversation on the far side of the room.

'Now then, my dear, isn't it time you had something to eat and met some of our local notables?' Moore took Laura's elbow in a proprietorial grip and led her into the crush around the laden table. 'I think we've got some real caviare here. I told them to lay some on. And there's certainly smoked salmon, if these trenchermen haven't got there before us.' He thrust a plate into her hand and began to pile food on it.

'Between you and me, it's pearls before swine,' he said confidentially. 'Half of them wouldn't know caviare from ruddy cods' roe.'

Half amused, half mesmerised, Laura let Moore lead her around the room, hailing this member and that member of the throng, in a whirl of names and flushed faces which she knew she had not a chance of remembering the next day. Occasionally she caught sight of Reg Fairchild and Jonathon West deep in increasingly animated conversation as the drink flowed freely and mince pies and thick cream succeeded the canapés and smoked salmon and artichoke hearts, the thickly sliced roast beef and

60

turkey, the potato salad and coleslaw heavy with mayonnaise.

She was, she knew, being used as Moore's prize exhibit, the only remotely attractive woman in the room, being displayed by the peacock of a man at her side, but she let it ride, keeping her ears open for any interesting gossip which might give her a clue as to whether Reg Fairchild's contacts here were as innocent as they seemed.

But she picked up little of use, apart from the tail end of a conversation about the unwelcome arrival of Fergal Mackenzie and his free-sheet.

'I've not met this man Mackenzie yet,' she said casually to Moore. 'I don't suppose he's on your guest list?'

'Bloody right he isn't,' Moore said dismissively. His voice hardened perceptibly. 'The man's a menace: all bullshit and innuendo. He's going to get clobbered for libel if he doesn't watch it. There's a few people getting very sick of that vicious little rag, I can tell you.' He glanced round the room again expansively.

'Now you should meet the long arm of the law, my dear. You never know when you may need it.' Whether there was any link between his dislike of Mackenzie and all his works and his sudden interest in the police, Laura could not guess. She stifled a sudden reluctance to follow Moore and smiled bravely as he led her towards a stocky, sandy-haired man with a square, obstinate jaw, and hard, bright blue eyes.

'This is Les Thorpe, Detective Chief Inspector Thorpe, who's our local CID.' Laura turned on the smile again, feeling her face beginning to ache after hours of forced conviviality. The policeman nodded with more suspicion than enthusiasm.

'You're the lass who got hurt by that Thurston woman in Bradfield, aren't you?' he asked. Laura nodded, not much wanting to be reminded of an occasion when the painful physical battering she had taken had been the easiest part of a personal tragedy to bear.

'Poking your nose in where you shouldn't, weren't you?' Thorpe asked unsympathetically.

'Depends on your point of view,' Laura said sharply, regaining her composure.

'One of Michael Thackeray's cases,' Thorpe went on, pursuing the matter into avenues where Laura was even more reluctant to follow. 'He's doing well in Bradfield, I hear. Bounced back.'

'Back?' Laura said quietly.

'He were lucky to still be in the Force at all when he left Arnedale,' Thorpe said dismissively. 'I'd have had him out if I'd had any say.' Moore had been listening to this exchange with unusual intensity.

'Drink, wasn't it?' he asked.

'At the root of it, aye,' Thorpe said curtly. 'I must be off, Barry. Pass my thanks on, will you. A grand do, as usual. And all the best for the festive season if I don't see you again.'

Laura suddenly felt very cold in spite of the sticky fug that she knew had built up in the crowded room. She could feel the effects of too many gins clouding her brain and knew that whatever she had intended she should not drive back to Bradfield tonight. She saw Jonathon West pushing through the crowd to join her.

'Are you ready to go?' he asked.

'I'm tired,' she admitted.

'Still not interested in going on somewhere?'

Laura shook her head. 'Do you get what you want by sheer persistence?'

'Usually,' West said. 'What about it?'

'No, I've had enough for tonight, but I'd be glad of a lift back to the office,' Laura conceded.

'Your wish is my command, ma'am,' he said, but his smile was not reflected in his eyes.

SIX

LAURA FUMBLED FOR THE KEY to open the side door to the *Observer* building, a door which led directly onto the staircase and up to the flat on the top floor. She had not noticed the dark car parked a little further down the road until she saw the door open and a tall figure get out.

For a moment she froze, looking anxiously in both directions and realising that the rest of the ill-lit street was almost completely deserted. Peggy's café was dark and firmly locked up for the night. There was not even a glimpse of the tail-lights of Jonathon West's car. The only signs of life appeared to be around a fish and chip shop far more than shouting distance away. If she was going to get mugged, she thought, she was on her own and would have to use those self-defence techniques which had seemed so easy on the mat in a gym and seemed so unfeasible now. Her stomach clenched for a moment before she recognised Michael Thackeray.

'Christ, you frightened me,' she said, taken aback by the depth of her own nervousness.

'I'm sorry,' he said.

'Oh, Michael,' Laura said, putting her arms around him uninhibitedly and kissing him full on the lips. 'I am so glad to see you. I thought you wouldn't come up to Arnedale.'

Thackeray shrugged slightly guiltily and drew back, not returning her embrace.

'I've got a couple of hours off,' he said. 'Unless there's some major development. I'm on my way up to High Clough to see my father. He's thinking of selling the farm.'

'Ah,' Laura said, with her key still in the lock, aware, in

spite of the alcohol which was clouding her judgement, of the distance he had put between them.

'Do you want to come in? It's pretty primitive, this flat they've given me. A single bed which reminds me of the one I had when I was a student – distinctly hard and lumpy.' The hard and lumpy bed had not deterred her from asking her first serious lover to share it with her on occasions, she thought, but decided that was a confidence best not shared with Michael Thackeray in his present mood.

'Come for a walk,' he said abruptly, turning away and leaving her little option. Laura glanced down at her high-heeled shoes and the thin black dress underneath her coat and considered the problem of staying upright. She was holding the bottle of Scotch which Jonathon West had won in the tombola and thrust into her hands as she got out of his car. Not, in the circumstances, she thought, something she could easily hand to Thackeray to carry.

'A very little walk,' she prevaricated. 'That was quite a party.'

'The fresh air will do you good,' Thackeray said unsympathetically. They walked side by side without speaking down one of Broad Street's wide pavements, past the closed-up shop fronts and the bags of rubbish waiting for the early morning collection, past the Bull, which cast an orange glow of conviviality into the street, together with the sour smell of ale and the sound of laughter, past the chippy, patronised by a collection of skinny youths and girls in black leather jackets, and then down a narrow alleyway which would hardly have been noticed by anyone unfamiliar with the town. Beyond a stone archway the alley broadened out into a lane lined with stone cottages, most of them in darkness and apparently unoccupied. Thackeray looked at them hard in the dim orange light from a Victorian street lamp and laughed.

'This used to be Arnedale's red-light district when I was on the beat,' he said. 'Such as it was. A girl called Annie and another who called herself Dolores, although when she was at school she was plain Brenda. But these cottages were pigsties. I wonder how they got tarted up?'

The answer came on a discreet board at the end of the

terrace which advertised Boatman's Holiday Cottages to let through the agents, Cheetham and Moore.

'Why Boatman's?' Laura asked, feeling confused.

'This is why,' Thackeray said, taking her elbow and guiding her round the corner onto a broad cobbled quay overlooking the black waters of a narrow canal where several houseboats and a couple of motor cruisers were moored. 'But the last time I saw this they were still unloading coal here, would you believe? Direct from the last pit in Milford.'

They were more exposed now and the sharp wind from the hills cut through Laura's light coat, but was still not enough to blow the cobwebs from her brain. She shivered convulsively and Thackeray put his arm around her.

'What is this? A trip down memory lane?' she asked. He did not reply and they walked to the end of the quay and up onto a steep humpbacked bridge where Thackeray stopped and leaned against the stone parapet, staring down into the dark water. It was a view into chilly depths he recalled very clearly. Laura stood close to him, resting her bottle of Scotch on the top of the roughly hewn stones.

'I met Barry Moore at the party,' she said as much for something to say to break into Thackeray's tense silence as because she was interested in the thrusting auctioneer. 'Did you go to school with him as well as Dolores?'

'He's quite a bit older than me,' Thackeray said, wondering if it was pure coincidence that Laura had raised a name that had come up in his own investigation, but by no means averse to taking up a subject which did not impinge on what was really bothering him. 'I think he was there when I started. I knew him better through the church. It's funny, that firm has grown enormously since he took over. It was just a little tinpot agency in those days. Nothing special. Now it seems to be turning the town on its head, redeveloping this and that. I wonder if he's still the bully he was when he was a kid.'

'Oh, I should think so,' Laura said, recalling how he had taken possession of her at the party.

They stood for a moment in a silence which was not companionable, each lost in their own thoughts.

'There's a great row going on in High Clough about

reopening a quarry,' Laura said recklessly at last. The combination of drink and the cold night air was making her feel quite light-headed. It was time to stop tiptoeing around Thackeray's sensitivities, she thought. She felt rather than saw him stiffen slightly.

'Have you been up there?' he asked.

'This morning,' she said, and told him about the accident involving the school bus. He listened in silence.

'Did you meet my father?' he asked at last.

Laura took his arm.

'No,' she said. 'Though someone pointed out the house to me. Michael, if I'm going to work up here for two or three months I'm inevitably going to meet people who know you. I can't avoid it.' She hesitated, recalling with immense clarity given her fuddled state, the policeman she had already met and the precise words Les Thorpe had used about Michael Thackeray. She knew that the ice beneath her feet was as thin as the brittle film beginning to form on the black immobile water beneath the bridge.

'Don't pry, Laura,' Thackeray said. 'That's all I ask.'

'Then talk to me,' she cried out suddenly, exasperated. 'I can't cope with these endless silences.'

He did not answer directly but turned away and began to walk slowly down the other side of the bridge.

'I'm thinking of getting out of the Force,' he threw back over his shoulder suddenly. Laura gasped.

'To do what?'

'I may take over the farm from my father,' he said.

'You can't,' she said, horrified. 'You're much too good a policeman for that.'

'It doesn't look as though they're going to want chief inspectors any more. I may not have the choice of staying on.'

She hurried after him, unstable in her high heels on the steep cobbles of the bridge. As she caught up with him she slipped and lost her grip on the bottle of Scotch which fell and smashed on the pavement. Fumbling in the dim light she crouched down to try to pick up the pieces of broken glass, surrounded by fierce fumes which made her eyes fill with tears. She brushed them away angrily, afraid of the jumbled emotions which threatened to overwhelm her.

'Oh, damn and blast,' she said.

'Laura, Laura.' Thackeray crouched beside her and helped her to push the broken glass to the edge of the road, laughing in spite of himself. 'What am I going to do with you?'

'You could try marrying me,' she said, throwing caution to the winds in the stinging, heady atmosphere, almost as though she was swimming in a giant Scotch on the rocks.

'You wouldn't say that if you knew me better,' he said quickly, helping her to her feet and disentangling himself from her impulsive embrace. 'Come on, I'll take you back. I think the Christmas spirit has been flowing a bit freely tonight, hasn't it?'

'Maybe,' she said dully, allowing him to take her arm in a fatherly sort of grip which was not at all what her body cried out for. They walked back the way they had come in a heavy silence. Thackeray turned his mind quite deliberately away from Laura to assess, and to some extent admire, the effect Barry Moore was having on the face of old Arnedale, while Laura walked beside him, bitterly regretting any number of things she had said and done that evening.

As they turned back into Broad Street it was obvious that the last revellers were being turned out of the Bull and the other hostelries clustered at the bottom of the hill to serve the market by day. Most were getting into cars but one solitary figure was weaving its way unsteadily up the hill towards them, coatless and hatless but apparently impervious to the bitter wind.

Laura was aware of Thackeray's grip tightening on her arm and she wondered if it was someone he knew and would rather not meet. Then she realised that it could not be, because it was someone she knew. As Gerry Lawrence drew level with them he gave an even more pronounced lurch towards the edge of the pavement as he tried to steer himself around them, lost his footing and fell in the gutter just inches from their feet.

She heard Thackeray curse uncharacteristically under his

breath as Lawrence, apparently none the worse for his tumble, struggled into a sitting position and smiled deprecatingly in their direction.

'Lookin' for a cab,' he said, in a voice thick with alcohol, hands waving as if he were conducting an orchestra. 'Should be a cab rank up here but I can't seem to find it.'

'Is there . . . ?' Laura began, turning to Thackeray and surprised to find him backing away from Lawrence with an expression on his face she found hard to read.

'You look as though you've seen a ghost,' she said.

'Perhaps I have,' he said, his voice thick. 'I must go. The weather's worsening. It could be snowing in High Clough by now.'

'That's where he's going,' Laura said, nodding towards Lawrence who had by this time painstakingly regained his feet but, apparently exhausted by the effort, was leaning unsteadily against a lamppost. 'It's Faith Lawrence's husband. They live next to the church. I expect you know the house. She inherited it from an aunt.'

'Dora Long,' Thackeray said mechanically. 'It'll be old Miss Long's place.'

'Can't you take him up with you? She's a nice woman and she'll be worried sick about him. She doesn't deserve this.'

'No one deserves this, Laura,' Thackeray said with sudden bitter contempt. Quickly he moved towards Lawrence, put an arm round his waist and hitched his other arm round his neck and steered him down the street towards his car and dumped him without much ceremony into the back seat.

He hesitated for no more than a moment with the driver's door open.

'I'll call you,' he said.

'Right,' Laura said, almost inaudibly as the car pulled away. As the tail-lights receded down Broad Street and disappeared round the sharp turn at the end towards the Lancashire road she shrugged dispiritedly. Some Christmas this is going to be, she thought.

Laura threw herself into work the next morning to dull the pain and dissipate the hangover of the night before. That week's edition of the *Observer* was out, with her own and Jonathon West's emotive description of the High Clough accident dominating the news pages. There had been two fatalities, a twelve-year-old girl and the lorry driver. Two other children were still in hospital seriously ill but likely to survive.

'A follow-up?' Laura asked at the morning's editorial conference. 'What are huge lorries like that doing on those narrow country roads? How many farmers are selling off their dry-stone walls? What's that doing to the environment in the Dales?'

Reg Fairchild was leaning back in his chair looking at her with a curiously unenthusiastic expression as though she had walked into his office carrying an unwelcome smell with her.

'We've done all that before, Laura,' Jonathon West said dismissively. 'You can't stop farmers selling off their own property when they're up to their eyes in debt. Nor lorries using the public roads either. It was the bus that was at fault, reversing like that. The police say they're considering a charge against the bus driver.'

'There's still a lot of feeling up there,' Laura said obstinately. 'It would make a good feature. Faith Lawrence says . . .'

The name was like a red rag to a bull. The normally mild-mannered Fairchild reddened and made a sound like a dog snarling.

'That woman's a menace,' he said. 'What have you been listening to her for?'

'She helped pull those children from the wreckage,' Laura said sharply. 'Who else would I talk to?'

'She's a stranger to these parts, knows nowt, full of hot air,' Fairchild said. 'What right has she to come up here telling folk how to live their lives? The Dales managed very well before she blew in and they'll manage very well long after she and her kind have blown out again. There has to be some change, or there'll be no farming left in these villages, and no jobs, nowt but holiday cottages and commuters nose-to-tail down the dual carriageway to Leeds and Bradfield every morning.'

'Isn't that a story?' Laura came back, equally angrily. 'The two sides of that argument?'

'There's no two sides to it,' Fairchild said flatly. 'What I'd like you to do for next week's paper is some Christmas features. This'll be our main festive edition coming up. We'll only get a token issue out the following week on Christmas Eve. Have a look through the files, will you, and see what we did last year and the year before. That's what our readers expect, Laura, so that's what we'll give them. If David Ross wants summat different he can do me the courtesy of waiting till I'm gone. While I'm editor of this paper, I'll run it my way. You can tell him that, if you like. I really don't care one way or the other.'

Dismissed and slightly discomfited at how close to home Reg's last defiant gibe had hit, Laura went back through the main office and into the small back-room where the *Observer* kept its files. It was not a big enough paper to have a proper library. Bound volumes of the newspaper going back twenty or thirty years were stacked on strong wooden shelves, while boxes and brown cardboard folders of cuttings and background material spilled higgledy-piggledy from bookcases from floor to ceiling. Finding anything after an interval of more than a few months, without going to the trouble of leafing through the heavy bound volumes of the paper, would be almost impossible, she thought, knowing that her inclination to hunt back through the files more than twelve months had nothing whatsoever to do with Christmas.

With a guilty sigh, she took down last year's volume from the shelf, blew off the dust, and did as Fairchild had asked. She made a few desultory notes on the previous year's rehearsals for Handel's *Messiah*, offered annually by the local choral society. Arnedale evidently worked on the premise that no true-bred Yorkshire man or woman felt properly prepared for the turkey and trimmings without having ritually stood to attention through however ragged a rendering of the 'Hallelujah Chorus'.

She read through a dreary interview with the local MP on the prospects for local trade and employment in the New Year, although as she noticed that this had been written by

Reg Fairchild himself she doubted whether she would be allowed to set pen to notebook on anything as serious as that. And she almost nodded herself to sleep as she read. The previous night, alone in her narrow and lumpy single bed to her intense chagrin, had been a restless one as she tried to convince herself that she and Thackeray had a future together and failed.

'Damn the man,' she said aloud at last, closing the heavy volume with a thump and springing to her feet. She ran her finger lightly down the spines of previous years' papers, leaving a faint trail in the accumulated whitish dust until she came to the volume for ten years before. 'Don't pry,' he had said, and she had known even as he said it that it was a request she would ignore.

The chances of stumbling across something or someone from his past must be very high in such a small town, she told herself in self-justification. All the more reason to discover the truth dispassionately now, rather than find herself defenceless when faced with possibly shocking rumour or innuendo, as she had been last night.

Something dreadful had happened to Thackeray in Arnedale ten years ago when he lost his baby son, and until and unless she discovered what it was she could see no chance of getting any closer to the man than their present prickly and deeply unsatisfying liaison. It was a high-risk strategy, she thought, as she opened the file and cast her eye down the column of death notices on the back page of the edition of January 5th.

She found what she was looking for six months into the volume where four short lines of tiny type spelled out the tragedy which he had briefly told her about. Ian, beloved son of Michael and Aileen Thackeray, aged eight months, the Requiem Mass to be held at the Church of the Sacred Heart, Arnedale, later that week.

Seeing the stark announcement in black and white caused Laura an almost physical pain. She had, she knew then with unexpected clarity, absolutely no right to pry. She was playing with the stuff of Michael's soul and the fact that she loved him was no excuse. Stop now, she told herself, though she knew she couldn't.

71

SEVEN

MICHAEL THACKERAY HAD DRIVEN BACK to Bradfield from his father's farm that morning in a state of deep depression. After ten years during which he had kept his life on an even keel through a combination of grim resolve and physical distance, he now found himself torn apart by forces he thought he had renounced for good.

Not long after dawn at West Rigg Farm on the moorland edge of High Clough, he had stood at the window of his mother's bedroom gazing at the huddle of sheep on his father's thin frozen pastureland outside. He had been watching the old man, the collar of his duffle-coat turned up against the wind, a battered tweed cap pulled low over his eyes, forking fodder from a trailer towards the wind-blown flock of hardy little Swaledale ewes who had been brought 'inbye' for protection from the worst winter weather.

He had told his father the night before that he could not do what he wanted. And now he hated himself for rejecting those reticent pleas for help, made in the teeth of a fierce pride which bitterly resented the asking. Farming on these hills was a tough job at the best of times, and these were not the best of times. Prices were low, the ticks which plagued hill sheep had been desperately troublesome this year, Joe had complained. But the real problem, only too evident to a relative stranger's eye, was simply that Joe was no longer a young man. Even with a wife who was whole and fit he would find it hard to cope. And in the bed behind him, motionless under the quilt, Thackeray's mother Molly lay dying.

In one sense she had been dying ever since Michael had been told as a fourteen-year-old that she had multiple

72

sclerosis, a diagnosis which meant little to him then. Molly was a fighter and for years had tried to ignore her increasing disability but by the time Michael had come back from university she had been in a wheelchair.

Michael had never been able to please his parents. Reconciled to the fact that he would not take on the farm, they had hoped he would go into the Church and then, as they watched his faith freeze over as his mother's illness progressed, that he would become a teacher. Neither chastity nor pedagogy attracted him. He had married Aileen, his first love, and joined the police force as soon as he graduated.

Thackeray had seen his mother and father very seldom since his son Ian had died, driven from the family by pride on his side and prejudice on theirs as his marriage and very nearly his life had disintegrated. But the shock of finding the indomitable linchpin of his childhood, whose bright blue eyes and dogged determination he had inherited, reduced now to a wizened, grey old woman, had kindled a grief he could barely contain.

But in spite of the pleading in those still-bright blue eyes behind him, Thackeray knew that he could not do what his parents wished. Even with the police force in a turmoil of reorganisation and his own future inevitably insecure, the sight and sounds of West Rigg had filled him with despair. There was a narrow, unforgiving quality here, not just in his parents' own rigid beliefs but deeply embedded in a community which closed itself to strangers and held intractably to the absolute rightness of its prejudices.

I've seen too much and been through too much to fit back into this, he had thought, as he gazed down the hill at the huddle of stone roofs to each of which he could still infallibly attach a family name. Incomers were still rare enough to be a novelty in High Clough, and not a welcome novelty at that, unlike some of the more accessible Dales villages which had given themselves over to tea shoppes and holiday cottages with enthusiasm.

The alternative, if he would not or could not come back to West Rigg, Joe had said harshly, out of Molly's hearing, was to sell the land which had been held by the Thackerays for four generations. There were, he added, folk who wanted to buy it, though he doubted it was to raise the lambs which he had painstakingly nurtured here for a lifetime.

Thackeray had turned to kiss his mother goodbye but found her eyes were fixed not on him but on her bedside table where her rosary lay beside her missal. He sat beside the bed, picked up the beads and threaded them gently through her lifeless fingers, one by one, silently rehearsing each well-remembered prayer to give her time to recall the words herself. '*Ave Maria, gracia plena . . .*' He was surprised at how easily the boyhood Latin came back to him.

He felt weary to the roots of his being. If it helped her to think the ritual meant something to him he would not disabuse her. There was enough cruelty in the world, he thought, without his adding to it. He had heard Joe come back into the kitchen below, the wheezing as he struggled out of his boots, and the thump as each one hit the dirty linoleumed floor.

'I'll come again when I can,' he said to his mother, whose eyes, mutely pleading, clung to him as he crossed the room and went out and down the stairs. Joe was putting the kettle on, his shoulders bowed over the stone sink, the rattle in his chest still audible.

'It's reet middling out theer,' the old man said, watching his son put his coat on. 'There'll be more snow, I reckon.' He held a spill of paper to the coal-fire range and lit a Calor gas ring for the kettle.

'Tha'll do nowt to help, then?' he said.

'I'll do anything I can to help,' Thackeray said sharply. 'If it's money you need, you only have to ask.'

'Money?' the old man said. 'It's not just money is it? Though there's little enough of that. But it's another pair o'hands I need, more than money. I'm gettin' on, lad, and thi mother needs me more than t'sheep do right now.'

Thackeray sighed and looked away, refusing to meet his father's eye.

'I can't give up my job. It's what I am. It's what I want to go on being, if I can. The Thackerays and the O'Donnells may have been farmers for generations but I don't seem to have inherited the gene. I'm sorry.'

74

'So I should sell out to yon sharp beggar, Barry Moore, then?' the old man said angrily.

'To Barry Moore?' Thackeray exclaimed, surprised.

'Well, not to him as such, to his firm more like. He'll have some scheme in mind, I don't doubt. Didst'a ever know a time when that lad didn't have some scheme in mind?'

'Is he offering you a fair price?' Thackeray asked suspiciously.

'Oh, aye. Given t'state o't'market, not a bad price at all. There's nowt to be made out o'sheep now, tha knaws,' the old man said. 'We don't get paid for doing nowt wi't'land like these set-aside Johnnies wi'arable farms. They're cutting our subsidies.'

'Now you tell me,' Thackeray muttered wryly, having spent hours the previous night listening to his father extolling the virtues of the farm as a going concern. 'I expect Cheetham and Moore will want to turn the land into a golf course or something, won't they? There'll soon be more golfers on these hills than shepherds.'

'Summat like that,' Joe Thackeray said bitterly. 'There's two farms over Netherdale way just abandoned in t'last year or so. No one wanted them when t'owd folk passed away.'

'So why does Barry Moore want this place?' Thackeray asked, more to himself than to his father, who was busy pouring boiling water into his old brown teapot.

The old man put it down on the heavy table, indented with years of accidental knocks and slashes and scratches from generations of careless Thackerays. It stood in the centre of the room where it had always stood, a monument to a family and a way of life which Thackeray and his father would both mourn in their own ways but he guessed they were utterly powerless to preserve. Thackeray accepted a mug of the dark tannic brew.

'I must get back to Bradfield,' Thackeray said slowly. 'I'm in the middle of a murder investigation. I can't be away any longer.'

'Aye, well, happen it's all for t'best. Tha'st made thy own bed. Tha'd best lie on it.' The old man had dismissed him without another word but Thackeray had been conscious of his eyes following him as he manoeuvred his car out of the snow-covered yard and out onto the lane.

There was, Thackeray thought, as he slipped the car into fifth as he reached the dual carriageway on the approach to Bradfield, no end to betrayal. He had never been able to satisfy his parents from the days when he roamed the hills around the farm letting his mind explore the ways he might escape from their suffocating embrace. This latest disappointment was just one more for them, disillusion piled on disillusion. But with Laura, he thought, it could have been different. With Laura he had perceived the possibility of a new beginning, the faintest glimmer of hope for himself, until panic had overwhelmed him the previous evening and he had seen her flinch from his rejection.

He put his foot on the accelerator and the speedometer flickered to eighty, as he switched his mind back to work, and the problem in hand, the unremitting challenge with which he filled his mind and blotted out the rest. If that went too, he thought, easing his speed back, he really would go mad.

Mower met him at the door of the incident room, dark eyes alight with triumph.

'They found some prints on the car, guv,' he said. 'Two hands, on the boot, where the bastard pushed it into the water.'

'Have they got a match?' Thackeray asked.

'Not yet, not from records, but I've sent what we found at Townsend's flat for comparison. Odds on they're his.'

'Time to tell the Press we'd like to talk to Mr Townsend, I think,' Thackeray said. 'I'll see Jack Longley about that.'

'He'll not get far,' Mower said. 'Unless he's got his pockets bulging with cash from somewhere, he's not got enough funds in his bank to fill his car with juice. He's skint.'

In the Church of the Sacred Heart, Father Frank Rafferty watched curiously as a slim young woman he did not recognise, her bright copper-red hair catching the coloured flashes of sunlight from the narrow stained-glass windows, wandered round his church as if looking for something. She was not a Catholic, that was obvious from the way she ignored the Sacrament reserved in the chapel to one side of the high altar. She neither bowed her head nor genuflected as she passed it. She screwed her nose up slightly at the unfamiliar smell of incense. She walked about thoughtfully, trailing a hand along the oak pews and glancing with some curiosity at the statue of the Virgin and Child and the Stations of the Cross as she went slowly by.

She paused only long enough to read the memorial tablets on the walls, and there were few enough of those. This was a modern church, built of pale concrete, spartan in its decoration and spare with its short history.

At the elegant wrought-iron gates of the Lady Chapel, a present from a local craftsman, she paused and Father Rafferty thought he heard her sigh. She stood for a moment by the flickering candles, looking at the half-dozen memorials there, all of them dedicated to children. She did not hear the priest come up behind her, his tread professionally soft, his cassock barely rustling, making no draught in the cold still air.

'Can I help you, my dear?' he asked quietly and was surprised at how quickly she turned and how startled she looked, like an animal taken unawares, or perhaps guilty.

'I don't think so,' Laura said, feeling her cheeks flush as if she had been caught in some childish misdemeanour. 'Unless . . .'

'Unless?'

'Unless you were here ten years ago, when Michael Thackeray's son Ian died?'

'Ah,' Rafferty said. 'And who would be asking?'

'Just a friend,' she said, and it was obvious to them both that he did not believe that was all she was.

'A friend of the family?' he asked. She shook her head.

'A friend of Michael's. I don't know his family.'

'Or his history, evidently,' Rafferty said. He hesitated for a moment, taking in Laura's pale beauty, the red hair which reminded him of a Dublin girl he had once admired and still dreamed of, and her frank grey-green eyes which pleaded with him for what she did not quite dare ask for, and he was filled with pity for her.

'If you're a friend of Michael's you must ask him what you want to know,' he said quietly. 'I can't help you.'

'Because you're his priest?'

'I was his priest. I don't think Michael calls on the services of priests any more,' Rafferty said.

'Since that happened?' Laura said, glancing behind her to where the memorial to Ian lay bathed in soft candle-light under the placid gaze of the statue of the Virgin. Rafferty did not answer, merely giving the slightest inclination of his head, which she took as agreement. Laura shook her head wildly at that.

'I can't get through to him,' she said. 'He won't talk about it, and it's breaking me apart . . .'

'I can't help you, my dear,' the priest said. 'I'll pray for you, for both of you. I would help if I could, but I can't break confidences, which is what you're asking. I can't tell you what you want to know. Only Michael can do that.'

Laura turned on her heel and walked swiftly out of the church without looking back. Rafferty watched her go with an expression of sadness, bitterly aware that when Laura discovered what she sought it would not be what she wanted to hear.

Why, he wondered, not for the first time, if God had wanted Man to be faithful, had He made the human heart so wayward? And why was it always the innocent who were hurt? Ian Thackeray had been the first to suffer because of Michael Thackeray but would evidently not be the last.

EIGHT

FAITH LAWRENCE SOUNDED BREATHLESS WHEN she called Laura Ackroyd at work early the next morning.

'There's all hell let loose at the travellers' site,' she said. 'Ray Harding's trying to evict them. There's a good story in it for you if you get up here quickly.'

Reg Fairchild looked dubious when Laura relayed the message to him but could find no adequate reason for refusing to let her go to High Clough to see what was going on. Jonathon West was out on another assignment and even Reg had to admit that the paper's trainee reporters were too inexperienced to handle what could turn out to be a violent confrontation.

'It's not our sort of story,' Fairchild prevaricated even as Laura was putting on her coat and boots. 'Our readers have no sympathy for those layabouts. They'd help evict them, most of them, given half a chance to get stuck in.'

'What happened to live and let live, then?' Laura asked irritably, but did not wait for an answer. She knew what it would be.

She put her foot down hard up the winding hill to High Clough, and found herself following a police patrol car with blue light flashing for the last mile of the journey, across the bridge, up the village street and over the half-mile of open country to the quarry. I'll qualify as a rally driver by the time I've finished my stint up here, she thought grimly as she braked hard and spun slightly on the last bend. She pulled in to the side of the road behind the police and followed two uniformed constables down the steep, narrow track into the quarry proper.

There confusion reigned. A heavy tractor was parked across the track, effectively preventing entrance or exit by any other vehicle. Beyond that the travellers' trucks and caravans, and an ancient bus painted blue and bright yellow were parked in a defensive circle. The scene was eerily reminiscent of all those films featuring a wagon train defending itself against Red Indian marauders. The only difference here, Laura thought wryly, was that most law-abiding citizens would be likely to see the roles reversed, with the 'savages' on the inside looking out, the 'good guys' outside looking in.

There was evidently some sort of heated exchange going on behind the tractor where a gesticulating huddle of people broke into two groups as the forces of the law approached. Laura recognised the tall figure of Rob Tyler and was faintly amused to see that it was he who strode confidently towards the police officers, with a straggle of unkempt men and women and dogs behind him. Most of the camp's children seemed to be watching events from the safety of the inner circle of vehicles.

'I'm glad you're here,' Tyler said expansively, taking in Laura as well as the policemen in his greeting. 'We have a problem with Mr Harding and his tractor.'

At the mention of his name, a stocky, belligerent-looking man with a mop of startling gingery hair also strode forward and began berating the police

'I want them off my land,' he said flatly. 'I brought t'tractor to tow 'em out. I want them gone by tea-time or I'll not be responsible for what happens. The whole village is fed up to t'teeth wi' 'em: hippies and layabouts and little hooligan brats. They've got to go. It's my land and I know my rights.'

'Mr Harding knows that I have an agreement with him which allows us to stay here for the winter . . .' Tyler began, only to be interrupted by Harding, who was backed up now by a phalanx of angry supporters, some of whom were carrying ugly-looking sticks.

'Bugger that,' Harding said. 'I never gave permission for all this lot. Every time I turn around there's another bloody van on t'site. Any road, things have changed. I've got other plans now for t'land. It's not surplus to requirements any more.'

Laura heard a sharp intake of breath just behind her and turned to find Faith Lawrence and Tim standing on the track, hanging on Harding's every word and looking indignant.

'So it's true then,' the boy said. 'He does want to reopen the quarry.'

'That's what I was afraid of,' Faith said to Laura quietly. 'Until now it was just rumour. Apparently he doesn't need planning permission, he can just re-start operations as and when he wants. How many more children are going to be killed when dozens of lorries start coming up and down through the village every day?'

Laura took out her notebook and began to jot down everything she had heard so far, an action which evidently did not meet with the whole-hearted approval of Ray Harding.

'Who the bloody hell are you?' he asked, breaking away from the heated conference which was still going on around the policemen, and making a thrusting grab at her notebook, which she easily evaded.

'I want nowt in the *Observer*,' he said flatly when she told him. 'It's between them and me. Nowt to do with anyone else, so you can get off my land for a start. And you, Mrs Lawrence. I don't want you poking your nose in neether.'

'What goes into the *Observer* isn't really up to you, Mr Harding,' Laura began reasonably enough, although the comment seemed to reduce Harding to an almost apoplectic rage. His face turned an uncomfortable shade of puce and he clenched his hands in impotent fury, obviously aware that lashing out at a woman would not do his case much good with the forces of law and order who were glancing in his direction.

'We'll see about that,' he said, turning on his heel and marching back towards the policemen as if to enlist their aid. The whole group turned towards the two women and after a brief altercation one of the constables approached Laura, followed by Rob Tyler.

'Harding isn't going to get us out just now,' Tyler said, nodding a greeting to Faith and her son, with a guarded look in his eyes which Laura did not quite understand.

'And I'm told that if I invite you into my van then there is nothing he can do about that either, so you're duly invited.' He grinned disarmingly, apparently unworried by the seething resentment of the group of local men only yards behind him.

'If he wants to overturn our agreement he's going to have to go to law to do it,' he went on. 'In the meantime, of course they've tried a bit of illegal harassment. We had bricks thrown through half a dozen windows last night. Par for the course, but it frightens the kids so I've made a formal complaint to the police. They won't do anything, of course, but it might just deter the yobs for a few nights. You never know. Come and have a look. It'll make you a good story.'

With total self-assurance Tyler put a protective arm around both of the women and shepherded them past the still furiously arguing group around the policemen and towards the circle of caravans and trucks. Tim Lawrence followed close on their heels and as he approached the circle of vehicles two young children ran towards him and clung around his knees.

'Melody and Flint,' Tyler said to Laura by way of introduction. There was no need to explain that they were his. Their looks proclaimed it. Within the protective circle were other women and children, most of them bundled up in a weird assortment of more or less tattered clothes worn layer on layer in a jumble of prints and plaids and hand-knitting. Rob led the way towards his converted bus, painted a cheerful blue and yellow, which was leaning slightly, one of its tyres evidently flat.

'They let that down,' he said, pointing to the puncture. 'How they expected to get us off the site in that state I can't imagine. And the windows – look.' He pointed to the windscreen of the bus which had been shattered on the driver's side. 'And there.' There were similar holes, roughly boarded up with cardboard and paper in several of the side windows. 'I think they're trying to freeze us out if all else fails.'

'Was anyone hurt?' Faith asked anxiously. 'Topaz is all right?'

82

'Topaz?' Laura asked.

'My partner,' Rob said, somewhat dismissively, Laura thought. He turned back to Faith as if reassuring her was his first priority. 'Yes, we're all fine,' he said. 'We sleep at the far end and they left that alone, although not for reasons of human kindness, I shouldn't think. When I heard the sound of breaking glass I got my shotgun and fired into the trees. That scared them off.'

'Was that wise, Rob?' Faith's anxiety evidently magnified itself at that, as she looked at the small tribe of young children who had gathered around them, eyes large with curiosity. 'You don't want to start a war.'

'We're not the ones who are starting a war,' he said. The two women's eyes met with the same thought: the travellers might not be starting the war but they were undoubtedly the ones who would lose it in the end.

Sitting across her kitchen table, to which she had invited Laura for yet another cup of tea, Faith Lawrence looked tired and drained. She pushed the fine silver-grey hair away from her face. Today, Laura thought, she looked her age.

'It will get more violent, that's what frightens me,' she said. 'There are an awful lot of children up there. Someone could get seriously hurt. And Tim hero-worships Rob. He spends half his time up at the camp. I'm half-afraid he'll go off with them when they move on. He's up to his eyes in ecology, green issues, you name it . . .'

'Village life,' Laura said, looking round the stone-flagged kitchen where the cats stretched luxuriously by the ancient Aga. 'It looks attractive but there seems to be all hell bubbling away beneath the surface.'

'It's not what I ever wanted,' Faith said sharply. 'It's a case of needs must. It's all been a complete disaster, if you must know.' She flushed slightly, obviously feeling she had said too much that was too personal. Laura smiled reassuringly.

'Tim gave me some idea. I gave him a lift up to the travellers' site.'

'He's a very unhappy boy and there's nothing I seem to be able to do to help,' Faith said. 'He walked out of school,

83

there are no jobs, he's bitterly angry with his father . . .' She shrugged. 'Perhaps the best thing would be if he did go away for a while. It would give me and Gerry time to straighten things out – if we can.'

She crumbled a biscuit between her fingers onto the table-top with an expression of near despair in her eyes.

'Talk, if it helps,' Laura said. 'I don't suppose there's anything I can do, but you know what they say about troubles shared.'

'I never thought reporters were like you,' Faith said. 'The only other journalist I've ever known was a smooth young man from the *Daily Telegraph* I met at the races at Ascot. Eton and Christ Church or something like that. You know the type? One of those who think the world owes them a living and that women owe them a favour. Gerry's firm had a box, corporate hospitality, all that stuff . . .' Her voice trailed away and she glanced around her kitchen with a look which was eloquent with regret for what she had lost.

'How did you get interested in the environment, then?' Laura asked. The background of the corporate wife which Faith had just sketched did not seem to mesh with her currently green concerns.

'By chance really. I had a friend who was head of a girls' school near where we were living and they wanted to run a link road to the M25 right through the grounds. It was such a philistine thing to do, across one of the most beautiful valleys in the area, I just got very angry and helped her with her campaign. We organised petitions and waved placards and a few brave souls lay down in front of the bulldozers. The travellers and hippies turned up, of course, from all over southern England, and got arrested and outraged the locals. That's where I first met Rob Tyler and Topaz. The planners took no notice, but it all seemed worth doing at the time.'

'And then you came to Yorkshire?'

'And then we had to come to Yorkshire,' she corrected, a touch of her normal asperity creeping back into her voice. 'Don't let's mince words, Laura. This house was our salvation. If it hadn't been for Aunt Dora dying when she did we'd have been out on the street.'

'The Lloyd's crash?'

'Oh, that was just the last straw. Gerry was on the skids long before that: friends and colleagues covering up for him, bouts of diplomatic flu when he drank himself insensible, the rows, the bottles hidden in the sock drawer, in the tool shed, you name it, the self-pity, the promises to give it up . . . I'm sorry, I'm not very good at the loyal wife bit any more. It's been going on too long.

'Originally I planned to come up here with Tim. Leave Gerry to find his own salvation when the house in Surrey had to be sold. But he discharged himself from the clinic where he was supposedly drying out, two days before we were due to move. I put him in the back of the car and brought him with me. A bit like a family dog you can't bear to part with.' She laughed without much humour.

'Is he getting treatment now?' Laura asked.

'He tells me he's going to AA meetings. He's lost his driving licence, of course, so he gets the bus down to Arnedale, but more often than not he comes back smelling of booze. He seems to be able to scrounge a lift back, usually. Some complete stranger brought him home the other night. Said he was Joe Thackeray's son. Had found him in Broad Street and brought him home. So I don't really know what he's doing down there, what to believe. He's shifty, evasive, you know what alcoholics are like.'

'Not really,' Laura said, appalled by what Faith was telling her and by the possibility, probability even, that this was the road Michael Thackeray had travelled too.

'What I would like to know is where he's getting the money from to drink,' Faith went on, the words flooding out now she had begun, oblivious of the effect she was having on Laura. 'It's certainly not from me. I'm running this place on the little bit of capital my aunt left me along with the house. But that won't last long. Very soon I'm going to have to get a job, or we'll starve.'

'I'm sorry,' Laura said, feeling helpless.

'Don't be,' Faith said. 'I'll get by. I don't give in easily. And there are some compensations up here, I've found.' She smiled a satisfied smile but did not elaborate further.

'In the meantime,' she said, 'let me tell you about the next stage of our campaign to stop Ray Harding reopening that quarry.'

Laura dutifully took notes about Faith's plans to join up with other anti-quarrying campaigners in other parts of the Dales. It was a good solid everyday story of protesting folk, the sort of campaign which had erupted across rural England as previously remote areas had been opened up by new roads and motorways to commuting and holidaying home-buyers, and established communities, threatened by the economic blizzard of the late 1980s, had sought desperately for new means of turning an honest penny.

She was about to go when the kitchen door opened and to her surprise the traveller, Rob Tyler, walked into the room with the familiarity of a frequent visitor. He seemed surprised to find Laura still there and for a moment Faith seemed to lose her composure.

'I came to tell you Tim has decided to stay up at the camp tonight,' Tyler said, his dark eyes amused now. He stood for a moment with a hand lightly on Faith's shoulder and she glanced up at him with a warmth which said all that needed to be said about the compensations she had found in High Clough.

'I must go,' Laura said, embarrassed by the intimacy that so clearly existed between them.

'Not on account of us,' Tyler said.

'On account of my editor.'

'Who probably won't print a word of what we've told you this afternoon,' Faith said drily.

'We'll see about that,' Laura promised.

Neither woman was entirely right. Reg Fairchild leaned back in his chair with his eyes half-closed and listened impassively to Laura's account of the confrontation at High Clough.

'It used to be genuine gypsies who stayed in these parts on their way to Appleby horse fair,' he mused. 'There'll be a chapter on them in my book.'

'Your book?' Laura said, startled.

'I'm writing a history of the Dales,' Fairchild said sharply. 'Though I doubt I'll get it finished until I retire. There's a wealth of oral history still in these remote villages, if you take the trouble to look for it.'

'I'm sure,' Laura muttered. 'But about this story . . .'

'*They're* not gypsies,' Fairchild said, returning sharply to the here and now. 'They're scrounging layabouts. Parasites. Did you get the farmer's side of the story? We can run it along the lines of an attempt to get rid of a threat to the local environment, with Harding as the local hero.'

'Harding's not a hero, he's a thug,' Laura said flatly.

'Aye, well, perhaps he's got a lot to be angry about. His brother blew his head off with a shotgun last Michaelmas because he couldn't make ends meet. Had a farm up Netherdale.'

Laura paused for a moment, but only for a moment.

'Throwing bricks through windows onto sleeping children could be lethal,' she persisted.

'Do we know Mr Harding threw the bricks?'

'Well, no,' Laura had to admit.

'Then what you are suggesting is defamatory. You should know that.'

Laura flushed. Fairchild was right and if she had been thinking more clearly about the events at High Clough she would have been well aware of that danger. It was only Rob Tyler's assumption that Harding was involved in the midnight harassment of the camp. No one had seen the assailants who had come and gone in pitch darkness. She cursed herself silently for a fool and knew she had weakened her own case irretrievably.

'Talk to Harding and get his side of the story,' Fairchild said. 'We'll give it a couple of paras. Then you'd better get on with the Christmas features.'

Furious with herself as much as Fairchild, Laura went back to the cramped and untidy desk she had inherited from Greg Winters. From across the room, Jonathon West gave her a malicious smile, as if fully cognisant that she had not got what she wanted out of her interview with the editor.

There were two scribbled messages on her typewriter, one asking her to telephone Ted Grant at the *Gazette* in Bradfield, the other simply with the name Thackeray and a local Arnedale number. The writing was West's and Laura knew that he was watching her intently.

She took the easiest call first. Ted was short and sharp, which was entirely predictable, and his instructions unwelcome, which was not – quite. David Ross was expecting a call from her, he said, by the end of the week. He was looking for results.

She broke the connection irritably and dialled the number Thackeray had left. A voice she did not know answered, a broad country voice, suspicious and unhelpful.

'He's bin and gone,' Joe Thackeray said. 'Gone back to Bradfield. Who's that?'

'Just a friend,' Laura said, although she sometimes wondered if she was even that.

'What's the name?' the old man persisted, but she hung up without answering and sat staring at the phone for a long time. West broke into her private thoughts with his usual directness.

'Have you seen this?' he asked, flicking a rolled-up paper across the room at her. Laura unfolded it slowly. It was the free-sheet, *Inside Info*, which appeared erratically, usually a few days before the *Observer* itself was published. The headline was the one she had wanted for herself: Quarry Threat to High Clough. And the story was the one she had wanted to write. But there was more. According to Fergal Mackenzie there was new speculation in the village that another farm was about to be sold to a mystery developer. The land in question was at West Rigg and belonged to Joe Thackeray.

Laura groaned, and West gave her a look of triumphant sympathy.

'Same Thackeray, is it?' West pressed remorselessly, his eyes flicking to the message he had taken for her.

'It's a common name round here,' she snapped. 'But this makes us look ill-informed.' She gestured at the free paper.

'Rubbish. No one's interested in these campaigns. The locals will be queuing up for jobs in the quarry,' he countered. 'They're not interested in the Greens and their airy-fairy nonsense.' He turned away and pecked half-heartedly at his typewriter for a while before renewing his assault.

'What are you doing for Christmas?' he asked, leaning confidentially towards her and speaking in a low whisper.

'What's it to you?' Laura replied, more sharply than she really intended, guiltily aware that she had made no preparations for the festivities which she would spend with her grandmother as usual. It was not a prospect which filled her with enthusiasm this year, mainly because she had not found the courage to ask Michael Thackeray what he would be doing, fearing one of his unpredictable and numbing rebuffs. West seemed to pick up her uncertainty because he persisted.

'I thought you might like to come up to my uncle's place. There's always a big party there, turkey and plum pud, carol singers, a bit of beagling on Boxing Day, all very traditional and jolly.'

'If I saw a beagle I'd be more likely to sabotage it than follow it,' Laura said tartly. 'I can never understand why you wildlife lovers can't leave the wildlife alone.'

'And I can't understand why you townies persist in interfering in what you evidently don't understand,' West snapped back.

'It's a kind thought but I'm spoken for at Christmas,' Laura said placatingly. She had, after all, to work with this insufferable young man and nothing would be gained by getting involved in overt hostilities.

'Ah,' West said knowingly. 'Say no more.'

Laura gritted her teeth, swallowed her pride and took his advice. This time.

NINE

FERGAL MACKENZIE WAS A HAIRY man. He peered at the world from beneath a thatch of thick, grizzled, dark curls and an equally thick bushy beard with bright knowing eyes that looked as though they had seen it all before and then some. Even his hands were hairy and Laura could imagine that if he ever divested himself of his grubby denim shirt his arms and chest would be equally thickly furred. If he had revealed pointy ears she would not have been too surprised.

But Mackenzie, whom she had tracked down in the tumbledown stone-terraced cottage in an unreconstructed lane near the canal where he evidently both lived and worked, was no fool. Amongst the piles of books and papers on his desk stood the latest in computer technology with all the electronic trimmings which could, and evidently did, link him to the outside world.

'To what do I owe the pleasure of a visit from the *Observer*?' he asked, the Scottish accent less pronounced than she had expected, more Edinburgh than Glasgow, the eyes gleaming impishly.

'If they find out I've been to see you I'm likely to be out of a job,' Laura said flatly, knowing that once she had crossed his threshold she was putting her future in his hands.

'Ah,' he said knowingly. He waved her towards a battered maroon plush armchair which in its better days would not have looked out of place in a Victorian house of ill-repute. 'Do I gather from that you are not an unqualified admirer of the sainted Reg Fairchild?'

'You could say that,' Laura said, with a faint smile.

'Any particular reason?' Mackenzie asked with a lack of

guile which was clearly feigned. His resemblance to a garden gnome was only heightened by this assumed innocence.

'I thought you might be able to give me a reason. You're dropping enough hints. How come you swan in from points north and sniff out local scandals that no one else seems to have noticed before? What are you doing here anyway?'

'Questions, questions,' Mackenzie teased, with a smile that could have belonged to a particularly fierce pussy-cat or a fairly benevolent tiger. 'I'll tell you a story,' he said. 'Are you sitting comfortably?'

Laura grinned, disarmed in spite of herself, settled herself back in the sagging plush and arranged her skirt decorously over her knees. There was no need, she thought, to give a man who would likely grab a mile if encouraged even half an inch.

'Once upon a time,' Mackenzie said, in all seriousness, 'there was an emperor who needed a new suit of clothes . . .'

'I know that one,' Laura countered.

'Well, what about the one about the little girl in the red hood whose grandmama lived in the woods . . . ?'

'Heard that one, too,' Laura said. 'How about a classical one: the nice wooden horse that the citizens pulled into Troy . . . ?'

'Very good,' Mackenzie said. 'And the moral is?'

'If you don't ask questions, the right questions, you are liable to be taken for a ride, if not gobbled up completely?'

'Exactly. I came to Arnedale six months ago quite by chance. I'd been running a radical weekly up in Scotland for years and it had folded so I decided to head south on my redundancy money. I stayed with a friend in Netherdale for a couple of weeks and started reading the Arnedale *Observer* and I couldn't help noticing that no one around here was asking the right questions, or any questions, come to that.'

'About?'

'About anything much. But in particular, about why this town is being ruined by inept redevelopment which seems to cock a snook at the planning laws, tramples over a national park, and looks set to repeat all the worst mistakes

91

of the sixties in the supposedly environmentally friendly nineties.'

'People are asking questions,' Laura said. 'The letters coming into the *Observer* are full of protests. They just don't get printed.'

'Nor do the views of the politicians and campaigners whose faces don't fit with the people who pull the strings around here. At least they didn't, until I turned up and gave them a voice.'

'Making yourself very unpopular in the process,' Laura said, thinking of Barry Moore's threats against Mackenzie at the Christmas party.

'Oh, aye, I dare say,' Mackenzie said. 'But if you're doing your job properly you don't expect to be popular, do you? Surely you've learned that by now if you're any sort of reporter.'

Laura nodded, thinking that it was an uncomfortable maxim that Ted Grant, who pulled no punches in Bradfield, would certainly subscribe to. She glanced at Mackenzie's bookshelves, recognising a few Marxist titles she had been impressed by herself as a student.

'And it all furthers the cause, I suppose,' she suggested. 'I wouldn't have thought revolutionary cadres were much in evidence in the Yorkshire Dales.'

'It's a long march, comrade,' Mackenzie said. 'A long march.' It was a topic he was evidently reluctant to pursue. 'And the next question is, Ms Ackroyd?'

Laura fell in with him again.

'Why are the protests not getting covered in the *Observer*, Mr Mackenzie?' she asked.

'Very good, Ms Ackroyd.' Mackenzie's face darkened suddenly and he dropped his bantering tone.

'If I knew that, I'd have published it. So in that sense, you're wasting your time. I don't sit on information. If I can prove it, I print it.'

'And what can't you prove yet?' Laura came back quickly.

'That Barry Moore is buying and bullying his way to becoming a millionaire – at least. Worse perhaps. And one of the people he is either buying or bullying is your esteemed editor. But I should think that's just a side-show, keeping the

Press sweet. Probably goes down under the heading of public relations on his tax return.'

'I need to prove it,' Laura said.

'*You* need to prove it?' Mackenzie said, surprised.

'Contrary to what you might think, the company isn't too chuffed at having its editors bought or bullied,' she said.

'So that's why you're here,' Mackenzie said, with a malicious grin. 'I thought it was a bit odd bothering to replace Greg Winters. The amount of news the *Observer* actually prints could be written by Reg and a couple of trained chimpanzees.'

'Ouch,' Laura said.

Mackenzie stretched luxuriously and tapped a few words into his computer.

'Reg Fairchild,' he said as text flashed up onto his screen. 'I've got a list of subjects he's written leaders on over the last twelve months and his stance. The bypass – straight through a watermeadow of special scientific interest, incidentally – "vital to Arnedale's future prosperity" – the extension to the industrial estate – "jobs boom for Arnedale" – the boom hasn't happened yet, needless to say – a golf course and leisure complex at Netherdale – "exciting new opportunities for the Dales". That was Ray Harding's brother's place, incidentally. Cheetham and Moore bought it for a development company after Dave Harding shot himself. The inquest is on Friday, as it happens. That should be interesting. Planning permission went through on the nod though I guess they paid agricultural prices for the land – in other words, next to nothing, given the state of the market for sheep.'

'Cheetham and Moore are major advertisers in the *Observer*. The paper survives on its property ads.'

'There's that. Withdrawing their ads is a weapon they wouldn't hesitate to use if it suited them, I'm sure,' Mackenzie agreed.

'Do you think that's all it is?'

'Oh, no, not all, not by a long way. My main query about Barry Moore is not whether he's breaking the law but how.'

'He seems to be on quite good terms with the law,' Laura

offered, remembering DCI Les Thorpe. 'At least with the head of CID.'

'Does he now? That's something I didn't know,' Mackenzie said cheerfully, tapping at his keyboard again. 'That deserves a favour in return.' He pulled out a bottle of Scotch from a drawer and when Laura nodded poured two generous measures. 'What do you want to know?' he asked.

'Everything you've got on Reg,' she said quickly, before her scruples got the better of her or, even worse, she was diverted into an inquiry she had even less right to pursue. Mackenzie took a healthy swig of Scotch and turned back to his screen, activating a printer which began to churn out page after page of close-typed script.

'It looks like a biography,' Laura said.

'Oh, believe me, it is,' Mackenzie said. 'I've got a large proportion of the population of Arnedale in here. Wonderful the connections you can make with a good data program.'

'Isn't that dangerous?' Laura said seriously. 'Anyone who found out about it could wipe it.'

'Don't worry,' Mackenzie said. 'I'm not as daft as I look. It's all backed up and the disks stashed away where not even someone as well connected as Barry Moore could find them. What did you make of Faith Lawrence, by the way, when you were up in High Clough? I noticed from your story on the accident that you interviewed her.'

Laura hesitated. She had no doubt that whatever gossip she passed on would be duly recorded in Mackenzie's computer for future reference.

'A very tough lady with a messy family life,' she said shortly.

'Aye, I fell over her husband one night in Broad Street – literally. You don't get many drunks as blatant as that down here. Edinburgh on a Saturday night in the old days was something else.'

'She thinks he's coming into Arnedale to get treatment,' Laura said, recalling her own encounter with the vertically-challenged Gerry Lawrence.

'She may think that. My impression is that there are people who prefer to keep him well oiled and a useful source of information about what his wife's getting up to. Poor bastard probably doesn't even realise he's being used. All good pals together in the Con Club I'm told.'

Laura drained her glass and stood up.

'You're very well informed,' she said coolly.

'Aye, and so should you be if you're going to survive and prosper in this town,' Mackenzie said. 'Don't kid yourself, lassie. These aren't country yokels you're dealing with here. Reg Fairchild may be a naïve old fool, but he's running with the wolves. Just mind you don't get gobbled up like Red Riding Hood for asking the right questions at the wrong time.'

Laura drove back to Bradfield that night. She felt unsettled and dissatisfied and, on a more practical level, craved a good night's sleep in her own comfortable bed. Dumping her overnight bag without ceremony, she glanced at her copy of the *Gazette* which had been lying on the hall floor and took on board the blurred photograph of the man she assumed must be Thackeray's prime suspect on the front page, alongside an appeal for him to contact the police so that he 'could be eliminated from inquiries'. He must be making progress, she thought, as she picked up the phone and dialled his home number. There was no reply. She tried Vicky Mendelson's number instead and it was answered immediately.

'I just got home. I need to talk,' Laura said.

'To me or to Michael?' Vicky asked. 'He's here. He invited himself to supper. Do you want me to put him on? Do you want to talk to him?'

Laura hesitated.

'Desperately, Vic,' she said, whispering in her anxiety not to be overheard at the other end of the line. 'But I don't want him to know that.'

'Oh, Laura, you're in a bad way,' Vicky said equally softly, her voice thick with emotion. 'He seems depressed, too. Why can't you two stop tormenting each other and get your act together? I'll tell him you're at home, shall I? Odds on he'll find a sudden excuse to leave.'

'I wouldn't bank on it,' Laura said soberly. 'How's Naomi Laura?'

'Blooming,' the baby's mother said proudly. 'Another tooth and a couple of quiet nights at last. Come over soon and see us.'

It was an hour before Thackeray arrived, by which time Laura had almost given him up. He strode into the flat with his coat collar turned up against the bitter cold, his face grey with fatigue, and slumped without ceremony onto her sofa, hands in his pockets, shoulders hunched.

'I thought I'd missed you,' she said, her own nervousness at what might have been decided at High Clough making her almost as reticent as he obviously felt himself. She longed to sit down beside him and take him in her arms but knew from experience that in this mood he would stiffen and resist her uninhibited attentions. He looked up at her, taking in the pale face, free of make-up, the cloud of red-gold hair which she had loosened from its clips, and the anxiety in her eyes, and wished he could make her truly happy.

'My father has a bad effect on me,' he said apologetically.

'And your mother?'

'She's dying,' he said simply. 'She lies there with a look in her eyes that's difficult to bear . . .' He shrugged, lost for words to describe the pain in that low bedroom where the sound of the wind had always moaned like a dirge even on the balmiest summer day.

'It's not a life,' he said, the anger and despair he had felt at West Rigg cracking his voice. 'My father would have condemned what I was thinking up there as mortal sin, but she'd be better off dead.'

'So what did you decide to do?' she asked quickly, to deflect that line of thought.

'To try to make superintendent if they go ahead with this reorganisation,' he said. 'I think I'm better chasing villains than lost sheep.'

'I think so too,' she said, with a sense of relief that surprised her. She had not realised how afraid she was of Michael Thackeray's returning to Arnedale, but his news seemed to lift an enormous weight from her shoulders. She was only half aware of why he hated the place so much but she was deeply sure that he would not be happy if he went back. The nightmares which occasionally disturbed his sleep were a clear enough indication of that.

'But your father's disappointed?'

'Bitterly,' Thackeray said.

'The farm will be sold?'

'Oh, yes. It's more than he can cope with now. And there's no money in it, a fact he neglected to tell me when he was trying to persuade me to take it on.' Thackeray sounded as depressed as she had ever known him, Laura thought, and she was not sure how to break through the barriers he seemed to be erecting again between them.

'The free paper is suggesting that it will go to a developer – Barry Moore, I shouldn't wonder.' She chattered on as much for something to say as because she thought it was of any real significance to Thackeray. Silence in his company never felt comfortable or comforting, she thought bleakly. It held too many threats.

But Thackeray looked at her sharply as she confirmed the suggestion which his father had already made about the fate of the farm.

'Why Moore?' he asked.

'Simply because he – or his clients – seem to be buying up everything they can for redevelopment. They're putting a golf course up in Netherdale, which seems bizarre, on a farm where some chap shot himself. Perhaps they've got designs on High Clough as well.'

'What else have you discovered about Barry Moore?' Thackeray asked, and Laura suddenly realised that he had a policeman's glint in his eye. She could not understand why.

'I told you I met him at the Christmas "do",' she said uncertainly. 'The free paper is hinting pretty openly that he's a crook and I think he's using some sort of influence to keep Reg Fairchild in his pocket. Not difficult to do, as he's a major advertiser.'

'There are some question marks over Cheetham and Moore at this end too,' Thackeray said. 'We keep running into them at every turn. The young woman who was murdered, and her boyfriend, worked there. Keep me informed, will you? If that isn't a breach of your reporter's ethics.'

'You don't like Moore, do you?' she asked curiously.

'I hated him as a lad,' Thackeray said. 'Which makes me a bit cautious now. Maybe I'm just looking for a way to settle old scores.'

'After all these years?' she asked quietly.

'They have long memories in Arnedale,' he said.

He paused, and the silence lengthened awkwardly.

'Can you stay?' Laura ventured at last. Thackeray groaned.

'I'm dead beat,' he said, and she had to believe him. There were dark circles of fatigue beneath his eyes and the grey in his hair looked more pronounced than usual.

She slipped onto the sofa beside him and took his hand, a square, capable hand which more than covered her own small freckled one.

Thackeray reached out to pull her towards him and kissed her gently.

'I'm sorry about last night,' he said. 'I don't think I deserve you.'

'Stay,' she said, with a grin. 'And I'll tell you afterwards.'

TEN

'THAT IS COMPLETELY OUT OF order,' Jonathon West said in a tight, controlled voice. His face went white and pinched when he was angry, Laura thought dispassionately, and this morning he was very angry indeed.

'You've only been here five minutes. You know nothing about this town. It's ridiculous.'

Laura was sitting in Reg Fairchild's battered swivel chair at Reg Fairchild's untidy desk, and, possession being nine-tenths of the law, she had no intention of giving up either. She had arrived at the *Observer* from Bradfield that morning later than she should, Thackeray having distracted her mind from work as successfully as he usually did when he stayed overnight, only to find that Reg had gone down with flu and West was intimating to anyone who would listen that he would assume the editor's mantle for the next edition of the paper.

'No, I don't think so,' Laura had said quietly when she had taken in what was going on and was able to attract his attention. For a moment he did not appear to understand what she had said, and went on giving instructions to Debbie, the young trainee, without looking at Laura. Laura stood by the door, slowly unwinding the scarf with which she had attempted to keep out the morning's bitter north wind, and said it again.

'No,' she said, rather more loudly this time. 'I was sent here to be deputy to Reg. If Reg is ill, then I'll stand in for him.'

This time West heard clearly enough. She could see the muscles at the side of his jaw tighten and his mouth open slightly in surprise. He turned away from the silent Debbie, who flushed in embarrassment and gazed down into her coffee mug to escape their eyes.

'In the office?' he said at length in a strained voice and lost the initiative immediately by standing back to let Laura go ahead of him into Reg's cluttered room and sit herself firmly behind his desk. Such old-fashioned manners were one of the disadvantages of that expensive public school education, she thought unsympathetically as she settled herself ostentatiously into her seat.

'So I'm ignorant, inexperienced and of course I'm a woman,' she said pleasantly as West dithered between subsiding into the visitor's chair, and thus conceding her status, or standing awkwardly over the desk in what could only be interpreted as a threatening posture. He sat down at last, and Laura relaxed a fraction.

'I never said that,' West said. 'Sex has got nothing to do with it.'

'But seniority has,' Laura said crisply. 'I was sent here to stand in for Greg Winters precisely because I'm not ignorant and I'm not inexperienced, even though I am a woman. And stand in for Greg is exactly what I'm going to do.'

'I'll ring Reg and ask him what he thinks,' West came back, his face sulky now under the floppy blond hair. Just like a little boy who's had his sweeties taken away, Laura thought.

'And I will ring David Ross in London to confirm my position,' she said. 'He sent me here. His will be the decision that counts.'

'I'll ring Reg anyway. He'll have some views about what he wants covered.' West was clearly very unwilling indeed to give way.

'I'm sure he has. I've no objection at all to talking to him about that, if he's well enough to talk,' Laura said. 'But be quite clear, Jonathon. If I'm editing the paper, I am editing the paper. And what I say goes. Okay?'

'If that's what your chums in London confirm then I suppose it'll have to be,' West conceded. 'I suppose you'll be running back to teacher telling tales if we don't all toe the line.'

'Sod off, Jonathon,' Laura said, suddenly irritated beyond measure. For the first time she understood and was glad of the editor's time-honoured privilege of cursing subordinates roundly. 'You just do your job and nobody will need to tell tales to anyone.'

The matter was settled quickly enough when she rang the group's headquarters in London and was immediately put through to David Ross.

'Can you cope?' he asked crisply, when she had explained the situation.

'Of course,' she said.

'Your colleague didn't seem to think you could when he called,' Ross said. Laura took a second to take in the implications of that remark before she flashed a glance of real dislike at Jonathon West.

'He wouldn't, would he?' she snapped. 'But if you really want to see some changes here, you'd better leave it to me.'

'Right.' Ross was obviously a man of few words.

'About the other matter,' she said, more tentatively. 'I've not got very far . . .'

'Why don't you take old Reg some flowers?' Ross suggested, and no one who had overheard him would have intimated anything other than solicitude from his tone. 'Cheer him up a bit. Have an old-fashioned heart-to-heart?'

'I might just do that,' Laura said. 'And thanks,' she added although she suspected Ross had already hung up. She leaned back in her chair and looked long and hard at West, whose chilly blue gaze eventually dropped.

'We've two days to produce a paper,' she said coldly. 'I'm going to work on the lead story, which will be about the protesters in High Clough and the other Dales villages. *You* can do the usual Christmas features. You'll find some notes about carol concerts and church services on my desk.'

Chief Inspector Thackeray was also gazing across his desk at a subordinate with less than total enthusiasm. Kevin Mower stood uneasily in front of him and Thackeray wondered if the detective sergeant had at last gone too far.

'Reputable solicitors don't make formal complaints about

harassment without good reason,' he said mildly, hoping that for once he was wrong and that Mendelson, Green and Macdonald had gone inexplicably over the top.

'Solicitors' clerks like Ronnie Shepherd do anything they think they can get away with if it's likely to get them a result, guv,' Mower countered hotly. He looked unusually rumpled, his silk tie loose at the neck of a creased shirt, the jacket of his fashionable grey suit flung carelessly across his desk, hints that all was perhaps not quite well with his conscience, Thackeray thought.

He wondered constantly what proportion of his salary Mower spent on clothes. Far more than was prudent, he was sure, even for a single man with, as far as he knew, no commitments, although with Kevin Mower you could never be sure even of that. For all Thackeray knew he could be living in fear of the advancing nemesis of the Child Support Agency which was tracking down absent fathers.

Thackeray had summoned Mower from the canteen as unceremoniously as the complaint in question had been flung onto his desk by an irate Superintendent Jack Longley. He smiled faintly at the notion that solicitors' clerks would push the spirit of the law any further than Mower himself, given the opportunity.

'For God's sake sit down, and tell it from the beginning,' he said more quietly, prepared to give Mower the benefit of the doubt for now. He had worked with the sergeant since he had transferred to Bradfield almost a year before, not long after Mower himself had moved north. He knew him to be intelligent, ambitious and physically tough. But there remained the faintest suspicion in Thackeray's mind that when push came to shove the bright young copper who had come from the Met trailing a cloud of 'personal problems' was ready enough to bend a few rules himself to get a result.

Mower slumped into his chair and ran his hands through his short, stylishly-cut dark hair, his eyes still bright with an indignation which did not wholly convince his boss.

'Darrell France,' he said crisply. 'Afro-Caribbean, about thirty, married, couple of kids, in a steady job, picture of respectability except that there's too much cash about. He works down at Frazers, that big warehouse on the industrial estate. Wife hasn't worked since the second baby was born. But he's running around in a Sierra Cosworth, and it's not the first fast car he's had, all paid for, completely legit. And buying a house on the new development at Southwaite.'

'How did he come to your attention?' Thackeray asked, interested in spite of himself.

'Routine. Traffic stopped him for speeding: black lad, fast car, you know how their minds work. Checked him out, searched the car, found nothing . . . but passed it on to CID just in case.'

'And?'

'It wasn't the car that interested me as much as the address. It was the estate where Linda Wright had been working. They go for around £100,000 a throw, those places. That seemed a hell of a lot for an honest warehouseman to be funding. So I made a few discreet inquiries at the sales office, said I was getting married, needed a place, you know?' Mower grinned suddenly at the recollection.

'The office Linda used to work in?'

'Right, guv,' Mower said. 'You know the sort of bimbos they have in these show houses? Linda was one. Good looks and not necessarily much upstairs. Her replacement, Jacquie Coates she's called, is in the same class, and it turned out she was a mate of Linda's. Quite chatty she was about Linda and Jimmy, though she didn't tell us much more than we knew already. What she did say was that she thought Linda had another man in tow – an older man, she said, plenty of dosh. She sounded quite jealous of Linda when I turned on the charm and she unbuttoned a bit.'

'You identified yourself, I hope?'

Mower shrugged non-committally.

'I told her I was from the Bill,' he said. 'Coppers need houses too, I said.'

'Go on,' Thackeray said, prepared to let the near-deception pass for now.

'Well, I dropped a few hints about neighbours, would they be the sort of people my fiancée would get on with.'

'In other words, were they letting the blacks in?' Thackeray said contemptuously.

'Well, it was more the Pakis I pretended to be concerned with – the smell of curry? And there'd be none of that, she assured me, though they had sold one house to a very nice West Indian family, moved in a couple of months ago, small children, very respectable. That, I told her, was fine. We could live with that. Very magnanimous, I was. But Pakis . . .' Mower shrugged eloquently, evidently still pleased with his performance, but he caught the chilly look in Thackeray's eye.

'You know they're hypocritical bastards, guv,' Mower said, placatingly. 'They play along with it. They know bloody well it's illegal. Anyway, I went on to mortgages then, and she was very helpful, said her firm could help with all that, I needn't worry if my income was okay, no probs.'

'And on the strength of that you pulled Darrell France in?'

'Not straight away, no. First off, I called all the mortgage companies who'd been taken for a ride before. Talked to the managers we had dealings with in the cases your friend David Mendelson won't prosecute the agents for.' That evidently still rankled with Mower, Thackeray thought.

'And sure enough, France had borrowed eighty per cent of the purchase price from one of the companies. He must have inflated his income to get that, but they said he was up to date with the payments so they had no reason to worry. Not yet, anyway.'

'And you brought him in on that basis? That's not just thin, it's bloody transparent,' Thackeray snapped.

'Just to answer a few questions, nothing heavy,' Mower protested. 'Just to help with inquiries into Cheetham and Moore's methods of business, how he found their service, what they suggested he do about a mortgage, who he talked to there. We are still interested in them, guv. We need more evidence, is what David Mendelson said.'

'And France called for a brief rather than answer questions?'

'He got rattled. I'm not sure why. I want to go over my notes again . . .'

'You didn't record the interview?'

'I didn't want to faze him. I hadn't cautioned him, he was there voluntarily, just for a chat. But as I say, in the end he demanded a solicitor and Shepherd turned up, and got very aggressive and started on about harassment and racism. If he thinks I'm racist he should meet a few of my old mates from south of the Thames.' Mower was genuinely aggrieved and with some justice, Thackeray thought wryly. Mower might cut corners but prejudice of that sort was not a sin anyone could lay at the Punjabi-speaking sergeant's door.

The phone rang on Mower's desk and he picked it up automatically, tucking it into his shoulder-blade as he reached for pen and paper to take notes. Thackeray watched him idly, confident now that the complaint would not stand up, even though it came from one of the town's most respected firms of solicitors, and one with which, through David Mendelson, he had some personal connection. Mower, he noticed, was smiling as he put the phone down.

'Bingo,' he said. 'That was the manager at the West Yorkshire Building Society. I asked them if they had loaned Darrell France any money on the house in Southwaite and they said they had no record of anyone of that name. But he says I roused his curiosity and he did a search on the address. They've loaned an entirely different applicant £80,000 on the same property.'

'I think you might safely ask Mr France to give us a little more of his time,' Thackeray said softly, satisfied.

Laura called Faith Lawrence to check some details and got more than she bargained for.

'Are you going to use the story?' Faith asked cautiously.

'Yes, I am,' Laura said. 'Reg Fairchild has taken to his sick-bed and I'm in charge, would you believe? I'll lead on it.'

'Right then. Get your photographer up here this afternoon. There's time, isn't there, for your next edition? We're going to block the road. There have been lorries up and down all day taking away another huge mountain of stone he's demolished: a complete barn gone and a couple of walls. We're going to stop the next one before the school bus arrives. We can't go on like this.'

'We?' Laura asked.

'The mothers whose children were in the accident, and some of the travellers.'

'That won't go down too well with Ray Harding.'

'No? Well, Rob wanted to help. A couple of the kids from the camp were involved that day, you remember?' Laura did remember the hostility the mention of the 'gypsy' children had caused.

'And the other parents don't mind?'

'I'm past caring,' Faith said sharply. 'If they want something done about Harding's schemes they'll have to swallow their pride and take what help they can get. When it comes down to it the locals are a passive bunch. It's incomers like me, and even the travellers they despise so much, who get things done, who take a stand.'

Laura had not heard Faith Lawrence so vehement before and she wondered what had happened to stiffen her resolve. She evidently hesitated too long, because Faith came back at her angrily.

'I suppose you disapprove of me and Rob?' she said. 'My toy-boy! How very bourgeois of you, Ms Ackroyd.'

'It's not for me . . .' Laura began, but Faith did not give her the chance to continue.

'You have no idea what it's like,' she said bitterly. 'You can't begin to imagine what it's like. Without Rob I don't think I would have survived the last few months. He's made it bearable . . .' She broke off and Laura could tell that she was crying.

'I'm sorry,' she said helplessly. 'Really I am.' There was another silence before Faith's voice came back, strong and firm again.

'Will you send a photographer? About four o'clock? It'll be nearly dark when the children come home on the bus, we don't have street lights, it's another accident waiting to happen.'

'I'll send someone,' Laura said, conscious that Jonathon

106

West was standing in the office doorway listening impassively to the conversation. She hung up and looked at the unfriendly, petulant face for a moment before she told him what Faith had said about the protest demonstration.

'It's not our sort of story,' he said, but the protest was half-hearted and she knew her battle with Jonathon was won.

ELEVEN

THE CORONER'S INQUEST INTO A violent death is almost as ancient as English justice and at times shows its age. The Arnedale coroner, Dr John Priestley, certainly made the most of his centuries-old right to conduct matters more or less as he pleased.

Laura Ackroyd sat at what had been optimistically designated the Press table in the cramped upstairs room at the Bull Hotel which served as temporary court for the inquiry into the death of David Harding four months previously, and marvelled at the idiosyncratic arrogance of the man presiding. Fergal Mackenzie, who had arrived late and earned himself a magisterial rebuke from Dr Priestley over the top of his gold half-moon glasses, sat at her side. His sharp eyes surveyed the gathering with amused cynicism.

The jury of six men and two women were seated on the left side of the room on chairs which looked as though they had been brought up from the bar below. The coroner's desk was covered with a yellowing damask table-cloth onto which the clerk who sat at the doctor's side seemed to have already smeared ink, and the Press had been provided with a polished round oak table which had even more evidently been brought up from downstairs without even having had the beer stains wiped off it. It was a makeshift court, but all that could be expected, Laura thought, in a town which probably needed no more than a dozen inquests in the course of a year.

Dr Priestley was dressed in what looked like the same hairy, brown tweed suit he had been wearing when she had first seen him at the Chamber of Commerce Christmas party, his generous paunch encased today in a floral burgundy brocade waistcoat, his fine check country shirt bizarrely set off by a flowered tie in purple and gold. He was not a man who flinched from personal distinctiveness, however ill-conceived, or, evidently, one who felt at all abashed by his own whims and prejudices. In a very real way they dominated the proceedings.

Priestley had overtly relished the medical evidence, presented by an exhausted-looking young doctor from the local hospital who constantly tossed lank hair out of his eyes as he gave evidence. To him had fallen the grim duty of examining David Harding's body and pronouncing him dead. Priestley jollied his colleague along with relentless cheeriness as the young man flinched almost as much as the jury did at the details of the shotgun blast which had been directed through Harding's mouth to blow most of his brains out of the back of his skull.

The coroner was now unmercifully bullying the dead man's widow who was standing at the side-table which served as the witness stand.

'Surely you know something about his finances, madam,' Dr Priestley said. 'I thought you women were emancipated now, equal partners, all that nonsense.'

The pale, thin, grey-haired woman, wearing a navy blue coat several sizes too large for her gaunt frame, twisted her hands together in embarrassment and distress. The dark circles under her eyes looked like bruises, Laura thought, and her pale eyes were pools of misery.

'He told me nowt about the farm affairs,' she said in a strained whisper. 'But I knew he were worried. I could tell that.'

'How could you tell?' Priestley asked. 'Moody, was he?'

'Aye, that's it, moody,' Mrs Harding agreed. 'He'd been coming into town to see folk, to talk about money. I knew that.'

'But not who he saw?'

She shook her head mutely.

'Speak up,' the coroner said.

'He's one for my little black book,' Fergal Mackenzie whispered into Laura's ear. She raised an eyebrow.

109

'Come the revolution, he'll be top of the list,' the Scotsman said with a malicious gleam of amusement in his eye. Laura grinned, careful not to let Priestley see her face. The man was quite capable of having unruly reporters thrown out of the court, she thought. And within his rights.

'But after he was dead, you knew the trouble he was in?' Priestley persisted. This time Mrs Harding nodded.

'He were bankrupt,' she said, in a voice the whole room strained to hear.

'Speak up, madam, please. So when he said in this note . . .' Priestley waved a sheet of cheap, lined writing paper in the direction of the widow. 'When he said that he couldn't go on because of the bills, that made sense?'

'Oh, aye,' Mrs Harding said resignedly. 'For him, it made sense. Though how he expected me and the kids to fettle on us own, I'll never know.'

Mackenzie's eyes were roaming restlessly around the small crowded room, Laura noticed, and she followed his gaze to the public seats behind them where to her surprise she found that she recognised more than one of those squashed onto a narrow bench near the door. Ray Harding, with whom she had clashed at High Clough, sat at the inner end, crushed against the brown painted wall in an ill-fitting dark suit, obviously his seldom-worn best, his face flushed red, his ginger hair bristling as he listened to this stark memorial to his dead brother.

Next to him were two conventionally dressed businessmen, bank managers, she surmised, or insurance brokers, certainly individuals whose impassive attention to the proceedings spelt an interest that was distanced from the emotion washing around the witness stand; financial, probably, rather than personal. But next in line, she was surprised to see the smartly dressed figure of Detective Sergeant Kevin Mower, who gave her a circumspect nod of greeting as she caught his eye. Finally, crushed against the sergeant, half-hanging off the outer edge of the bench, was the grim-faced local CID chief, DCI Les Thorpe, looking hot and uncomfortable and distinctly ill-disposed.

'Are you running the High Clough story tomorrow?'

Mackenzie whispered in her ear fiercely as she turned her attention back to the proceedings, her mind full of questions she had no chance of finding answers to just now. She nodded to Mackenzie, giving him a complicit smile.

'All safely put to bed,' she murmured. The *Observer* was already being printed for distribution overnight and would appear in the local shops the following day.

'Quite a little fracas they had up there, I gather, when they blocked the road,' he said. 'Well done. You'd better mind your back though. You'll not be popular.'

'I thought you said that it wasn't our job to be popular,' she said.

'Aye, but I didn't say it would be any fun being unpopular.'

Mackenzie broke off suddenly, aware that they had attracted the attention and the displeasure of the coroner, who was glaring in their direction. They both turned dutifully back to their notebooks as Dr Priestley began advising – although it sounded more like instruction than advice – the jury on their options in reaching a verdict. He had not read out the note David Harding had written before he shot himself, but he left the eight jurors in little doubt that their only feasible conclusion was that the farmer took his own life.

It was a verdict with which the jurors clearly had little difficulty in concurring because they returned it within ten minutes of leaving the room to confer. Dr Priestley made no comment after the verdict was delivered and dismissed the court abruptly, leaving Mrs Harding weeping onto the shoulder of a friend.

'So that's that then,' Fergal Mackenzie said, running a hand with difficulty through his bushy dark hair as they made their way down the back stairs of the Bull and out into the pale wintry sunshine of Broad Street. 'Not a lot of doubt, even without hearing what was in the note. I wonder why he was so reluctant to read that out, though,' he mused half under his breath. Laura flashed him another smile.

'I'm sure you won't be slow in trying to find out,' she said.

'And you won't?'

'Oh, I think I've got enough on my plate for now,' Laura

111

said as she noticed Chief Inspector Thorpe, with Kevin Mower in half-hearted attendance, bearing down on her. The local man had a distinctly unfriendly look on his face and Mower, a step or two behind, raised a quizzical eyebrow in what she could only interpret as a warning of trouble in store. She felt, rather than saw, Fergal Mackenzie melt away into the jostling market-day crowds behind her, a prince who was obviously not in dragon-slaying mood today, she thought wryly.

'A word, Miss Ackroyd?' Inspector Thorpe said, putting an officious hand on her arm in a way which was guaranteed to cause maximum irritation.

'What can I do to help, Inspector?' Laura asked through gritted teeth.

'You had a photographer up in High Clough, I think, when some attempt was made to obstruct the highway yesterday.'

Laura nodded.

'You wouldn't expect the *Observer* to ignore a story like that, would you?' she asked, although she knew very well that was exactly what far too many people in Arnedale did seem to expect. The news, in Reg Fairchild's book, appeared to mean what he wanted it to mean, Humpty Dumpty style, and it was clear this was a policy which had a lot of support in the town.

'Traffic is not my responsibility, Miss Ackroyd, but criminal conspiracy might be, if it came to that.'

'I'm sorry?' Laura said, thoroughly startled by the turn the conversation had taken. Mower, she noticed, was keeping well in the background, his face impassive. Another bashful prince, she thought.

'You must have known what was going to happen before it happened,' Thorpe said. 'Did it not cross your mind that if you'd been informed that a crime was about to be committed you should have told the police?'

It crossed Laura's mind briefly that Thorpe must be joking, but looking at the square, sour face she realised that he was not a man to whose thin lips a joke would ever spring, unless it were a malicious one, perhaps.

'A crime?' she said stupidly. 'It's hardly a crime to stop the traffic for half an hour.'

'Indeed it is, Miss Ackroyd, as are a lot of other things these direct action protesters get up to. Intimidation. Harassment. Violence of one sort and another. One thing leads to the next and before you know where you are you're getting letter-bombs through the post from people who claim to love pussy-cats. Very nasty. Very dangerous. That's precisely why the law has been changed to curb their activities. Perhaps you'll bear that in mind next time you're in communication with these people. Will you be using your pictures?'

'Yes, of course,' she said.

'I'll be looking at them quite closely,' Thorpe said. 'If I need any other help, such as the unused photographs, I'll let you know.'

He was gone as quickly as he had approached her and, as far as Laura could see in the jostling crowds which packed the pavement, Mower had gone with him.

'Jesus wept,' she said to herself softly, knowing that she had been warned to back off as clearly as she was likely to be, even before her edition of the *Observer* had seen the light of day.

She went back to the office in an extremely thoughtful mood and stood at the window of the empty newsroom looking down on the packed street below, where the entire population of Arnedale appeared to be engaged in a sort of shuffling minuet as they scanned the laden market stalls for a Christmas bargain, or loaded themselves up with anticipatory provisions for the day itself, still a week away.

She had given the rest of the staff the afternoon off to get on with their Christmas shopping now that the paper had gone to press at the printers on the other side of the town. There was nothing she or anyone else could do now to prevent her extensive description – with graphic pictures of the human barricade which had held up Ray Harding's stone lorry – of Faith Lawrence's campaign at High Clough thudding onto doormats around the district the next morning. And she had no doubt at all that Faith's motley crew of supporters, half a dozen mothers with push-chairs and toddlers and a dozen unkempt New Age travellers, including Rob Tyler and his family, would

113

be instantly recognisable spread across four columns of page two.

There could be no more warnings, only retribution of some sort, perhaps. There had been cases where newspapers had become legally entangled with the police over the use of photographs as evidence so she did not take Inspector Thorpe's veiled threats lightly. She did not think that David Ross would be too pleased if her brief occupation of an editor's chair thrust the company into a legal wrangle which could go on for months if not years. She began to think that Fergal Mackenzie's precautions to protect his information were not quite as paranoid as she had supposed.

She spun round suddenly as a door behind her opened quietly, setting her heart thudding. She was surprised to see Kevin Mower in the doorway smiling his particular knowing smile.

'The door downstairs was open, so I came up,' he said.

'Yes, perhaps I should lock it. I'm not sure I want your lot in here without a search warrant,' she said, more sharply perhaps than she intended, still smarting from Les Thorpe's verbal assault, though she was pleased enough to see a familiar Bradfield face.

'What the hell was all that about?' Mower asked. 'He was pushing it a bit.'

'You may well ask. Didn't he enlighten you?'

Mower shook his head.

'Inspector Thorpe didn't seem too delighted to see me at the inquest either,' he said. 'I was left in no doubt that I wasn't very welcome on his patch, although it'd all been cleared higher up. There's not much love lost between him and Michael Thackeray, apparently.'

'No, I'd already got that impression the first time I met him,' Laura said.

'Do you know why?' Mower persisted, but Laura shook her head sharply, not willing to venture down that avenue with Thackeray's sergeant when she hardly dared tread it herself.

'So why were you at the inquest? I thought you were up to your eyes in a murder investigation,' she asked, her question being in many ways as illegitimate as his. She was not surprised when he too equivocated.

'Pursuing inquiries,' he said vaguely. 'We're looking at fraud as well. Harding could have been involved, or a victim, or a bit of both. There could possibly be a link with Linda Wright's death.'

'And was Inspector Thorpe helpful?' she asked. Mower looked at her thoughtfully for a moment.

'As I said, there's not much love lost . . . Do you fancy a drink? A little Christmas celebration for old times' sake?'

Laura grinned in spite of herself and knew that she was still admired in this quarter, although it was an admiration Mower would not now dream of following up except in jest.

'Some old times,' she said. She had been out to dinner with him once and the evening had ended with an almost chaste embrace.

'Well, the old times that might have been, if a chief inspector hadn't pulled rank,' Mower persisted.

'Not now, Kevin, thanks,' she said a shade wearily, wondering whether if she had opted for the sergeant rather than the chief inspector when the choice was there, her life might not have been a deal less complicated. 'I've got some work to do here before I go back to Bradfield tonight.'

'Ah,' he said softly, reading far more into her statement than was justified. She was returning to Bradfield that evening to see her grandmother, but did not see any particular reason to tell Mower that.

He blew her·an ironic kiss and left, leaving a waft of some exotic aftershave behind him. Laura smiled faintly as she listened to him clatter down the stairs far more noisily than he had climbed them. She would always have a soft spot for the good-looking Kevin, she thought, but she had learned the hard way that it was no wiser to trust him with her secrets than to confide in her worst enemy.

She cleared her desk desultorily now that the adrenalin of getting the paper out had drained away. She wanted to be on the valley road, well out of the town, before the evening rush. But twice the phone delayed her. The first time she was surprised to hear the smooth tones of Barry Moore.

'Have lunch with me at the Bull tomorrow,' he said in a tone which clearly did not anticipate any sort of rebuff. He was not a man who took no for an answer.

'Why not,' she said sweetly. 'We like to keep on good terms with our advertisers.' Though she did not think for a moment that it was advertising that the auctioneer wanted to talk about.

The second call was almost as brief.

'It's Fergal, princess. You remember the two suits at the inquest? They were from mortgage companies. Two different mortgage companies. Our deceased Mr Harding had been a naughty boy and done a fiddle. That's what it said in the suicide note they wouldn't read out.'

'Why are you telling me all this?' Laura asked.

'Insurance,' Fergal said. 'My next edition is due out before yours but I got the feeling that you and I both are becoming increasingly unpopular around here. See you around, princess. I hope.'

'So I helped a few folk do their own conveyancing? There's nowt illegal about that.' Ronnie Shepherd, solicitor's clerk and a frequent thorn in police flesh, leaned back in his chair in the interview room, the picture of injured innocence. 'I don't do it *for* them. I just advise.'

'Just a social service, is it?' Chief Inspector Thackeray asked sceptically. 'Do your employers take that view?'

'It's nowt to do with them,' Shepherd said. He was a big man, running to fat, heavy-jowled and sharp-eyed, and much more used to calling the shots at police interviews, at which he regularly represented various of Bradfield's villains, than having them called for him. His unexpected situation, pulled into the police station as he left work to help with inquiries, clearly made him deeply uneasy.

'I should have thought the loss of potential clients you happen to have made contact with was very much to do with them,' Thackeray said. 'Anyway, I'd like a list of people you've kindly "helped" in this way.'

'What the hell for?' Shepherd said. 'I told you it's not illegal. A lot of folk can't afford a solicitor for that sort of job. You know the fees they charge: an arm and a leg and your balls as well, some of them. It's helping people out, that's all. What's it got to do with you, any road? What's all this about? Been getting too many of your suspects off, have I, so you've got to cause trouble for me, is that it?'

Thackeray ignored this outburst and waited for Shepherd to subside back into his seat, breathing heavily.

'Who recommends this useful social service you've got going?' Sergeant Kevin Mower continued, when it was clear that the chief inspector had no intention of explaining anything to the indignant Shepherd. For a second his eyes narrowed.

'I've got contacts,' he said evasively.

'Would Linda Wright have been one of those contacts?' Mower snapped, suddenly aggressive.

'Aye, one of 'em,' Shepherd muttered. 'She was very helpful when she was working at the show house up at Southwaite.'

'Tell me about your relationship with Linda, Mr Shepherd,' Thackeray broke in quietly. 'A close one, was it?'

'Relationship?' Shepherd exclaimed, obviously outraged. 'I didn't have a relationship with Linda Wright. I hardly knew the girl. I met her once in a pub with some friends and we got chatting about property and that, as she was in the trade, and I said that if she had clients wanting a cheap conveyancing service, to put them in touch. Every now and again she did just that.'

'Do you also "help people out" with their mortgages, Mr Shepherd?' Thackeray switched the subject abruptly. 'Did Linda put people your way for a very advantageous mortgage deal as well?'

'No, I bloody don't,' he snarled. 'And no, she bloody didn't. I know nowt about mortgages. It's not my scene, nothing I know my way round at all.'

'But perhaps you know a man who does?' Mower suggested.

'Everyone knows a man who does,' Shepherd said. 'They're not hard to find. They're called estate agents, in my experience.'

'But if I wanted to borrow a bit over the odds? Not a single legal mortgage, but two – or perhaps three? Where would I turn then, Mr Shepherd – in your experience?' Thackeray asked conversationally.

Shepherd scowled.

'So that's what this so-called chat is about, is it?' he said. 'I thought there was more to it than a bit of conveyancing on the quiet.'

'It's not going to be difficult to discover whether you advised on the paperwork for some of the people we know have been involved in mortgage fraud, Mr Shepherd,' Thackeray said. 'We've already charged four people and there's more to follow.'

'What if I did?' Shepherd came back. 'I told you, I know nowt about anyone's mortgage arrangements.'

'Well, I'm sure your boss will be able to confirm all the details, won't he?' Thackeray said.

Shepherd sat very still for a moment, knocking his fist on the table in front of him in time to some urgent rhythm in his head.

'You don't need to do that,' he said at length, almost to himself. 'Do you?' he demanded. 'You don't *have* to talk to my boss about me doing something which is perfectly legal?'

'Even if a bit dodgy as far as your employer is concerned,' Mower said. 'I suppose we could turn a blind eye to your little scam – if you could help us with some other matters that are of more interest.'

'Like someone else's mortgage deals, you mean?' Shepherd suggested, as if the notion had never crossed his mind before.

'In which, of course, you played no part,' Mower said eagerly, too eagerly.

'Though if we found you were involved, I'd throw the book at you, you know that, don't you?' Thackeray said.

'I hear things,' Shepherd muttered. 'In my job you hear things.'

'And as a law-abiding citizen – even if you do cheat on your employer – you'll be only too pleased to tell us what you've heard about mortgages, won't you?' the chief inspector said kindly.

'Linda would put them in the right direction,' Shepherd said. 'I guessed it was the boyfriend actually doing the deals. He'd be the one with the know-how. Linda just provided the ambition.'

'You mean Jimmy Townsend?'

'Aye, Jimmy. That's his name,' Shepherd conceded reluctantly.

'So they worked the fraud together?' Thackeray persisted.

'He'd need to do summat to keep that lass the way she'd like to be kept,' Shepherd said. 'Thought she was summat special, she did.'

'Did she now,' Mower murmured, remembering Linda's unexpectedly luxurious wardrobe and expensive jewellery.

TWELVE

BY THE STANDARDS OF THE *Daily Mirror*, or even the *Bradfield Gazette*, it was not much of a headline, but even so Laura was proud of it for the ground it broke if not for its verbal felicity. 'Anti-traffic campaign hots up' ran across the top of six columns on page two, above a photograph of Faith Lawrence, and an assorted band of village mothers and children and New Age travellers flagrantly breaking the law, if Inspector Thorpe was to be believed, as they blocked the main street at High Clough.

If the police seriously wanted evidence of wrong-doing, Laura thought ironically, she had certainly provided it for them. Every determined face in the protesting band was instantly recognisable, every word on their placards legible. Every plea for a ban on lorries in memory of Alison, the child who had been killed, came straight from the heart.

Laura sat at Reg Fairchild's desk early the next morning admiring her handiwork and waiting for the inevitable reaction. It was not slow in coming. Fairchild's voice was hoarse, though whether with emotion or the virus which had laid him low she could not tell.

'Don't make any plans for the next issue,' he croaked. 'I'll be back.'

'Good,' Laura said non-committally. 'I was thinking of coming out to see you this afternoon. Will that be okay?' It was high time, she thought, to take Reg on, and although attacking a man on his sick-bed might be thought to be not quite cricket she did not think that David Ross was an aficionado of the gentleman's game. Australian rules football was more his style, and if she read it right that meant grinding

120

an opponent's face into the mud when he was down rather than helping him up.

Faith Lawrence was the next to call, full of thanks for the coverage and optimism about the outcome of the campaign.

'I don't think I'll be able to keep it up,' Laura confessed. 'Reg Fairchild is threatening to come back next week even if he has to come in by ambulance.'

'Well, perhaps you'll have shamed him into doing an honest job,' Faith said.

As she hung up, she saw Jonathon West come into the office and it was obvious he was not best pleased with the result of her labours, for reasons of his own.

'I really liked your Christmas shopping feature,' Laura said kindly. Debbie, who had come in quietly and was already at her desk, sniggered into her copy of the *Daily Mail*. West scowled indiscriminately at them both.

'I gather Reg will be back soonest,' he said. 'To do the Christmas Eve edition?'

'I'm sure he will,' Laura said, feelingly. 'I'm going to see him tomorrow.'

'Well, the best of luck,' West said insincerely. 'I should think he'll have you back in Bradfield by Christmas Eve.'

'Oh, I doubt it,' Laura said, tossing a cloud of red hair back from her face, though she did not feel as confident as she hoped she sounded.

The Bull Hotel was packed with pre-Christmas revellers, market traders and shoppers and farmers in town for the last auction before the holiday. Laura struggled through the crowd, buffeted by tweedy elbows and blocked by quilted gilets as she tried to locate Barry Moore in the low-ceilinged restaurant beyond the bar.

The Bull was one of those old inns which would never need the services of a brewer's architect to convince the public that it was ancient. Centuries of accretions and alterations, windows blocked off and walls knocked down, had created a maze of old oak and yellowing walls, unexpected steps and stairs and jutting ceilings that cracked the crowns of the unwary. The place creaked under its own weight, smelt permanently of wood smoke and warm beer, its beams pickled black in ale and brandy fumes and tobacco smoke. It threw a close, welcoming fug around anyone who crossed its worn stone doorstep.

Given a cursory scatter of holly boughs and tinsel it announced that this was how Christmas ought to be and almost never was. If Mr Pickwick and Sam Weller had strolled in and demanded a boiled leg of mutton with the usual trimmings, no one would have raised an eyebrow. In spite of her anxieties, Laura had felt her heart lift as she crossed the threshold. Lunch at the Bull today could not be all bad.

She spotted Moore eventually, already settled at a corner table, deep in conversation with a wiry, grey-haired man in a tweed cap and dark duffle jacket. Moore caught her eye across the crowded room, which was already wreathed in smoke, and apparently made a dismissive comment to his companion, who also glanced in Laura's direction before moving back into the bar and picking up a half-full pint glass.

'Laura, my dear,' Moore said, half-rising to his feet as she approached, waving her into the old oak chair opposite his own and greeting her with an enthusiasm that she did not imagine for a moment was genuine. 'They're doing a Christmas lunch if you're fond of turkey. I prefer the roast beef myself. And they keep some excellent Stilton for a few favoured customers, if you'd like that?'

'May I look at the menu?' Laura asked, as much to make a point as because she would be unhappy with the beef. Moore did not miss the implication and passed her the large leather-bound volume with mock courtesy and an ironic smile. His colour was high, and his mood ebullient, and she guessed that he had come straight to the Bull from the morning's cattle mart. The farmers who packed the pub, many with money in their pocket from the sale, were taking this last opportunity for a convivial celebration before the holiday.

'So you're editing the *Observer* now,' Moore said thoughtfully, eyes narrowing as he watched her study the menu with ostentatious care. 'That's an unexpected pleasure for the readers.'

'Is it?' she asked sceptically. 'Some of the readers seem a little disconcerted to be presented with the unvarnished truth for once.'

'Ah, I see we have a woman of principle here,' Moore said. 'You musn't be too hard on old Reg, you know. He's been in Arnedale a long while. He's almost an institution himself, you might say.' Laura turned back to the menu, not to be rushed.

'Is it a job you'd like to inherit?' he persisted. Laura guessed it was a question he would dearly like a definitive answer to.

'I'd give it some thought,' she said non-committally. 'If it fell vacant. Which I'm sure it won't.'

He ordered the salad she indicated with no more than a raised eyebrow at her choice and chatted inconsequentially about Arnedale and its 'characters' while they ate their way through a main course. She went on abstemiously to coffee while he was brought a whole crumbling Stilton from which he scooped himself a generous portion to accompany a glass of port.

All the time, though, Laura was conscious of being weighed and assessed by Moore's considering gaze, from the top of her copper head to the tips of her black lace-up boots. By the time they had finished their meal, she was aware that he had, in the course of an apparently casual conversation, inspected her antecedents, her career and her prospects. If she had a price, she thought, the auctioneer would probably work out what it was to the last penny. As she didn't, she could see he was thrown.

Eventually he leaned back in his chair as the waitress poured second cups of coffee. He took out a cigar and waved it cursorily in her direction.

'Do you mind?' he asked. She wondered what his reaction would be if she claimed a desperate allergy to cigar smoke.

'Not at all,' she said sweetly, knowing that now they would be getting down to the real reason he had invited her to lunch. She decided to get her retaliation in first.

'So what are your plans for High Clough, then?' she said. He did not answer at once, a sudden stillness coming over his face and tightening his jaw, as he drew hard on his cigar to get it going satisfactorily. Barry Moore's conviviality was less than skin deep.

'High Clough?' he asked, at length. 'Have I got plans for High Clough?'

'I was told that you – or your firm – were interested in buying Joe Thackeray's farm. I didn't suppose you intended to raise sheep on it.'

Moore's eyes flickered across the room to the bar where the farmer he had been talking to earlier was still leaning with his cronies over very slowly diminishing pints of beer.

'We have an interested client,' he said shortly. 'That's what Joe Thackeray was discussing when you came in.'

Laura's eyes followed Moore's with a surprised look she could not disguise. There was no family resemblance, she thought, between the small, wiry farmer and his tall, broad-shouldered son. She knew she had betrayed herself when Moore turned the conversation sharply away from matters of property in High Clough in a more unwelcome direction.

'You don't know the father – Joe – then?' Moore said, clearly not expecting an answer but confirming that he was aware there was another Thackeray she did know. But he did not press his advantage straight away.

'So how long do you think poor old Reg Fairchild will be off sick?' he asked instead.

'I've no idea,' Laura said. 'I'm going to see him tomorrow. As far as I know it's just flu.'

'He's chesty, is Reg,' Moore said. 'It could keep him out of action for a while. Of course, it won't do you any harm, editing the paper, will it? Impress your boss in Bradfield, no doubt.'

Laura smiled to herself, knowing how unlikely Ted Grant was to be impressed with anything she could do with the weekly *Observer*.

'You give a lot of coverage to these troublemakers in Bradfield, do you?' Moore pressed her, more aggressive now. 'The Greens, the hunt sabs, the New Age travellers?' The litany was loaded with contempt.

'We don't pick and choose,' she said, although she knew that was not strictly true. Ted had his own list of unmentionables which overlapped with Moore's but was not exactly the same. Gays and 'reds', which in Grant's book meant anyone much to the left of Genghis Khan, were bottom of the pops on the *Gazette*.

Unexpectedly Moore was distracted by something or someone behind Laura's back and he offered a thin smile which had about as much friendliness in it as a piranha.

'Afternoon, Gerry. You're out and about early,' he said as Gerry Lawrence hove unsteadily into view and drew up at a precarious angle above the table.

'Barry,' Lawrence said indistinctly. 'Merry Christmas, Barry. And a Happy New Year.'

'And to you, Gerry,' Moore said heartily, but with a wariness in his eyes that made Laura wonder what he was afraid of.

'Have you sheen . . . have you seen what my wife's been up to now?' Lawrence asked. 'All over the newsh-papers? Silly cow.'

'You ought to get her to take up quieter hobbies, Gerry,' Moore said, rising slightly from his seat to steady Lawrence as he tipped dangerously close to the candle lamp in the centre of the table. Lawrence nodded owlishly, and with a great effort, stood upright again.

'On my way to the Con Club,' he said solemnly. 'Shee . . . see you there later, Barry. Buy you one . . .' Nodding his head in approval of his own generosity, he turned away to weave back through the restaurant tables and into the crowded bar.

'You know Gerry Lawrence?' Moore said. 'It'll be me who buys him one, of course, poor sod.'

Laura nodded. 'We've met – briefly.'

'Doesn't know when to stop,' Moore said. 'But with a wife like that, who can blame him?'

Laura froze, unwilling to let the insult pass but not wanting to get into any sort of discussion with Moore about Faith Lawrence.

'He needs help, doesn't he?' she said neutrally.

'His wife thinks he's signed on with AA,' Moore said contemptuously. '"My name's Gerry, and I'm an alcoholic,"' he mimicked viciously and Laura flinched, feeling the conversation veer in directions she would give anything to avoid. 'In my experience there's no cure for what Gerry's got, short of a new wife. But even that might not do the trick. Once a drunk always a drunk, in my experience. Of course, it runs in professions, doesn't it? Journalism's not immune, is it? Publicans? The police?'

Laura took a sip of her coffee and hold of her temper. She was being provoked, she knew, although she was not at all sure where the provocation was intended to lead.

'Are you a Catholic then, Laura?' Moore asked unexpectedly. She must have let her surprise show because he smiled at her sympathetically, the smile of a boa constrictor about to swallow its prey. She shook her head, a slight tingle of fear warning her that the conversation was now heading in a direction she would like even less.

'Funny,' Moore mused. 'Someone I know thought they'd seen you up at the Sacred Heart, talking to old Father Rafferty. Thought maybe you'd popped in to confession, temporarily one of his flock while you were up here.'

Laura's mouth felt very dry and she drained her coffee cup quickly. She might pride herself on not having a price, but she had a weakness that Moore seemed to have targeted like a guided missile. If he knew she had foolishly talked to Frank Rafferty who else knew – or could be told?

'Are you a Catholic, then?' she asked, avoiding Moore's indirect question, and recalling that Michael Thackeray had said he had known the young Barry Moore at church.

'A cradle Catholic, but in name only now,' Moore said dismissively. 'Though they do say you never really lapse. When it comes to the crunch you'll be there, seeking absolution, just in case. I was an altar boy when I was a lad. With young Michael Thackeray, Joe's son, though he's another who's fallen by the wayside, I hear. I see the old man occasionally when I go to Mass. Easter, Midnight Mass at Christmas, you know? Chew the fat, talk over old times. We're a close little group, the left-footers. Everyone knows everyone else's little peccadilloes – venal sins, and a few mortal ones too, now and again. It all gets around. Like Chinese whispers.'

There was no mistaking the threat even though Moore was gazing airily around the bar again, looking in every direction except at Joe Thackeray and his friends.

'I must be going,' Laura said quietly.

'Oh, must you? I was enjoying our chat,' Moore said heartily. 'And I'm really looking forward to reading your efforts in the *Observer*. Such a breath of fresh air you've brought up from Bradfield. Such a pity you'll be with us such a short time.'

'Damn, damn, damn, damn,' Laura said to herself as she pushed her way through the increasingly merry crowds around the bar and made her way out into the equally congested Broad Street, where the Christmas shoppers were becoming ever more frantic in their search for the best – or the cheapest – gifts as the first flakes of snow began to fall from a leaden sky. She had, she thought, no one but herself to blame. She had taken a chance, made herself vulnerable, and lost. Just how much she had lost she did not even dare think.

'Of course, Sydney Cheetham's not a Bradfield man, any more than you and I are,' Superintendent Jack Longley said thoughtfully as the two senior detectives waited in Thackeray's car for the electronically controlled gates of Cheetham's mansion to open for them.

'I thought you were born and bred here,' Thackeray said, surprised. He had tiptoed delicately amongst Longley's extensive and celebrated acquaintances in the town once before and feared that the decision to interview Sydney Cheetham would stretch his limited reserves of tact and diplomacy again. Which was no doubt why Longley had abruptly announced his intention to accompany him to talk to the senior partner in Cheetham and Moore, a decision that Thackeray decided to take less as an insult than as insurance against distraction from the task in hand.

'I was born a couple of miles into Derbyshire,' Longley

127

said gloomily. 'Your predecessor Harry Huddleston never let me forget that. If you weren't eligible to play cricket for Yorkshire then you weren't much cop, in Harry's book. I came to Bradfield as a lad. Just an adopted son.'

Thackeray eased the car into gear as the iron gates swung smoothly open and drove sedately up the curving gravelled drive towards the house partly hidden amongst trees. He had little time for professional Yorkshiremen and knew that in former Chief Inspector Huddleston's case it was a bluff façade behind which a man of iron lurked. Although handicapped by birth, Longley too came from the same mould.

Sydney Cheetham, like himself an off-comer from Arnedale, had made a better job than he had of settling comfortably into his adopted home in Bradfield, Thackeray thought, as he and Longley climbed the stone steps to the front door of Manningham House, a dour stone double-fronted Victorian villa of stolid grandeur. Cheetham himself came to the door to greet them, a thin elderly man, though still with a sprightly step and a bright eye, and an evident taste for the sort of elegant country clothes which Thackeray knew seriously understated their expense.

Cheetham greeted Longley affably, nodded with somewhat less warmth at Thackeray when he was introduced, and led his two visitors into a room at the back of the house which clearly served as library and home office, the walls lined with books from floor to ceiling, the mahogany desk bearing an expensive-looking computer system with a geometric pattern repeating endlessly on the screen.

'How can I help you, gentlemen?' he asked, waving them into armchairs close to the glowing log fire and lifting a silver coffee pot from the tray on the small table beside the mantel-piece. Longley nodded imperceptibly at Thackeray. He was, he had told him already, content merely to observe his inter-view with Cheetham. He had sanctioned it quickly enough once it had become apparent both from Ronnie Shepherd, and as a result of a rather more forceful discussion with Darrell France, the young warehouseman from Southwaite who had now been charged with obtaining a mortgage by deception, that at least two of the firm's employees had been engaged in an extensive mortgage scam.

'I am astonished,' Sydney Cheetham said, when Thackeray had outlined the police case against Jimmy Townsend and Linda Wright. 'I have to say that I had the merest acquaintance with them both, although naturally I was very disturbed to hear what had happened to Linda. I have sent my condolences to her parents, of course. Townsend I have met a couple of times in the office. He came to us from our Arnedale office, you know. Linda I've met perhaps once.'

'We're told that Linda might have had another boyfriend, an older man,' Thackeray said. 'You wouldn't know who that might be?'

Cheetham looked at the chief inspector blandly.

'I have no idea at all,' he said. 'As I expect you realise, I'm semi-retired, and only go in once or twice a week. I hardly knew the girl. Her main function, I'm told, was to work in the show houses on new developments – and very good at her job she was, Stephen Stokes tells me.'

'Do you trust Mr Stokes, Mr Cheetham?' Thackeray asked. 'Is there any possibility that he is involved in this fraud?'

'I'd be astonished if he were,' Cheetham said, a slight flush reaching his thin cheeks this time. 'I have found him absolutely trustworthy.' Which proves nothing except that he'll watch your back if you are involved in this as well, Thackeray thought.

'You realise, Sydney, that to take this to court we will need to look at the records of clients Townsend has handled during the time he had been with you?' Jack Longley broke in, forgetting his self-denying ordinance for a moment.

'Anything you need, Jack, anything you need. I'll talk to Stokes about it,' Cheetham said agreeably enough, but his eyes were chilly and flickered for a split second to his desk and the dancing computer screen.

'This is a long-established firm, you know,' Cheetham said, suddenly bitterly angry. 'To have these young people destroying its reputation grieves me deeply. It really does. And do you think it has ended up with Townsend killing the girl?'

'It's really too early to say,' Thackeray said non-committally. 'We're trying to trace other connections of Linda's. But I don't suppose that is anything you would know about?'

And that was a question to which Sydney Cheetham responded with nothing more than an affronted and emphatic shake of the head.

Back in the car, ten minutes of inconclusive questioning later, Thackeray glanced at Superintendent Longley with a slightly mocking smile.

'What do you reckon?' he asked.

'Oh, he's grieved all right,' Longley said. 'And maybe it is because Townsend and Wright were taking the firm for a ride. On the other hand it could be nowt to do wi'that. It could be that we're getting too close to him as well.'

'For someone retired he's got a very sophisticated work station there,' Thackeray said thoughtfully. 'We should have brought Mower with us. He's a damn sight more computer literate than I am.'

'Any road, you'd better get yourself up to Arnedale and find out what Townsend got up to when he worked up there,' Longley said.

'Ah,' Thackeray said softly, as he swung the car back into the main road leading down the hill to the town centre. It was the challenge he knew must come sooner or later, and from which he now had no excuse to flinch.

'Do you have some difficulty with that?' Longley asked coldly.

'No, sir,' Thackeray said impassively. 'If you fix it with DCI Thorpe, I'll go up there tomorrow.'

Back in his office, Thackeray had no time to reflect on the commitment he had made. Sergeant Kevin Mower was at his desk.

'Right, guv,' he said. 'D'you want the good news or the bad news?'

'The good,' Thackeray said grimly. 'And don't muck me about, Kevin.'

He listened quietly as Mower filled him in on a telephone chat he had had with a sergeant at Arnedale police station.

'Thorpe wouldn't tell me anything, so I rang his sergeant,

Armstrong, this morning, saying I wanted to check some details on the inquest on David Harding in Arnedale. What I really wanted was to know what was in the suicide note.'

'And?' Thackeray prompted impatiently, feeling Arnedale closing in on him inexorably.

'He hadn't simply gone bust,' Mower said. 'He'd gone bust because he'd taken out more than one mortgage on the farm. I knew that already from the building society investigators who turned up at the inquest. What I didn't know was that he was about to be arrested for fraud. The societies had found out what had been going on and were pressing Thorpe to act.'

'Right,' Thackeray said when he had absorbed the implications of that. 'And the bad news?'

'Forensic say that the fingerprints on Linda Wright's car are not Jimmy Townsend's,' Mower said. 'They don't match anything we picked up at his flat. Whoever shoved that car into the reservoir, it wasn't Jimmy.'

THIRTEEN

LAURA DROVE DOWN NETHERDALE TOWARDS the office the next day in a turmoil of emotion. The snow had already taken a grip of the dale at this height and the hills stretched away in a patchwork of brilliant white, divided by the snaking stone walls and broken here and there in sheltered spots by black clumps of trees and the occasional square barn and farmhouse isolated by the glittering blanket which had appeared overnight. The sky was a delicate eggshell blue and only an occasional cloud obscured the wintry sun and threw a fleeting shadow across the unsullied hillsides. It was a scene she would normally have exulted in, but this afternoon's trip had not left her capable of anything but a bitter sadness at the unfairness of life.

The snowfall had eased up here before dawn and the roads had been cleared, but she drove carefully, not trusting the uncertain surface in the still bitter cold. The narrow lane she was descending eventually wound its tortuous way up more than a thousand feet to the top of the dale. Reg Fairchild lived in one of the last cottages in a sheltered hillside fold, just before the road took a final vicious twist to the top of the pass which led to Swaledale. It was an isolated spot, a hard three-quarters of an hour's drive from Arnedale in good conditions. Today it had taken an hour or more to negotiate bends where fine frozen snow was already beginning to drift back across the tarmac on the most exposed corners.

Fairchild had come to the door himself when she let the dull brass knocker fall onto the solid wood of the front door. He was wearing a faded, checked dressing-gown with a woollen scarf tucked in at the neck, and looked grey-faced and haggard. Laura realised as she had not before that Fairchild was not a young man, that his sprightly step into the office and around his familiar haunts in the town might well be concealing a fragility which he would never admit. It was apparent now, though.

He waved her into the cottage's main living-room to the right of the narrow hall where a coal fire burned in the grate, and a low table covered with books and papers was pulled up to the sagging armchair in which he had evidently been sitting. Laura was very conscious that she did not know whether there was a Mrs Fairchild, but looking round the cluttered room, almost overwhelmed with bookcases, the contents of which overflowed in ragged steps onto the floor, she guessed that there was not.

'Can I get you anything?' she asked. 'Make a cup of tea, or something?' Fairchild dabbed at his reddened nose with an enormous handkerchief and nodded gratefully.

'That would be kind,' he said. 'You'll find everything you need by the kettle. Kitchen's across the hall.'

She took off her coat and ventured into the kitchen where the clutter on every available surface convinced her even more certainly that Fairchild lived alone. She sighed, turned the hot tap onto the dirty dishes filling the sink and switched on the electric kettle for tea.

She took the teapot, cups and a plate of slightly stale currant scones which she had found in a bread-bin back into the living-room where Fairchild had returned to the book he had evidently been reading before she arrived. She put the tray down on top of the piles of papers on what passed for a dining table and poured out two cups.

'You seem to be working as hard at home as you do in the office,' she said as she passed him a cup and he reluctantly let go of his book.

'Time's winged chariot,' he muttered, wolfing a scone and reaching for another.

'Are you getting regular meals?' she asked.

'Oh, aye. The woman next door's been in and out, bringing me a pie and a casserole and so on. I've not been able to get down to the shops.' He broke off as a fit of coughing shook his

133

thin frame. It took him several minutes to recover, dabbing his eyes dry on his handkerchief.

'Have you seen a doctor?' she asked, and he shook his head impatiently. 'You're really not fit to come back to work, you know.'

He nodded a gloomy acquiescence to that.

'There's nothing they can do for flu, is there?' he said hoarsely. 'I don't like to drag them all the way up here just for a virus they can't treat.'

'You should take care,' she said non-committally, not knowing him well enough to bully him as she might have bullied her grandmother in the same situation. 'Is all this for your book?' She nodded at the mountains of papers which surrounded them, the notebooks carefully set out on the dining table, the photographs laid out on the floor, the cassette tapes stacked amongst the books.

'There's so much to record,' he said vaguely. 'No one's ever done it properly, you know. Not a proper oral history. It's a lifetime's work, really, and I don't think I've got a lifetime left. I started too late. I've done most of the interviews and transcribed the tapes. It's all a question of collating it and writing it up now. But I'm afraid it will never be finished, just like poor old Casaubon.'

'You should use a computer,' Laura said idly, and was surprised when Fairchild gave her a slightly sly look in return. 'They're more efficient than a wife,' she said with feeling. Dorothea Casaubon had never been one of her favourite heroines, eager as she had been to act as an intellectual skivvy for her husband.

'Yes, yes, that's what Barry Moore says,' Fairchild said, his guard evidently down now. 'He's going to advise me. Find me some young computer buff to help,' he said.

'Barry Moore,' Laura said wearily, surprised that she should even be surprised that the name had come up again. 'A man who believes everyone has a price,' she said. 'Or a weakness.'

'A weakness?' Fairchild said sharply, aware now that he might have said too much.

'Oh, don't worry,' Laura said bitterly. 'You and I are in the same boat. It's my weakness he's found. Just to curb my over-enthusiasm for honest journalism. Stories about High Clough two weeks running seem to have really got up his nose. Presumably your price is all the help you can get with this.' She nodded at his life-work on which time was so evidently running out.

'He's always been very helpful,' Fairchild said quietly. 'You wouldn't understand. You're too young.'

'Oh, I understand a passion all right,' Laura said. 'Only too well. Not this sort of passion, perhaps, but something that runs your life in its own way, takes you over, and maybe destroys you in the end. I understand that perfectly.'

'You can go away again, Laura,' Fairchild said sharply. 'You don't have to stay in Arnedale. This is my whole life. I don't have anything else to look forward to except finishing the book. What's the harm in humouring Barry with his schemes? They're mostly harmless, some of them actually improve things for people in the end.'

'Only as long as they make Barry a fat profit,' Laura said. 'And no questions asked. He's ready to exploit anyone's tragedy, isn't he? Like the farmer up here who shot himself, Dave Harding. Moore moved in pretty quickly there to snap up the land for a song. And he's set to do the same in High Clough, though he denies it. I'd put money on his buying Joe Thackeray's farm when it comes on the market. He's a sort of vulture, isn't he, waiting for people to hit hard times and then moving in, scavenging whatever's worth scavenging?'

'Joe Thackeray's farm?' Fairchild said. 'He's selling up, is he? I don't suppose the son's much interested in coming back to Arnedale after what happened.'

Laura froze, a lump in her throat almost preventing her from asking the question she knew she had to ask.

'What did happen?' she said, so quietly that she did not think that Fairchild had heard her. But he heard and seemed to find nothing odd about the question.

'Oh, the wife went off her head and killed the baby,' he said. 'Dreadful business. Dreadful.' To Laura's relief, he dissolved into another fit of coughing and she guessed that he did not even notice her stricken look. By the time he had mopped his eyes again she had composed herself and leaned back in her chair, drained of all energy and emotion.

'So will you go running back to Bradfield – or is it to David Ross himself? – to report on all this,' Fairchild said sharply, nodding at his notebooks.

'You knew that's what they wanted?' She had had too much of lies and subterfuge, she thought, to bother denying what Fairchild had evidently worked out for himself.

'I guessed. We're not all inbred sheep-shaggers up here, you know,' he said with uncharacteristic venom. 'We can recognise a spy without a Mata Hari name-plate when she walks through the door.'

'I have to report back to Ross,' she said soberly.

'So report,' Fairchild said flatly. 'I dare say you'll lose your job if you don't. And you've got the makings of a good reporter. I liked your High Clough story. It had the right balance of fact and feeling. It's not everyone can do that.'

'But you'd not have run it?'

'Oh, no, I'd not have run it. You understand now why not. Barry Moore's always had a genius for manipulating people to get what he wants. I've known the family since he was a lad. I don't think he's ever forgiven the world for the fact that his mother ran off and left them when he was about eight or nine. He's treated it all like a game of Monopoly ever since, calling in the mortgages when it was to his best advantage. And very successful he's been at it, too.'

'At what cost?' Laura asked.

'Oh, the cost isn't too high if you play along with him. You pay in self-respect but there's usually a quid pro quo. He keeps his promises.'

'And if you don't go along?' Laura asked, desperately wanting to know.

Fairchild looked at her from rheumy, speculative eyes.

'His father once told me that his mother always sent him a Christmas and a birthday present, every year, without fail. He always passed the parcels on to the boy, not wanting to encourage him to bear a grudge, but Barry took them off to his room and never mentioned them again. Years later, when the house was being sold, and Barry was away working in Bradfield, the old man found a couple of suit-cases hidden in the attic. Inside them was every single present Mrs Moore had sent, smashed or ripped into a hundred pieces, wrapping paper and all.' Laura shuddered, suddenly cold.

'So you see my dilemma?' Reg said. 'Don't they say to understand all is to forgive all? David Ross won't forgive, but perhaps you will. You've got the capacity for it.'

Trying to understand all, Laura thought sadly, putting her foot hard on the accelerator as the road widened out on the approach to Arnedale, she had given her curiosity free rein and bitterly regretted it, hopelessly uncertain of what to do with the burden of Michael Thackeray's tragedy that she had uncovered.

An accidental death would have been hard to bear, she thought, but murder, infanticide, whatever John Priestley had concluded at Ian Thackeray's inquest, must have led Thackeray and his wife into labyrinths of guilt and recrimination which she could not even begin to imagine and which she guessed he would never be willing to share. He had warned her not to pry and, now she knew why, she wished with all her heart she had taken him seriously.

It was mid-afternoon when she got back to the office, the street lights already flickering into life over the still-crowded Christmas market in Broad Street, the fluorescent tubes bleaching Debbie's pale face as she met her in the doorway of the newsroom.

'Thank goodness you're back,' the girl said breathlessly. 'I didn't know what to do. Jonathon's gone down to Eckersley to interview someone, he said, and I'm here on my own.'

Laura hung up her coat, not taking much interest, until Debbie got to the point.

'There's been a murder,' she said. 'That woman up at High Clough, the one's whose picture we had in this morning, Faith Lawrence? She's been shot.'

The news hit Laura like a blow to the stomach and she sat down suddenly in Jonathon West's swivel chair, her knees refusing to support her.

'Say that again slowly,' she demanded.

'Someone rang from the police,' Debbie said distinctly. 'Thought we'd want to know. They've found a body on the moors. They're treating it as suspicious. They're searching for a gun.'

'Dear God,' Laura said faintly, wondering if she had in a single day's work demolished her own future happiness and brought about the death of a woman she admired. 'Surely not because of the demo we reported,' she whispered. 'It couldn't possibly be because of that? Could it?'

Chief Inspector Michael Thackeray had driven into Arnedale that morning with painfully mixed emotions. He had come up the valley to work, with a dispensation to move outside his own division to pursue the fraud inquiry, which had now quite probably turned into a murder investigation. He was driven partly by the anger which had first seized him at the mortuary as he and Amos Atherton had stood above Linda Wright's body, stretched out like an alabaster statue on the slab.

Thackeray had turned away, disgusted by the waste and by the casualness of death. He had learned to cope with it but never to take it for granted. It had touched him too closely to ever become a familiar.

His mood on his solitary drive worsened as the tumbling river, which ran alongside the main road, narrowed and the morning traffic eased, leaving a broad clear road for the last few miles to the market town. He had not been able to avoid Arnedale entirely since he left it, but he had never returned, officially or unofficially, to the police station where he had risen swiftly to the rank of detective sergeant. He had been the bright young Oxford graduate destined for higher things, until he had pulled disaster down upon himself and his family out of an apparently clear blue sky. The day's work ahead filled him with foreboding.

He knew there were people at the Arnedale nick who would not have forgotten Detective Sergeant Thackeray and the manner of his leaving, not least Les Thorpe himself, whose wife had borne a third child within months of Aileen Thackeray's first and had taken it upon herself to act as confidante to the newer mother.

There had been a night, he recalled, soon after Ian had died, when he had been sitting in the Bull at someone's leaving party drinking himself insensible and Betty Thorpe had screamed at him across the crowded bar, putting into words what he knew most of his colleagues felt.

'It was your fault, not Aileen's,' she had said. 'You're the bloody murderer.' In the agonising silence that followed not one of his colleagues had tried to deter him as he bought a bottle of whisky and left the bar. He had headed for the dark coal-encrusted banks of the canal where he had systematically set about drinking enough to give himself the courage to jump into its freezing waters and put an end to the nightmare once and for all.

But he had failed even that test, he thought, being found unconscious with his empty bottle and hauled before his senior officers and told to dry out or get out. And in the end the job which had nearly destroyed him had finally saved him, absorbing his energies and satisfying his intelligence and enabling him, most of the time, to push what he had lost into the farthest recesses of his mind, the stuff of nightmares, but bearable.

For ten years he had survived alone on the other side of the county, ten reasonable years of long hours and hard-won promotion and a careful avoidance of commitment, until he was posted to Bradfield and met a self-willed young reporter who had shaken his carefully nurtured equilibrium. He was often infuriated by Laura but he knew he could not change her and would not even try. He liked her very much the way she was. What he dreaded more than anything was to see Betty Thorpe's bitter accusation reflected in Laura's frank green eyes. That, he knew, he would not be able to bear and did not know how to avoid.

He was greeted at the desk at Arnedale police station by a fresh-faced sergeant he did not know and directed to Chief Inspector Les Thorpe's office on the first floor. His former colleague stood and offered his hand but there was little enough warmth in his smile.

'I can spare you a DC for a couple of hours, but that's all,' Thorpe said unhelpfully. 'I'm up to my eyes wi'this shooting at High Clough.' Thackeray had picked up the news of Faith Lawrence's death on the local radio and he wondered how Laura Ackroyd was dealing with it.

'I've arranged to see Barry Moore at two,' Thackeray said. 'It would be helpful to have back-up for that. Otherwise I'll be fine, thanks.'

'And I don't suppose you're going to tell me why you want to talk to Barry Moore. You should know he'll play merry hell if he thinks he's being harassed – especially by you.'

'I saw Sydney Cheetham in Bradfield yesterday and he wasn't too pleased, either,' Thackeray said mildly. He did not elaborate further and Thorpe scowled his frustration.

'This girl in the car, is it?' he asked. 'I thought you'd got someone lined up for that. I saw the photograph in the *Bradfield Gazette* of someone you want to talk to.'

'Jimmy Townsend? Oh, I want to talk to him all right,' Thackeray said. 'But I'm not sure yet that he killed his girlfriend. It's not as simple as it looked at first. What about Mrs Lawrence? Domestic, is it?'

'Couldn't say,' Thorpe said non-committally. 'She was well-known as a troublemaker, was Mrs Lawrence, so she could have got up any number of noses.'

'I want to get up to Netherdale later,' Thackeray said. 'And call in on my father in High Clough, if there's time. But the weather doesn't look too promising.' The two men glanced out of the window where the snow was now whirling down from a leaden sky, blown in gusts by a wind which seemed to be rising even as they watched.

'Forecast's bad,' Thorpe said. 'You'll be lucky to get up to Netherdale and back today. It'd be Mrs Harding you'd want to see, would it? Mortgage fraud?'

'You're not following it up?' Thackeray asked casually.

'The man's dead and buried,' Thorpe said. 'What's the point? There's no evidence the wife was involved.'

'But he couldn't have worked a fiddle like that on his own.'

'Mebbe, mebbe not,' Thorpe said. 'But with David Harding dead, his evidence gone, there was no mileage in it. As far as we were concerned it was a one-off, minor league.'

'And as far as we were concerned, too. A bit less minor, perhaps, as we had four cases to go on. But we ended up with a young woman dead,' Thackeray said. 'So it's not minor league any more, it got promoted to the first division, the chief constable's concerned, and I don't like having my witnesses knocked off to protect bigger fish, if that's what's happened.'

'Barry Moore could make life very unpleasant for you, one way and another,' Thorpe said.

'Do you think I don't know that?' Thackeray said. 'Why do you think I came up to Arnedale personally, Les, if it wasn't to prove that you bastards don't scare me any more?'

Chief Inspector Thackeray and his borrowed detective constable, Brian Able, were already settled in Barry Moore's office when the auctioneer returned from what appeared to have been a bibulous lunch at the Bull. Moore apologised fulsomely and with complete insincerity for keeping them waiting as he shook the snow off his sheepskin jacket and scarf, hung them up and settled himself behind his enormous walnut desk. His weather-beaten face was even ruddier than usual, his blue eyes almost disappearing into a forest of creases and sandy eyebrows, the mouth disconcertingly thin-lipped and unforgiving. Under his outdoor clothes he was wearing a light tweed suit over a silk shirt and tie, with the heavy gold jewellery he favoured confined today to a couple of rings.

'It's been a long time, Michael,' he said to Thackeray. 'Will you have a drink?' The hesitation which followed was clearly deliberate. 'Coffee, I mean, or tea? Something hot?'

Thackeray shook his head impassively. 'Your secretary already offered,' he said.

'So what can I do for you?' The auctioneer spread his arms expansively. 'Anything I can do to help the police, it goes without saying, although I can't imagine what brings you up from Bradfield to see me. You're not moving back to Arnedale are you? Old stamping grounds and all that?'

When Thackeray shook his head again almost imperceptibly, Moore nodded sympathetically.

'No,' he said. 'I don't suppose that would do at all, would it?'

'David Harding,' Thackeray said, refusing to be provoked. 'A client of yours?'

'Not mine personally, of course,' Moore said. 'The firm's. I can find out who dealt with him for you, if you like. I believe he came in wanting to sell the holding about two years ago.' He put a finger on the intercom switch on his desk and waited a second for Thackeray's reaction.

'In a minute,' Thackeray said. 'First tell me what you know about the Hardings, how they got into such a mess financially.'

'All these hill farmers are getting desperate,' Moore said. 'I thought you knew that. The subsidies have gone down, some silly beggars don't want to eat meat any more, you name it. Your own father's planning to sell up, isn't he? Harding was just a bit further down the line, that's all.'

'And tried to buy time by getting involved in a mortgage fraud?'

'So I'm told,' Moore said. 'You know nothing stays secret long in Arnedale, Michael.'

Thackeray swallowed his fury again and let it pass.

'So would you – the firm – have advised him on that?' he persisted.

'On a legitimate package, yes,' Moore said sharply. 'Assuming the valuation was sufficient to leave room for a second mortgage.'

'And he could afford the repayments?'

'Of course. That's what these people so often forget,' Moore said, as if discussing a lower form of life. 'Loans have to be repaid. Harding seems to have over-extended himself hopelessly, from what John Priestley, the coroner, says.

'It didn't all come out at the inquest,' the auctioneer went on blandly. 'To save Mrs Harding's distress, of course. But it was in the note. You remember John Priestley?' Moore finished, fixing Thackeray with a crocodile smile.

'Of course, you would,' he added quickly, answering his own question and leaving Thackeray white and speechless with anger. He wondered what alternative career would be open to him if he smashed his fist into Moore's face, as he was tempted to do.

'I'd like to see the person who dealt with Harding now, please,' he said at length, when he had controlled his breathing and unclenched his jaw, and this time Moore did flick the intercom and instruct his secretary accordingly. The two big men sat in uneasy silence, with the bemused detective constable behind them, fiddling with his pencil and notebook, aware of the intense emotion swirling around him but oblivious to its cause.

Seeing Moore again after all this time reminded Thackeray of the Barry he had known, the big-boned sandy-haired prefect and altar boy eight or nine years his senior and never slow to take advantage of his size. His greatest joy had lain in provoking younger children into all sorts of mischief at school and at church, his greatest talents being able to talk his own way out of trouble with an entirely spurious air of injured innocence, and to enforce silence on others by a combination of threats and the sort of violence which left no mark. The child was father to the man, Thackeray thought, and it was high time Barry Moore earned the reward long due to him as a sadist and a crook.

'Are you staying in Arnedale for Christmas?' Moore asked conversationally, as if nothing had happened. 'Will we see you at Midnight Mass?'

Thackeray shook his head in irritation, refusing to answer, and within minutes the pretty blonde woman who had looked anxious when Thackeray arrived came into the room looking even more anxious.

'Jimmy Townsend handled the Harding remortgage before he moved to the Bradfield office, Mr Moore,' she said.

'Well, well,' Thackeray said, satisfied, although Moore looked entirely unfazed.

'I read that you were looking for Townsend in connection with the murder of what's-her-name? Linda Wright?' Moore said, his gaze unblinking.

'And a series of mortgage frauds in Bradfield,' Thackeray conceded. 'So let's start with everything you know about that young man, shall we? He worked here for some time, I believe.'

'He came here when he left school,' Moore said easily.

143

'Gave complete satisfaction, as far as I was concerned. Soon became a canny young negotiator, keen, smart, ambitious, everything you'd want in this business. I thought he'd go far.'

'As far as Armley gaol, if half of what we know about him is true,' Thackeray said grimly. 'You had no idea he was on the make?'

'Absolutely none, Michael,' Moore said earnestly. 'He'd have been out of the door like a shot if I'd even suspected. He'd been brought up in Arnedale, father had a shop in Broad Street – you probably remember it, fancy goods, tourist bits and bobs. Did one or two A levels at the grammar school and then came here. Seemed a good lad, on the face of it. Then there was a vacancy in the Bradfield office and he said he'd like to move. I'd no hesitation in recommending him to Sydney Cheetham. None at all. I don't think I've seen him since.'

'And Linda Wright? The girl who was killed? I believe she worked here too for a while?'

'Oh, a couple of weeks as a trainee, that's all, must be two years ago. It was never intended she should stay here. A pretty little blonde thing, as I remember.'

'That must be when she met Jimmy Townsend?'

'Yes, I dare say it was,' Moore said. 'I can check all these details for you if you like.'

'Yes, I would like,' Thackeray said flatly. 'Everything you've got on file about the two of them, please.'

He stood up, startling the secretary who had been hovering behind Moore, and bringing a wary look to Moore's expansive features.

'I need to speak to that young man, and I need to speak to him urgently,' Thackeray said.

'I don't suppose,' he went on conversationally, 'that you knew Linda Wright socially at all? Took her out for a drink or anything like that?'

'Socially?' Moore said in a strangled tone, glancing at his secretary who looked away, embarrassed. 'No, I bloody didn't know her socially. From what I heard she was a little tart with more lads sniffing after her than dogs around a bitch on heat.'

FOURTEEN

LAURA TURNED TO MICHAEL THACKERAY that evening because she could not think who else she could turn to. Her usually incisive brain seemed to have been curdled by the day's disasters, and she could not decide what to do next. But Thackeray proved to be elusive. He was not at his flat or his office in Bradfield, where an unhelpful sergeant she did not know seemed reluctant to locate him for her.

He might have gone back to High Clough if his mother had taken a turn for the worse, she thought, and she sat at her desk staring at the telephone number for West Rigg Farm for a long time before she could bring herself to dial.

'I didn't want to intrude,' she said when he came to the phone. 'But I need to see you.' He hesitated and she could imagine his irritation at being disturbed at the house he only visited out of a sense of duty.

'There's a pub on the Ribblesdale Road, the Drover, on the left before the turn up to High Clough,' he said at length. 'Meet me there in about an hour?'

She drove out of Arnedale and into the hills for the second time that day, spinning the journey out but still arriving at the pub before Thackeray. She parked and went inside to an unwelcoming and chilly bar where a surly landlord looked her over for a moment before serving her the vodka and tonic she requested. The pub was an isolated one, and clearly did not attract many customers on an evening when more snow threatened.

She took her drink to a corner table and sat down with her coat on. The old stone fireplace showed remnants of a log fire but had been neither cleaned out nor re-lit recently.

She shivered, not entirely as a result of the cold, and took a sip of her drink, avoiding the landlord's unfriendly gaze as he leaned on his bar and engaged in desultory conversation with a couple of men in working clothes who had come in just after her.

She had finished her drink by the time Thackeray arrived, coming in from the car-park in a flurry of snow and a blast of cold air. He glanced at her glass without speaking, and went to the bar to get her another, before settling down opposite her.

'How is your mother?' she asked automatically, staring into her drink to avoid his eyes.

'Dying,' he said. 'Slowly. I don't think she should stay up there much longer but my father doesn't want her moved.' He shrugged, as preoccupied with his own emotions as she was with hers, and as reluctant to share them.

'You know about Faith Lawrence?' he asked quietly, after a pause. She nodded, not trusting herself to speak.

'I'm sorry,' he said. 'She seemed a pleasant woman. Took my delivery of her husband the other night in her stride – no recriminations, not to me, anyway.'

'I liked her a lot,' Laura whispered, thinking of that delicate, pale face half-hidden by the sweep of silver hair, the determined lines of the mouth and the occasional humour in the clear eyes, a woman who had come late into her full powers, and found a tentative sort of happiness before she died. Laura felt defeated by the events and revelations of the last two days.

'She couldn't have been killed because of the campaign, could she? Because we reported it? There's an awful lot of angry people up there.'

'Come on Laura, you don't get shot for getting your picture in the papers,' Thackeray said dismissively. 'But if she's made enemies, it will all be investigated. It's all been pretty public, hasn't it?'

'Some of it,' she conceded after she had fortified herself with another sip of vodka. 'That's what I needed to talk to you about. She told me some things which I suspect no one else knows about, private things . . .'

146

'Nothing about Faith Lawrence is private any more,' Thackeray said grimly. 'A murder victim becomes public property, no secrets, no privacy.' Amos Atherton, he thought, would no doubt already be on his way to Arnedale hospital, if he had not already arrived, ready to expose Faith's body to the indignities of a post-mortem, but he did not think that Laura would want to know that.

'It was definitely murder? She didn't kill herself? You know that?'

Thackeray shook his head at that.

'Inspector Thorpe's DS came up to West Rigg earlier this evening to see if anyone had seen or heard anything unusual. He was quite chatty when he discovered I was there. There was no gun near the body, he said. They're still scouring the moorland round where she was found – or they were until it got dark. The snow's not helping, of course. It's already covering tracks, and may cover the weapon for weeks if it hangs about.'

'A shotgun?'

He nodded.

'What about the boy, Tim?' Laura said, remembering the unhappy, lovesick adolescent Faith had been so worried about.

'I don't know, Laura. It's not my case. I can't get involved even if I wanted to, which I don't. I've got enough problems of my own in High Clough, and Les Thorpe is no friend of mine. And I have to go back to Bradfield first thing in the morning. I've a murder of my own to investigate.'

'Faith was having an affair,' Laura said bluntly. 'She told me about it – briefly. I'm not sure anyone else knows.'

Thackeray looked at her and wondered what it was about her that seemed to persuade the most unlikely people to confide in her. He had done it himself in the first days of their relationship, telling her something – but not everything – of a past he had not discussed with another living soul for years. Faith Lawrence, on his brief acquaintance with her on her doorstep when she had taken reasonably gracious delivery of a semi-comatose husband, did not appear to be a woman

147

who needed a shoulder to weep on. But with Laura on hand to provide it, you could never tell.

'Who's the boyfriend? Did she say?'

'Oh, yes. I met him. It was one of the travellers up at the quarry. She'd met him before, on some anti-road protest down south, and then he turned up here.' Laura seemed to be having trouble getting the words out, and Thackeray guessed there was more to tell, and something of more significance too, judging by her reluctance to confide.

'Come on, Laura,' he said. 'You're going to have to tell Les Thorpe everything you know. There's no choice about that. The woman's dead. You can't protect her now. Or him?' The last was a shot in the dark but evidently hit home because Laura drained her glass and deliberately looked away.

'You think the boyfriend killed her?' Thackeray persisted. 'What makes you think that?'

'Don't interrogate me, Michael,' Laura objected fiercely. 'You said it's not your case. Leave it alone. I'll go to see Chief Inspector Thorpe tomorrow.'

'Most murder victims are killed by people they know,' Thackeray said sombrely, and Laura gave him an anguished look that he did not understand. There was so much she wanted to say, and not the remotest possibility that she could even begin, she thought.

'He had a shotgun,' she muttered at last. 'Faith's toy-boy, that's what *she* called him herself. But I can't believe he killed her. I can't believe that.'

'You must tell Thorpe now, straight away,' Thackeray said flatly. 'Anything could happen overnight. He could make a run for it, dump the gun, anything. Go down to the police station in Arnedale. There'll be someone there to take a statement.'

'Everything's always so clear-cut with you,' Laura said angrily, knowing she was being irrational but seeking any excuse to dodge doing what she knew she had to do. 'You live on a different moral plane from the rest of us. Everything's black and white, no fuzzy edges.'

Thackeray winced at that, it was so far from the truth, but she did not seem to notice his reaction.

'I don't think Rob killed Faith. They seemed so happy. She thought I disapproved, but I didn't. With all she had to put up with from that appalling drunken husband I was happy for her . . .' She broke off, aware that the ground beneath her feet was the thinnest of crusts over a very deep crater, and all the fires of hell beneath.

'You must go,' he said again, his expression stony. 'It doesn't matter what you think. You're in possession of material information and if you don't pass it on promptly Thorpe would be quite within his rights to take action against you. And knowing him, he'd probably enjoy it.'

Thinking of her own most recent encounter with the Arnedale chief inspector, Laura knew that Thackeray was closer to the truth than he could know. She stood up and buttoned her coat with shaking fingers.

'I'll go,' she said bleakly. 'Good-night, Michael.'

'I'll call you,' he said, but he did not think she heard as she swept out of the bar without looking back. There was a shout of ribald laughter from the men at the bar which Thackeray guessed was directed at him in the light of Laura's sudden exit. He sat for a moment, wondering bitterly if he could ever escape from the long shadows of the past, before he too put his coat on and set off back up the steep hill towards his father's house.

The last thing Michael Thackeray wanted that night was to get involved in DCI Les Thorpe's murder inquiry. He drove back through the village consciously ignoring the two police cars still parked on the verge close to where Faith Lawrence's body had been found. The night was very dark, with snow flurries occasionally hurling themselves against the windscreen, and it was impossible now to see the gulley which the police had cordoned off with blue and white tape.

Back at West Rigg he found his father sitting at his mother's bedside, holding her limp hand in his gnarled one, the two farm dogs asleep together at the foot of the bed. Thackeray raised an eyebrow at that.

'I thought they weren't house dogs,' he said.

'She likes to see them about,' Joe Thackeray said.

'Have you eaten?'

The old man shook his head. It seemed to Thackeray that food was the last thing which ever entered his head, and his bony frame was being held together by some sort of psychic energy, like a marionette on wires which would snap as soon as, or even sooner than, Molly's life finally drained away.

'It's snowing,' Thackeray said, knowing that if he were concerned for nothing else he would worry about the safety of his sheep.

'The ewes are all inbye in t'bottom field,' Joe said. 'They'll be reet if there's owt less than a blizzard.'

'I'll get us some tea,' Thackeray said and went downstairs again to the big kitchen which, with its open fire in the old-fashioned black range, was the warmest room in the house. He took the iron poker and stirred the coals before stoking them up even higher. It was going to be a bleak night.

He peered around his father's frugal larder and collected up bacon, a couple of cans of baked beans and half a dozen eggs, realising that however long the old man could go without food he himself was ravenously hungry. Cooking took his mind temporarily off his own disenchantments and the room was soon filled with the smell of frying bacon, bringing the dogs down the stairs, tails wagging frantically and looking so curious that he wondered how long it was since his father had had a hot meal at all.

Their feeding dishes were in the stone-floored lobby by the back door which led out into the farmyard. He opened two cans of dog food for them, which they wolfed down hungrily, and replenished their water, before opening the door to let them out. The wind had risen and the snow was blowing in swirling gusts with such force that the dogs almost turned tail back into the house but he booted them gently over the threshold regardless. If they needed shelter he knew they could gain access to the barn on the other side of the yard.

The door closed again, he put two plates on the solid old table which dominated the room and called his father from the bottom of the stairs. The old man came down slowly, holding tightly to the banister with a white-knuckled grip.

'The nurse'll not get up here tonight,' Thackeray said. The

150

community nurse was supposed to call twice a day to see to Molly Thackeray's toilet.

'I'll manage. It'll not be t'first time she's not come,' the old man said. He sat at the table, poking a fork into his egg desultorily.

'You must eat. You need to keep your strength up,' Thackeray said, feeling helpless to sustain a situation which appeared to be rapidly spinning out of control. His mother, he thought, had to be moved and moved quickly, but he flinched from making the point to Joe again for fear of reopening the wrangle about his own future. It would be a bitter irony, he thought, if he let his father sell the farm and then the reorganised police force decided it could dispense with his services.

They finished their meal and Joe went back upstairs to make Molly comfortable for the night, refusing all offers of assistance.

'She'd not want that,' he said flatly, and Thackeray had to admit that he was probably right. Instead he settled down in the single high-backed chair close to the fire with the previous day's *Arnedale Observer*, re-reading Laura's fierce prose and wondering whether it could, as she feared, have had any connection with Faith Lawrence's death. That the increasingly vocal protests she had been leading had made her powerful enemies in Arnedale he had no doubt. But murder seemed an unlikely reaction.

He must have dozed, because the next thing he was aware of was the sound of the dogs barking frantically outside. He glanced at his watch and realised it was already ten o'clock. The fierce wind which had been whipping around the house earlier, finding endless cracks in its defences through which to whistle and moan, appeared to have dropped and when he went to the lobby door and looked out he was faced with a virgin expanse of snow, gleaming in the single bar of yellow light from the door. The dogs were nowhere to be seen, but the sound of their barking was coming from the barn on the other side of the yard.

He forced his feet into a pair of his father's wellington boots, took a flashlight from its hook by the door and waded

151

through the crisp new snow to investigate. The two black and white sheepdogs greeted him ecstatically in the half-open entrance to the barn, which was used as a store for winter feed, but they soon ran off again towards the darkest corner and crouched there, quivering, tails moving uncertainly as they faced whatever was hidden there. Thackeray focused the flashlight and made out a human figure half-hidden behind a couple of bales of hay.

He approached cautiously behind the dogs but soon realised that the man offered no threat. He was hunched, shivering, into the hay for warmth, with an arm across his face to protect it from the bright flashlight beam. A tramp caught out by the sudden snowfall, Thackeray assumed.

'You'd better come into the house,' he said. 'You'll freeze to death out here tonight.' Awkwardly the unexpected visitor scrambled to his feet, staggering slightly as if one leg would not easily bear his weight. Thackeray flashed the light downwards but could see no signs of injury.

'I had a fall,' the stranger said, his voice faint, slightly slurred, as if speech were a great effort. 'I don't know how long I lay in the snow.'

'Put your arm round my neck,' Thackeray said. 'It's not far.' Hopping and stumbling, the two of them made erratic progress across the snowy yard and in at the back door where Thackeray lowered him into the chair close to the fire and stood back to take stock.

He found himself facing a surprisingly young man, who lay back in the chair, shivering convulsively, with his eyes shut. A gypsy rather than a tramp, Thackeray concluded quickly, taking in the swarthy weather-beaten complexion, and the dark hair tied back in a pony-tail, but a gypsy hopelessly ill-equipped for the moors in the bitter weather which had suddenly swept in from the north and which might well have killed him if he had not found shelter in the barn when he did. He was dressed in soaking wet jeans and trainers and a plaid jacket on which caked patches of snow were now beginning to melt in the heat of the fire.

'You'd best get out of those wet clothes,' Thackeray said. He went upstairs to fetch a couple of blankets, but when he came back the young man had made no effort to undress, but was sitting hunched forward towards the fire with his head in his hands.

'Where am I?' he asked dully, when Thackeray put a hand on his shoulder to urge him to take his sodden jacket off.

'You're at West Rigg Farm,' Thackeray said. He turned to the oak dresser which filled one wall of the kitchen and unearthed the small bottle of brandy which had been in a cupboard there almost as long as he could remember. He poured a small measure and offered it to the stranger who took a sip and choked on it as a touch of colour began to return to his sallow cheeks.

'Christ, what a mess,' he muttered. A sound behind them made Thackeray spin round in surprise. His father was standing in the doorway in his pyjamas, a shotgun in one hand.

'I heerd t'dogs carrying on,' he said, by way of explanation. 'What's he doing here?'

'Do you know him?' Thackeray asked, surprised.

'Aye, he's one o't'lads from t'camp in t'quarry. What's he strayed up here for?'

The visitor said nothing as he slipped out of his jacket and wrapped the blankets Thackeray had brought around himself. He drained the brandy and gradually his convulsive shivering began to subside but his eyes remained wary.

'I set off over the tops to Netherdale before the snow started,' he said. 'I had a fall, wrenched my ankle and then got well and truly lost in the blizzard. I'd no idea where I was when I found the barn, just thankful to get under cover. You must be Joe's son?'

He gave Michael Thackeray an equivocal look before he eased his left foot out of his trainer, rolled off his sodden sock and poked experimentally at the puffy flesh of his ankle. He winced.

'Tha'll not be walking far on that,' Joe Thackeray opined, leaning over the damaged foot. 'Tha should teck more care, lad. It's an old-fashioned neet to be out on t'fells.'

Too old-fashioned, Thackeray thought, for a casual trip after dark up the exposed track which took a tortuous ten-mile course to Netherdale. He glanced out of the window at the frozen snow.

'I'll not get my car to the quarry in this,' he said. 'You'd best stay here until morning if my father doesn't mind.'

'He can sleep on t'sofa in t'parlour,' Joe said. 'It'll be a sight better than t'barn, any road.'

Thackeray glanced at the stranger with a faintly mocking smile as he met those dark, suspicious eyes.

'No,' he said. 'I'll sleep down here and our guest can have my bed. He'll be more comfortable there with that ankle. And the dogs won't bother him upstairs.' The young man's shoulders slumped at that, as Thackeray had thought they might. Conscious of the sudden tension, the old man gave them both a steaming mug of tea and announced his intention of returning to bed.

'I'll leave t'gun theer,' he said meaningfully to his son, nodding his head to the corner where he had left the shotgun leaning against the wall, but Thackeray shook his head.

'Lock it up again,' he said. 'Mr Tyler's not going anywhere.'

'You know my name,' the young man said faintly. 'Of course, you're the policeman. I'd forgotten that. I chose the wrong barn, didn't I? Mind, if I'd ended up in one of Ray Harding's outhouses he'd likely have shot me first and asked questions after.'

He sipped his tea dejectedly for a moment while Thackeray watched him, wondering if he had inadvertently caught a murderer. If he had, it would be one of the easiest arrests of his career.

'So what do you think you know, anyway?' the young man said with a touch more spirit as the tea warmed him.

'I don't know anything,' Thackeray said quietly. 'I just guessed you must be Rob Tyler. But I reckon no one without a very powerful reason sets off across the moors to Netherdale on a night like this. And as there's been a brutal murder not half a mile away, I can think of one very powerful reason that might apply. You didn't make it, and you're not going to make it now with that ankle, so you might as well tell me what it's all about.'

'Confession time, Inspector? It is Inspector, isn't it?' Tyler said, acknowledging Thackeray's assessment with a shrug and a faint smile. 'It wouldn't be admissible evidence, would it, just you and me? Not that I suppose that would worry you.'

'You're well informed about the law,' Thackeray said.

'You need to be, believe me, if you step out of line these days. But it makes no difference. I didn't kill Faith, though there are plenty of people round here who would be only too pleased to see me go down for it anyway.'

'You just ran away in a blizzard for the hell of it?'

'I don't trust the police, Mr Thackeray. People like me have no reason to. So when I heard they were coming up here mob-handed I decided to make myself scarce for a bit. I'm not easily scared but the idea of sitting in gaol for a dozen years for something I haven't done frightens me. And don't tell me it couldn't happen, because we both know it could.'

'Heard?' Thackeray said sharply, wondering how such a significant piece of information had reached the quarry encampment so conveniently.

'We have a mobile phone,' Tyler said. 'You don't have a monopoly on new technology, you know. It's very useful when you're on the move a lot.' And trying to dodge the police as a way of life, Thackeray thought.

'And who did you hear from?' he persisted, concerned that police security in Arnedale was evidently so lax, but Tyler merely smiled and shook his head.

'You wouldn't expect me to tell you that.'

'No, but DCI Thorpe might when he gets his hands on you.'

Tyler ran a hand wearily across his face at that and groaned.

'I didn't kill her,' he said quietly. 'I was very fond of Faith. She was very special. I would no more have harmed her than I would harm my kids. But I don't think anyone's going to believe me.'

'You had a shotgun,' Thackeray said, remembering what Laura had said. Tyler looked at him consideringly for a moment and then nodded.

'You're well informed too,' he said. 'But I got rid of it after the attack on the camp. I know that doesn't sound very credible, but I fired it that night and I reckoned someone would complain, tell the police, and they'd come looking. It was a stupid thing to do, to use the gun, but everyone was terrified, in a panic, so I took a shot into the air and it drove them off.'

'Got rid of it?' Thackeray said sceptically.

'Threw it into a bog up beyond East Rigg.' If that were true there would be no chance of ever retrieving it. Both men knew that. But it could as easily have been thrown into a bog after the murder as before. Both men knew that too. Thackeray suddenly felt very weary and disinclined to venture further into a case which was officially no concern of his.

'You'll come with me to Arnedale to see Inspector Thorpe as soon as the road's passable in the morning,' he said. It was a statement, not an invitation, and Tyler nodded resignedly. Hardly able to walk, he had no choice.

Thackeray went over to the phone by the kitchen door and dialled the police station in Arnedale where he was quickly connected to Detective Chief Inspector Thorpe, who was in a decidedly angry mood.

'You'll not get up here tonight. There's been quite heavy drifting and no one will attempt to clear the road before morning,' Thackeray said when Thorpe expressed the intention of coming to fetch Tyler there and then. 'He's not going anywhere. I can guarantee that.'

'You did what?' Thackeray exclaimed, not sure that he had heard Thorpe's next angry outburst correctly. 'The Armed Response Unit? What the hell for?' He was too surprised to mince his words.

He listened in astonishment as Thorpe explained why he had called out the Force's élite firearms group because he believed that the travellers' camp was harbouring an armed murderer. His embarrassment at finding no weapons when the camp was searched, and no suspect either, explained his fury. That his humiliation was exposed to a senior officer in another division, and one who had apparently achieved on his own what Thorpe's small army had failed to do, merely added fuel to the flames. It took Thackeray five minutes to convince his colleague that he did not need to re-run the evening's exercise and that Rob Tyler would be safely and peacefully delivered for an interview the next morning as soon as the road down from West Rigg Farm was passable.

When he had put the receiver down, Thackeray looked at Tyler with something close to sympathy in his eyes.

'You're not very popular down at the nick,' he said.

Tyler sighed.

'I didn't kill her,' he said. 'But I've no cast-iron alibi. I'll never prove it. Do you believe me?'

Thackeray shook his head dismissively. To his own surprise, he found he wanted to believe Tyler innocent perhaps as much as Thorpe was evidently determined to believe him guilty but he knew neither reaction was rational.

'I haven't seen the evidence. I can't help you. I'm sorry,' he said, meaning it. 'Now let's get some sleep. I'll help you up the stairs.'

Alerted by Debbie, who had made an early call to the police station, Laura Ackroyd crossed Broad Street herself soon after nine the next morning to check out what progress the police inquiry had made into the murder of Faith Lawrence. The overnight snow had been much lighter here and the street and pavements had already been swept and sanded by the market traders anxious to get on with the urgent business of selling on the busiest Saturday of the year.

She went up the worn stone steps and under the blue lamp for the second time in just over twelve hours with a certain sense of misgiving. She had not enjoyed the previous evening's brief interview with DCI Thorpe.

In spite of what Michael Thackeray had urged, she felt that she was in some way betraying Faith Lawrence by disclosing the confidences she had shared about Rob Tyler. She supposed miserably to herself that it was possible that Rob had shot Faith, in the grip of some emotional turmoil she could not even guess at. Yet she was still haunted by the moment of tenderness she had witnessed at Faith's house, a moment she could not believe could be connected in any way with her brutal death.

Thorpe, of course, had had no such doubts or inhibitions,

complaining bitterly that she had delayed in coming forward, and taking her over every scrap of information she could dredge up from her memory again and again.

He had been particularly insistent in his questioning about Rob Tyler's shotgun. Had she seen it? he asked. Did she know where he kept it? Was it single- or double-barrelled, pump-action, sawn-off? She merely looked confused at his questions, knowing little enough about shotguns generally and nothing at all about Rob Tyler's, and unsure whether the murder weapon could be identified, as she knew other weapons could, from whatever traces it left behind.

He had shown no interest at all in her suggestion that maybe Faith's death was connected with her campaigning.

'She had made enemies,' Laura had said. 'In the village and down here in Arnedale.'

'So have you, lass,' Thorpe had come back quickly. 'But no one's tried to blow your head off.'

The whole episode had left her feeling unhappy and dissatisfied and she had slept badly in the hard, narrow bed 'above the shop' at the *Observer*, wondering what action Thorpe would take later that evening as a result of her statement. That question had been answered soon enough by Debbie, who had come in on the early shift and told Laura briefly of the raid on the travellers' camp and the failure to find either Rob Tyler or his shotgun. Chief Inspector Thorpe, she thought, would not be best pleased.

She was astonished to meet Michael Thackeray on the way out of the police station as she went in.

'What are you doing here?' she asked.

'I bumped into your friend Rob Tyler last night, and gave him a lift in to see DCI Thorpe,' Thackeray said succinctly and with scant regard for accuracy. He did not feel like adding to Laura's disillusion by describing Tyler's abortive attempt to escape from the police, and his own role in thwarting it.

'Has he charged him?' Laura asked and was relieved, though not much, when Thackeray shook his head.

'Not yet,' he said. 'But I think it's only a matter of time.'

'Can't you do anything to stop it?'

Thackeray took Laura's arm and led her back down the police station steps.

'You know I can't, Laura. It's not my case, not my patch. Thorpe is already pretty angry that I got involved inadvertently last night. Now I have to go back to Bradfield for a meeting with the super about my own murder case. If you want my advice, which I'm sure you don't, I wouldn't wear my heart on my sleeve in there. Thorpe thinks he's got an open and shut case against Tyler and won't take kindly to you, or the *Observer*, suggesting different.'

'I'm going up to High Clough,' Laura said, an obstinate expression which Thackeray knew only too well appearing on her face, her eyes angry. 'Thorpe's got it wrong, Michael. I know he has. I've got one more edition on Christmas Eve, just a token to get the TV listings out, but there's time to put something together for it if it's as important as this. I can't not try, can I?'

Even if it wrecks whatever it is you and I have got together, she thought bitterly, but she knew there was no contest. Barry Moore might threaten but when it came to the crunch she would have to let him do his worst.

Suddenly her eyes were pleading for support and Thackeray caught his breath, shaken with a sudden desire simply to take her in his arms and tell her all the things he regularly told her in his head before he went to sleep. But a uniformed policeman brushed past them clumsily, taking the steps two at a time, and the moment slipped away.

'Be careful,' Thackeray said, giving her a swift and unsatisfactory embrace before disappearing into the swirling crowds of Christmas shoppers.

FIFTEEN

THE MOOD IN THE QUARRYMAN that Saturday lunch-time was sour. The pub was crowded with High Clough residents who could number the generations of their family who had held cottages or farms in or around the village on the fingers of more than one hand.

'Off-comed'uns' were notably absent, perhaps well-aware that they would hear no good of themselves as recent events were chewed over with increasing indignation. The blame was being apportioned equally between the strangers who could afford to pay daft prices for damp stone cottages and those who could not but who arrived anyway in their motley collection of broken-down vans and buses. The 'old village' had closed ranks against the new and there was almost no crime too dire for suspicions not to be bandied around that morning.

The atmosphere in the public bar was almost fetid as the steam from damp and sweaty clothing and snowy boots mixed with the swirl of tobacco smoke from half a dozen pipes and as many cigarettes, the fumes from chips frying in beef-dripping and the hoppy smell of frothing pints of Tetley's. Saturday was not a working day for the men of High Clough, who had let the women take themselves off to Arnedale market once the road had been cleared, while they chewed the fat at length after two days of almost unrelieved sensation.

'It's time they bloody went,' Ray Harding said loudly into his fourth pint of Tetley's and there was a murmur of approbation around the bar. 'T'police should have shifted them last night when they had them surrounded. I couldn't believe it when they buggered off empty-handed. There must

160

have been summat up theer there shouldn't have been. Drugs, if nowt else. They're all on bloody pot or worse. LSD, cocaine, heroin – I reckon they've got the lot if you know where to look. I thought when they got this new law passed the police wouldn't have to bugger about like this. They'd have 'em out, and the bloody vans confiscated, as soon as look at 'em.'

'It were Tyler they were looking for,' another burly farmer offered. 'I heard someone saw Joe Thackeray's lad driving him down t'hill early on.'

'Aye, he were up theer again last night, were Michael. I saw his car,' Harding said. 'His mam's right poorly, I understand. But they were snowed in till I got t'tractor down t'lane at seven. He'd not have got a car down here again else. So you reckon t'police have got Tyler, do you?'

There was a murmur of approval at that but still with an undercurrent of deep dissatisfaction.

'One down, t'rest to go,' a voice muttered to vociferous assent.

'It's time they bloody went,' Harding said again, to another general murmur of approval.

'Just say the word, Ray,' the landlord said encouragingly.

The arrival of Laura Ackroyd and Fergal Mackenzie silenced the packed bar as if a steel shutter had been drawn down. The two journalists had met by chance in the car-park after a treacherous drive up from the main valley road. Fergal's complicit smile among the curling whiskers had cheered Laura up in spite of herself.

'Still chasing, princess?' he asked.

'Naturally,' she countered. 'I've got time to get something in the Christmas Eve edition.'

'Tut, tut. Surely that's just for stuffing recipes and an appreciation of this year's James Bond movie. You can't be putting news in on Christmas Eve,' he mocked. 'You breathe a word about that and Reg'll be back on Monday, mark my words. That'll cut you down to size.'

'Don't bet on it,' she flashed back.

'Well, it'll all be wrapped up by Monday if they charge Rob Tyler,' Mackenzie said, deadly serious all of a sudden. 'All you'll get is the magistrate's court appearance and there's never much copy in that.'

'Do you think they'll charge him?' Laura asked.

'Shall I tell you what I think?' Mackenzie said. 'I think Barry Moore engineered this but Tyler pulled the trigger.'

'That's your conspiracy theory run wild,' Laura said, horrified.

'Well, then tell me why I saw the two of them deep in conversation down at the auction mart the other day. Your jolly green giant Tyler certainly wasn't debating the ecology of hill farming with Moore, that's for sure. They seemed to be on very good terms to me. Good enough to take themselves off into the Lamb together for a wee dram afterwards.'

'Have you told the police that?'

'What's to tell, princess? I couldn't hear what they were saying. I was yards away, there were a couple of flocks of sheep and six trailers between them and me. I just thought it was odd at the time. I think it's even odder now that the lovely Faith has been killed. But it doesn't prove anything at all.'

'Oh hell,' Laura said. 'I don't know what to think. I saw Rob Tyler and Faith together and it just seemed to be very touching, somehow. I can't believe he killed her.'

'Your trouble is you let your heart rule your head, princess,' Mackenzie said dismissively. 'You need to develop a healthy cynicism. Think of them all as specimens in a menagerie, all of them with unpleasant habits of one kind or another. You'll be much nearer the truth. That's the basis that snake Barry Moore works on and look where it's got him. Now are you coming in for a dram or are we going to freeze ourselves solid out here while you come to terms with reality?'

Laura gave him a wan smile of assent and followed him into the bar, where they were met by a wall of silent, suspicious faces. Ray Harding was the first to thaw by a degree or two.

'Nah then,' he said, by way of greeting. 'Enough excitement for you newspaper beggars is there?' He addressed himself to Laura as they inched their way towards the bar. 'Pity they didn't let me finish t'job o'clearing that lot out when I tried to get started t'other day. Happen your precious Missus Lawrence might not be food for t'worms.'

'Are the police still up here?' Laura asked, swallowing her disgust.

'Aye, but cussing t'weather,' Harding said. 'Spoils their evidence, does snow. They've still got half t'moor fenced off up theer and a dozen men tramping about in wellies.' He laughed unsympathetically.

Mackenzie bought Laura a Scotch without bothering to ask whether she preferred an alternative to his national drink, but she sipped it gratefully, the spirit warming her a fraction emotionally as well as physically. They found seats in a corner of the tiny lounge bar where the press of locals was not quite so thick and listened for a while to the theories being bandied about, none of them flattering either to the dead woman or to the travellers they all seemed to have convinced themselves were responsible for her death.

'I think I want a word or two with Rob Tyler's friends up at the camp,' Mackenzie said softly after a while, and without attracting much interest they made their way out of the pub's side door and back into the car-park.

'They've tried and convicted him,' Laura said, outraged. 'And her, for that matter. "No better than she should be".' She mimicked the bar's cruel verdict, furious at their censorious prurience in a situation which did not touch them in any way that mattered.

'You should know what happens to women who step out of line,' Fergal said soberly. 'They used to burn them at the stake or duck them in the local pond. As for Tyler, he's one of the rogues and vagabonds they used to beat out of town. Read your traditional tales, princess. Nothing changes.'

'They'd hang him if they got the chance,' Laura said.

'Of course they would. And draw and quarter him too if they could get away with it. And all his mates. I think Rob Tyler might be better off safely down at the police station for the time being, whether he actually killed Mrs Lawrence or not.'

Tim Lawrence was sitting on the steps of Rob Tyler's bus when Laura and Fergal Mackenzie arrived, after struggling down through the snow on the steep track from the road with some difficulty. Behind him, through the open door of

163

the bus, Topaz's bells jingled gently in the wind. The boy looked up dully, hunched up into a duffle-coat, his jeans tucked into wellington boots, a shrivelled, shrunken figure, hollow-cheeked and dark-eyed with grief.

'Is Topaz here?' Laura asked gently. The boy shook his head.

'She went down to Arnedale to see about Rob,' he said. 'To get him a solicitor. I'm supposed to be looking after the kids.' He nodded to where Melody and Flint were playing snowballs with half a dozen other pink-cheeked and breathless children on the snowy edge of the camp. 'They don't really need me, but it's something to do, isn't it?'

'Shouldn't you be with your father?' Laura asked but the boy glared at her in return, a touch of angry colour returning to his cheeks.

'He's asleep, snoring like a pig,' he said. 'He got smashed last night. Typical!'

'Are you all right?' she asked, but he merely shrugged. The question was superfluous, she thought, and she guessed he might never be all right again.

'He didn't do it, you know,' Tim said, suddenly fierce.

'You mean Rob Tyler?' Mackenzie asked.

'Of course Rob Tyler,' the boy said. 'He didn't kill my mother. They were lovers, you know.' It was said with apparently casual sophistication, as though it were the most normal thing in the world, but Tim's eyes, pools of misery, bright with tears he could not bring himself to let go, said something else entirely.

'How long have you known?' she asked, thinking that perhaps he had picked up what had that morning become malicious gossip, whipping around the village like garbage on the cutting edge of the wind.

'Oh, for weeks,' the boy said. 'I saw them together one day when I was walking up beyond West Rigg. They were sitting up in the heather, with their arms around each other, just like Cathy and Heathcliff, you know.' Laura drew a sharp breath. It was difficult to tell whether he recalled the scene with grief or a hint of jealousy. Tim had hero-worshipped Rob Tyler, Faith had said, but perhaps it was more than that.

'Have the police talked to you and your father about what happened?' Mackenzie, who had been listening to the conversation with a sardonic look on his face, broke in.

'Only when they came to tell us when they found her. They talked to me. My father wasn't in a fit state to be talked to. He never is. They had to get a neighbour to do the identification. They said I was too young and he was too pissed.'

'Did you tell the police about your mother and Rob?' Laura asked, wondering if it was guilt at pointing the police in Tyler's direction which was adding to the boy's grief. But he shook his head at that. He looked away, sunk in such misery that Laura could hardly bear to look at him and it was Mackenzie who followed up.

'Did you tell anyone?' he persisted and almost imperceptibly Tim nodded in response.

'I told Topaz,' he said. 'I hated what they were doing. I thought she ought to know.' Laura looked at the face of fierce teenaged rectitude and flinched. Tim's illusions lay in shards about his feet and could not make the loss of his mother any easier to bear. Even Mackenzie seemed reluctant to ask the obvious question next.

'Did the police know Rob had a shotgun?' he asked instead. Tim looked mutinous but shook his head and Laura guessed that he was telling the truth. The information she had given Inspector Thorpe herself the previous evening had been greeted with the sort of sharp interest which implied that it was what he had been waiting for, not mere confirmation of what he already knew.

'So what? Everyone round here's got a shotgun,' he said. 'They're always at it. They shoot rabbits. They shoot dogs, if they worry the sheep. Ray Harding shot some inoffensive little terrier only a week or so ago, hardly big enough to worry a rat let alone a sheep.'

'And someone shoots people,' Mackenzie said brutally. 'If you think it wasn't your friend Tyler, your best course is to work out who you think it was, laddie.' Tim hunched himself even deeper into his coat at that, his eyes glazed. Laura guessed that even if he knew who had committed the crime, if it were someone to whom he was attached he would find it very hard to put his suspicions into words.

'How do I know who it was?' he muttered. 'They all hate Rob. Maybe it was a way of getting at him. I wouldn't put anything past Ray Harding. And they hated my mother too. Harding almost hit her at the Christmas carols.'

'What did she do to provoke that?' Laura asked, astonished, and hesitantly Tim described how Faith had taken Rob's unhappy daughter out of the church and earned the bitter reproach of the locals.

'It's the sort of thing she does,' the boy said, half-embarrassed and half-proud at the memory. 'Always doing things for people, like that day after the accident, when Alison was killed.' He looked at Laura and Fergal Mackenzie for a frozen moment before the tears finally came.

'What am I going to do without her?' he asked, distraught.

The December dusk had long ago closed in by the time Laura wearily pushed aside her papers on Reg Fairchild's desk and decided to call it a day. Depressed as she was by Faith Lawrence's death, she still had a newspaper to bring out, and only half the normal time to do it in. It would be a slim edition, with advertising scarce just before Christmas, but even so she was determined that it would be a good one, with the murder the inevitable lead story.

In spite of Fergal Mackenzie's prediction, she did not believe that the editor would be back in his own office before the holiday. A brief phone call to find out how he was had provoked a fit of coughing, which worried her. The doctor was coming, he had conceded breathlessly. He would, he had assured her reluctantly in the face of relentless concern, look after himself and not rush back.

Stretching wearily she glanced out of the office window into Broad Street where council workers were energetically clearing the debris from the day's market and hurling piles of cardboard boxes, rotting fruit and vegetables and discarded, dog-eared branches of holly into trucks. The milling crowds of Christmas shoppers had long gone and the customers for the pubs and the bingo palace which had once been the town's only cinema had not yet turned out for the evening's entertainment. The wind was rising, blowing some of the market rubbish into the air before the cleaners could corral it. A few spots of sleety rain speckled the window-pane.

At the far end of the street she could just see the blue light of the police station, and the yellow rectangles of windows still brightly lit. Somewhere behind that façade she knew that Rob Tyler was still helping Chief Inspector Thorpe with his inquiries. She wondered bleakly if he would ever come out a free man, and if he did whether he would survive the reception which threatened in High Clough, where he had already effectively been tried and condemned in his absence.

She glanced at the phone again consideringly. There was still time to drive back to Bradfield tonight if she could summon up the energy, she thought. Tomorrow she was committed to the trip anyway to see her grandmother, tonight was a blank sheet – a choice between a meal in Arnedale and the narrow bed upstairs, or going home to her own empty flat.

In the event the decision was made for her. The phone rang and she picked it up quickly, anticipating she did not know quite what. For a moment there was nothing but silence at the other end in answer to her increasingly anxious queries, but then she was horrified to hear a voice which she recognised only with difficulty as Fergal Mackenzie's, so faint and strangled did it sound.

'I'm glad I caught you, princess,' he said. 'The big bad wolf has blown the house down.' With that, the line went dead.

Almost without thinking, Laura grabbed her coat and ran down the office stairs, across the street and down the narrow alleyway which led into the back street where Fergal had his office. The door which led straight into the main room of the tiny terraced cottage was swinging open when she arrived, allowing a clear view of the shambles within. When she tried the light-switch it did not work, and at first she could not see Fergal himself amongst the scattered destruction of his room.

At length, her eyes growing accustomed to the gloom, she saw an outstretched arm and hand protruding from behind

167

his desk, where his computer lay smashed and books and papers were strewn in disarray. Cautious now, she picked her way across the littered floor and found him, doubled up as if in pain, still clutching the mobile phone in his other hand, his hair and beard matted with what she could see, even in the dim light from the street, was blood. His eyes were closed and he did not move as she approached.

'Oh, Fergal, Fergal,' she said to herself, sick with apprehension as she felt below his ear where she knew there ought to be a pulse. 'You stuck your neck out so often that you were bound to get your head chopped off one day.' Relief flooded her as she found a vein strongly beating away beneath the surprisingly silky hair of his beard. She took the phone out of his hand and called 999.

They let her go with him in the ambulance where, to her immense relief, he groaned and began to regain consciousness during the short trip to the casualty department of Arnedale hospital. The casualty staff were kindly and efficient, unmoved by the bruises and so much blood that it seemed to cover his face and head and had soaked his clothes with huge rusty stains. She sat for what seemed like an age in the waiting area with one of the uniformed police constables who had responded to her phone call for help and who wanted to know far more about what had happened than she was able to tell him.

'He was unconscious when I got there,' she said repeatedly. 'I don't know what happened. I honestly can't help you.' The young constable looked as though he did not believe her, his face still full of the suspicion which had flooded it as soon as she told him and his colleague that she was a journalist.

'So you don't know what might have been stolen?' he asked stubbornly.

'I have no idea. It was too dark to see much in there anyway. The lights weren't working.'

'Did he have any enemies?'

Laura looked at the officer, hardly more than a boy, she thought, and smiled faintly.

'Fergal probably had more enemies than you've had hot dinners,' she said. 'He went out of his way to seek them out.

It was his mission in life.' And she suddenly admitted to herself for the first time since his phone call that she would be utterly devastated if Fergal had come to any long-term harm from the vicious assault he had suffered.

The Fergals of this world are without price, she thought. He was the grit in the oyster, one of the awkward squad, one of the endlessly curious, pig-headed, infuriating seekers after truth who were all that stood between a complacent public and a rising tide of corruption. If Barry Moore had done him serious harm, and she assumed without even thinking about it that Moore was behind the night's events, then she would personally take over where Fergal had left off and she would not be content until Moore had got what he deserved.

A nurse came looking for them.

'Are you with Mr Mackenzie?' she asked Laura. 'You can see him now.' The police officer got to his feet as well, but the nurse waved him away impatiently.

'He's not fit enough for you yet,' she said dismissively. 'We're keeping him in overnight. He should be okay to answer questions in the morning.'

She thinks I'm his girlfriend, Laura thought to herself with quiet satisfaction. What she wanted to find out from Fergal was something that she was sure he would not want the police to know.

'It looks worse than it is,' the nurse said, leading the way. 'Mainly bruising. A nasty cut across his forehead which went very close to the eye but fortunately missed it. That's what caused all the bleeding. Concussion, of course, but no fracture. We need to keep an eye on him after a head injury, but he should be out and about in a day or so.'

Mackenzie was half-sitting up in bed, a dressing covering his temple and his left eye, his beard shaved away from the left side of his face to reveal the swelling and technicolour bruises, but his good eye gleamed when Laura came in.

'Five minutes,' the nurse said. 'And don't talk too much,' she added severely to Mackenzie, who managed a lopsided apology for a smile in return.

'You're my fiancée,' he said, his voice hoarse. 'I had to think of some way of getting them to let me see you. Sorry, they hit me across the throat, amongst other places. It seems to have left me lost for words.'

He was putting on a brave front but Laura could see that he was still in shock, his face pale and haggard where it was not purple and red, his hands clenching and unclenching restlessly on the hospital counterpane.

'That'll make a change,' Laura said, finding her own voice curiously husky. 'So what happened?'

'They were waiting for me,' he said. 'I walked in, all unsuspecting, and they jumped me. Two of them, perhaps three, it wasnae easy to tell in the dark. But they were very well informed. Knew exactly what they wanted.'

'Burglars? The police are putting it down to robbery. They took your TV and stereo.'

'Aye, I know all about that,' Mackenzie said, shaking his head irritably and wincing. 'But they werenae ordinary burglars, though I didnae tell the bobbies that.' His Scottish accent seemed to have thickened as he struggled to speak through an obviously painful larynx.

'You don't trust the police?' The question sounded naïve to Laura as soon as it had passed her lips. In Arnedale she was not at all sure that she trusted the police herself.

'I certainly dinnae trust that rat Les Thorpe and I've certainly no intention of telling him and his merry men why those bastards beat me senseless.'

'Which was?'

Mackenzie did not reply for a moment. He shut his good eye and eased himself back on the pillows, breathing heavily and for a moment Laura thought that he had fallen into a restless doze. She was on the point of getting up to go when the Scotsman suddenly thrust out a hairy hand and grabbed her by the wrist.

'I'll not be able to write this story,' he said in a fierce whisper. 'Will you do it, Laura? Have ye the bottle?'

'I don't know what story you're talking about,' Laura objected, pulling away from Mackenzie's surprisingly tenacious and clammy grip.

'I was going to keep it for my Hogmanay edition, start the New Year in style, but now I'm not so sure. I think it would be best used sooner rather than later, before anyone else gets hurt. Reg Fairchild wouldnae run it, but he's on his sick-bed too, so will you?'

'If it's a good story. If it's legal,' Laura said cautiously, though she could feel the excitement of the chase stirring.

'Och, aye, it's legal enough,' he said.

'So what were your burglars after? The disks?'

Fergal shook his head and then grimaced, realising that was a serious mistake.

'They found my back-up copies easily enough, and smashed up the computer so the hard disk will be a write-off.'

'You've lost all that information?' Laura said, horrified.

'No way,' he said with an attempt at a grin. 'I made another back-up set. But it wasnae just the disks they were after. They were looking for something else. But I passed out before I told them. They hit me a wee bit too hard.' He did not pretend that in the end he might not have told his visitors what they wanted to know.

'If you go up to Grange Farm in Netherdale, you'll find a laddie called Andy Butler, an old friend of mine from student days. He's got a package addressed to me. The back-up disks are there, and some plans. It's the best story you'll come across while you're in Arnedale, I promise you that.'

The effort of speaking eventually seemed to exhaust him and he subsided into his pillows in a fit of coughing. A nurse came round the flowered curtain of the cubicle anxiously.

'I think your time's up,' she said to Laura. 'He's not really in a fit state to be talking like this after a bang on the head.'

'Try and stop me, lassie, try and stop me,' Mackenzie muttered into the ruins of his beard, but weariness was evidently overtaking him and the light in his uncovered eye was fading fast. He did not object as the nurse took his pulse. She looked worried when he coughed again and a fleck of blood-speckled froth appeared at the corner of his mouth. Laura caught her eye and was not reassured.

'I think you'd better go now,' the nurse said quietly. 'I want the doctor to look at him again.'

Laura took Mackenzie's hand. It felt cold. She squeezed it as she leaned over and kissed him gently on the forehead.

He was sweating and beginning to toss painfully against his pillows.

'I'll come in again tomorrow when I've been to see your friend,' she said softly, but was not sure that he heard. Almost imperceptibly it seemed he had lapsed back into restless semi-consciousness. She left, with a sick feeling that she might not see him again.

If Laura felt she had had enough of hospital visiting, the fates decreed otherwise. As she made her way out through the almost deserted reception area she was surprised to hear her name called. She turned to discover Reg Fairchild lying on a trolley, covered by a hospital blanket. He raised himself up weakly on one elbow to try to attract her attention.

'Whatever's wrong?' she asked, her horror at seeing him there magnified by what had already happened that evening and all sorts of malign scenarios rushing through her head.

'Pleurisy,' Fairchild said bitterly, his voice at once husky and petulant. 'I'm waiting for a bed. May be here all night, they said. My GP sent me in, said I wasn't looking after myself properly . . .' He lapsed into a fit of coughing and Laura realised with some relief that here at least were natural causes.

'You'll be in here over Christmas?' she said, thinking of his cluttered, inhospitable cottage.

'I wanted to get back to work to do the next edition,' he said. 'But then . . .' His voice trailed off again and his eyes became distant. Laura waited, aware that he wanted to say more. At length he sighed and lay down again on the trolley, pulling the covering up to his chin and shivering.

'I'm finished, Laura,' he said.

'Nonsense,' Laura said, with automatic cheerfulness. 'They'll soon have you fit again.'

'You don't understand,' he said. 'I was so sorry to hear about the Lawrence woman. Devastating, devastating . . .' His voice trailed away for a minute and his eyes glazed over.

'There are so many things you don't know about, my dear. So many things. And in the end the price was too

172

high.' He turned his face away, and she waited, not knowing what questions to ask.

'I'll lead page two on the Lawrence murder,' she murmured at last.

'Yes, of course,' Reg said. 'We don't get many murders in Arnedale. Poor Mrs Lawrence. She didn't deserve that. She really didn't deserve that. She can't have known what she was taking on.'

'Or who?' Laura asked softly, her brain swinging back into gear, alert to every nuance of Fairchild's voice, aware that here was a man who knew everything there was worth knowing about Arnedale, if only he could be persuaded to tell. She had failed with him once, but now it seemed that sickness and deep depression might unlock his secrets.

'Barry Moore?' she prompted, terrified of frightening him back into silence but even more terrified of not being able to unravel the web of deceit which she was convinced had claimed Faith Lawrence as its victim and might yet claim Fergal Mackenzie.

'He wanted me to run a story about her misdemeanours,' Fairchild said with the ghost of a smile which split his sunken cheeks like a sword-slash.

'You mean her affair with Rob Tyler?'

Fairchild nodded, with an expression of distaste.

'He wanted a real *Globe* exposé, tabloid style. Wouldn't take no for an answer. Said he wanted her out of High Clough, out of the district. I didn't know what to do. I daren't say no and yet I couldn't say yes. It would have been impossible in the *Observer*. Character assassination? Muck raking? I could never have held my head up again.'

'How did he find out about it? Do you know?' Laura asked.

'How does Barry find out about anything?' Fairchild said. 'He cultivates people, listens to them, buys their confidences if he has to.' Laura nodded, knowing all too bitterly the truth of that. Barry Moore's grapevine was extensive and efficient and he used it ruthlessly. She could vouch for it personally.

'All this happened before you were ill, did it?' she asked.

'Just about the time you arrived in Arnedale. After the

173

accident in High Clough and the fuss that caused up there. He wanted me to put something in this week's paper. He wanted her discredited.'

'But you got flu and couldn't. And he must have known I wouldn't.' Barry Moore's resentment of her sudden promotion had more than one source, she realised. Not only was she printing what he would rather not have printed, she was also blocking what he wanted exposed.

'Do you believe all this psychological stuff about stress making you ill?' Fairchild asked querulously. 'Perhaps that's why I'm here.'

Stress or guilt, Laura thought. Take your pick.

'Is there any pie in Arnedale that Moore hasn't got his fingers in?' she asked angrily.

'I doubt it,' Fairchild said, and turned his face to the wall.

SIXTEEN

THERE WERE NOT GOING TO be enough hours in the day, Laura thought impatiently as she sprayed her car windscreen with de-icer and scraped off the resulting slush at eight o'clock the next morning. She felt as hyped up as Hercules with half a dozen labours to complete before breakfast.

It was bright and very frosty, the low sun casting long shadows across one side of Broad Street which lay deserted at this hour on a Sunday, and throwing the pastel-washed houses on the other side into sharp relief. There had been another scatter of snow in the night, frozen now into diamond crystals which gave a sparkle to the roofs and trees. The air was like wine, and as she worked and warmed herself inside her quilted blue ski-jacket and bright green scarf and gloves, Laura began to feel exhilarated in spite of herself.

She had rung the hospital as soon as she had wakened and had been told that Fergal Mackenzie was 'poorly but stable' after an operation to remove a ruptured spleen. It had been missed during his first examination, the ward sister had to admit when pressed, but it seemed he had been badly kicked in the stomach and there was internal damage.

Laura ground her teeth in impotent fury, wanting to blame the inexorable decline in the once great Health Service but knowing it was more probably sheer bad luck. Her grandmother would not have been so ready to give the doctors the benefit of the doubt, she told herself as she had flung on jeans and a thick Arran sweater, grabbed her jacket and scarf and clattered down the stairs from her poky flat at the top of the *Observer* building, her hair flying in an unrestrained copper cloud around her face.

But she knew she would never have her grandmother's single-minded certainty. Don't get mad, get even, she thought, as she got into her car and as usual thanked German engineering for the decrepit little Beetle's infallible ability to start on even the most unpromising morning. Though in Fergal's case, she thought, perhaps getting mad on his behalf would help settle the score.

She was heading for Netherdale, driving fast along the deserted main road out of Arnedale between silvered hedge-rows and snowy fields, when she spotted a figure in a plaid jacket she recognised limping slowly along the road in the same direction.

'They let you out then?' she said with some relief to Rob Tyler as she drew up beside him and opened the passenger door. He hesitated for a moment before getting into the car and Laura guessed that it was only the exhaustion which showed darkly around his eyes and his obviously painful ankle which persuaded him to accept a lift.

'Bastards,' Tyler said, and Laura did not have to ask who he meant. He looked unshaven and dishevelled, his hair hanging loose around his face in dark strings instead of in its usual pony-tail, his hands, as he fastened his seat-belt, shaking slightly. He swore softly under his breath as Laura started the car again.

'He gave you a rough time did he, Inspector Thorpe?'

'He's out to get me one way or another,' Tyler said. 'And he doesn't much care how.'

Laura glanced at her passenger curiously. There was a bruise half-hidden by the lank hair on the left side of his face and he was sitting awkwardly in his seat, as if his left arm and ribs were hurting him.

'Did they beat you up?' she asked, suddenly taking in the full implication of what Tyler had just said with a sense of shock.

'Not exactly,' he said. 'I just "happened" to take a fall going down the steps to the cells. Pure accident. It's all written up in the custody record. The only trouble is, it's a pack of lies.'

'Have you been in trouble with the police before?' she asked.

He smiled grimly.

'D'you remember the fuss in Wiltshire about the new motorway? The chap who took up residence in a tree for weeks to stop the road going through? Topaz and I were with the Crystal Tribe. We held them up for two months before they brought in the heavy mob, moved us all out by force, brought the bulldozers in to take down the tree and the cottages beyond. All sorts of people got charged. A mate of mine was accused of carrying an offensive tin whistle. They did a school-crossing lady for causing an affray with her lollipop. A bloody joke if it wasn't so serious. I got six months for assaulting a security man.'

'And did you? Assault him, I mean?'

'In so far as anyone assaults anyone in a mad bundle to stop people putting up a razor-wire fence,' Tyler said flatly. 'I'd just watched Topaz dragged off the site by her hair, so I wasn't exactly in a mood to go limp and do a Mahatma Gandhi when they grabbed me.'

'Did Faith Lawrence know about all this?'

Tyler laughed, genuinely amused now.

'She was taking lessons, flower,' he said. 'Wanted to know the best strategy to stop the lorries, and anything else Ray Harding decided to throw at High Clough. I told her she wouldn't like gaol but she didn't seem to care. She was a very, very determined person, was our Faith.'

'Inspector Thorpe threatened to do me for conspiracy for not telling him about her demo,' Laura said feelingly. 'I thought that was a bit over the top. Have you convinced him that you didn't kill her?'

If she was wrong about Tyler, she thought, she was driving a brutal murderer down a deserted country road and she guessed that if Michael Thackeray found out he would accuse her of taking a perilous gamble with her own safety.

'He's checking out my alibi,' Tyler said bitterly. 'But he's taking his time about it. Twenty-four hours I've been at that police station and even now he's not really satisfied. I was in Arnedale that day. I've got witnesses but I'm not sure everyone will be sure about the timing. I'm sure the only thing that stopped him charging me was that he can't find my gun. He won't either, because it's at the bottom of a bog and has been since well before Faith died. Anyway, sod them. I've had enough. They won't get me back in there again.'

He slumped into his seat and into a moody silence which Laura found impossible to penetrate again. At the fork where the Netherdale road left the main Lancashire road, she pulled in to the side.

'I'm not going your way,' she said.

He made no attempt to get out of the car, sitting hunched in his coat as if he was cold. Laura waited.

'I didn't kill her,' Tyler said at last with explosive force. 'Though it won't just be Chief Inspector Thorpe who doesn't want to believe that, will it?'

'I didn't suggest you did kill her,' Laura said quietly, pulling on the handbrake. She guessed there was more.

'Do you know who did kill her?' she ventured at last as Tyler seemed to be having difficulty in speaking again. He swallowed hard and shook his head.

'For God's sake, d'you think I wouldn't tell the police if I knew?' he said.

'Perhaps, if it was someone close . . .'

'You mean Topaz?' Tyler said with such incredulity that Laura had to believe him innocent of protecting the mother of his children. 'She couldn't shoot anyone,' he said thickly. 'She'd rather let a wasp sting her than kill it, lets the ants run all over the food . . . daft cow. Anyway, we didn't have a gun. I kept on telling Inspector Thorpe that I ditched the shotgun, threw it in a bog after I got mad with the intruders that night. He didn't believe me, didn't want to believe me, just kept on with the same questions. On and on and on. Said he knew I was lying.'

Tyler suddenly slumped forward against the dashboard, resting his head in his hands, in apparent despair.

'I owed Faith, after everything else I did to her,' he said in a voice so muffled that Laura was not sure that she had heard him correctly. She held her breath, waiting for him to continue and in the end he lifted his head up and gave her a wry smile.

'I conned her,' he said. 'She was looking for a shoulder to cry on and I provided it, told her what she wanted to hear, that she was still young enough to be fanciable. It was one of

178

Barry Moore's little schemes. He wanted to discredit her and her campaign so he set her up with a lover, the sort of lover who'd start a riot round here: a gyppo, a scrounging traveller, the next worst thing to a lezzie, they'd reckon. And did.'

'Moore paid you?' Laura tried to keep her voice neutral, swallow the disgust she felt. Tyler nodded.

''Fraid so,' he said. 'I needed cash. Times are hard, the bus needs repairs if we're ever to get away from High Clough, kids need clothes, even travellers' kids . . .'

'But he didn't pay you to kill her?'

'I may be a bastard, but not that much of a bastard.'

'And Topaz?' she asked, less unwilling now to trample over Tyler's susceptibilities. 'Did she know about this?'

'About me and Faith?' he said. 'She found out. I think young Tim told her. Said she could live with it. But she didn't know about the money. She'd have killed me.'

'Wasps notwithstanding?' Laura said. 'Why are women such fools?' she asked, and it was not Topaz she was thinking of.

Grange Farm stood at the foot of Netherdale, a ramshackle collection of barns and outbuildings surrounding a farm-house which was little more than a cottage. It could have been pretty, given a serious injection of capital and tender loving care by the sort of country-dwellers who have no more interest in farming than in flying to the moon. Instead, it was tatty, comfortably lived in and liberally decorated with posters on the gate and the side of the barn which ran alongside the road. They advertised free-range eggs, goat's milk, the services of an astrologer, a protest meeting against the golf course in Upper Netherdale and several meetings of an ecology group in Arnedale.

Laura was met at the gate by a motley collection of dogs which followed her exuberantly as she picked her way amongst wandering hens and a somewhat tatty cockerel towards the farmhouse door. It stood wide open to the morning air, letting out a welcoming smell of toast. At her knock a pretty blonde woman of about her own age, smaller and plumper and carrying a pink-cheeked baby of about eight months old on her hip, came to the door.

'Hi,' she said. 'What can I do for you on this lovely morning?' The accent was not local, more northerly, Laura thought, though not quite Scottish.

It was indeed a lovely morning, Laura had to admit, although she had hardly noticed the sparkling sunshine on the frosted snow of the fields as she had tried to absorb the flood of disquieting information which had come her way in the last twelve hours.

'I'm looking for Andy Butler.'

'Come away in,' the woman said. 'We're in the kitchen.'

Laura followed her down a narrow hall and into a spacious room at the back of the house where a young man with a sweep of blond hair down to his shoulders, dressed in jeans and a frayed sweater, was sitting at an elderly pine table. He gave Laura a friendly glance before turning his attention back to the two young children he was encouraging to eat toast and jam. With two small mouths contentedly full and chewing, he swept a sleepy black cat off a chair and waved Laura into it and looked at her interrogatively. His pale blue eyes under the irrepressibly tumbling thatch were warm and guileless.

He nodded, apparently unsurprised, when she explained why she had come, all the while tempting his small sons with carefully cut slivers of toast, while his wife lifted her sweater without embarrassment and began to feed the baby.

'Fergal will be all right, won't he?' he asked and his expression tightened as she shrugged her shoulders helplessly and told him what the hospital had told her.

'So who can vouch for you?' he asked then, his frank blue eyes looking her up and down more non-committally now. 'How do I know you're a friend of Fergal's and not one of the other lot?'

Laura could not answer that. She looked around the cluttered kitchen, with its bunches of herbs and dried flowers and bottles of preserved fruits and jams, at the three glowingly healthy children enjoying their breakfast. She glanced through the open door which led onto the farmyard with its jumble of implements and livestock and dogs playing amongst bales of straw. And she thought of Fergal Mackenzie, kicked and beaten unconscious, and suddenly she knew the answer.

180

'You know Fergal far better than I do,' she said, aware that the friendship went back to their student days. 'You know he wouldn't have sent anyone here to do you harm.'

Butler glanced at his wife, who smiled and nodded across the contented baby's downy head.

'That's true,' she said.

'Aye,' Butler said, doubtful still. 'Do you know what's in the package he left here?'

'No,' Laura said truthfully. 'Do you?' Butler shook his head and got up from the table. He took a small brown paper parcel from the top of the dresser where it had been in open view and handed it to Laura. She weighed it in her hand thoughtfully.

'What's he got himself into?' Butler asked quietly. 'He always was a chancer.'

'I think it's better if you don't know,' Laura said. 'Safer.' She was suddenly uncomfortably aware that by being here herself she was putting the Butlers at risk. She had not seriously considered that she might have been followed to Netherdale and knew now that she had been culpably careless.

'Hostages to fortune,' she said quietly, glancing at the two toddlers who had scrambled down from the table and were playing with the cat on the floor. Butler nodded, understanding instantly.

'I'll go and see him in the hospital,' Butler said, but Laura shook her head quickly.

'Not yet,' she said. 'Not if you want to stay out of it. Wait until I get the *Observer* out on Wednesday. If I get Fergal's story into that, it will all be out in the open and there shouldn't be any more risk. Until then I should stay away from Fergal. I'm not at all sure he's safe to know.'

Laura made it back to her flat in Bradfield in record time, with Fergal Mackenzie's package lying like an unexploded bomb on the seat beside her. She glanced in her mirror nervously as she skirted Arnedale without going back into the town centre and ignored the speed limit on the almost empty dual carriageway down the Maze valley, pushing the little Beetle until it shuddered in protest, but as far as she could see she was not being followed. Slightly reassured she took the stairs up to her third-floor eyrie in a converted Victorian villa two at a time, and closed the front door behind her slightly breathlessly.

Without even taking her coat off she flung herself into a chair and tore the wrapping paper off the package. As she expected, it contained a box of computer disks, which she could not explore without a suitable machine to feed them into. But there was more. With nervous fingers she unfolded a sizeable sheet of photocopying paper and spread out a detailed plan on the table in front of her.

It took her a few minutes of careful study before she understood why Fergal was so anxious to publish what the document contained and why Barry Moore, because the document came from the Arnedale office of Cheetham and Moore, was so anxious to prevent him doing so.

The village of High Clough took up the lower edge of the map spread out before her, with the farms at East and West Rigg and Ray Harding's adjacent quarry firmly in the centre. The map was not at all easy to read at first, because the area was criss-crossed not only with the black outlines of what already stood on the edge of the wild moorland beyond the village. Superimposed over the existing roads and buildings were blue lines indicating a substantial development around the farms and the quarry. In any rural area it would cause a storm. In a national park it would cause a national outcry.

What Barry Moore, or his clients, evidently had in mind when he acquired the land was a holiday village, with golf course, tennis courts, restaurants and a lake where the quarry had been. The final outrage, as far as local opinion would be concerned, Laura thought, would be a new access road across the top of the bleak fells from Netherdale. The traffic would not have gone past Faith's front door, but would desecrate one of the most beautiful parts of the Pennine hills instead. Faith would not have found that an acceptable alternative, Laura was sure.

She whistled quietly to herself. This was the story of a lifetime for the little local paper. It would have the whole town of Arnedale and the countryside for miles around incensed. There would be protests and campaigns enough

182

to fill the columns of the *Observer* for months to come and not even Reg Fairchild would be able to ignore them.

But was it a story to die for? Fergal Mackenzie had evidently thought so. She could not imagine how he had come by the copy of Moore's plan but he had risked his life to protect it. Now it was down to her to defy Moore and she knew with a miserable certainty what at least part of the price would be if she did.

She looked at her watch. She was due to collect her grandmother at twelve and bring her back to the flat for Sunday lunch and she suddenly felt a craving for Joyce Ackroyd's trenchant advice. She hid the plan and Fergal's disks behind the books in her bookcase and rushed into the kitchen to defrost a chicken in the microwave and set it to roast.

But by the time Joyce was sitting comfortably in an armchair after lunch Laura had still not found the words to discuss what had cast a shadow over their usual lively debate on the issues of the day. The Sunday papers lay around virtually unread. Joyce was a political animal, a war-horse – and she probably would have revelled in the description if anyone had been foolhardy enough to use it to her face – who had battled for the poor and deprived of Bradfield for the best part of her life.

Her disappointments were twofold: that her only son Jack had turned to business and made a fortune, on which he had promptly retired to Portugal when the going got tough, and that Laura, in whom she had had even greater hopes, had turned away from the socialist certainties of her student days and decided to watch the political fray from the sidelines with a reporter's scepticism instead.

Joyce watched her granddaughter pour the coffee with a faint frown of concern. Her physical fragility and the white hair which had once been as red-gold as Laura's own belied a combative toughness which surprised people half her age.

'Are you going to tell me about it, then?' she said. Laura handed her a cup and sank into the chair opposite, wrapping her hands around her knees in a tight knot, unsure where to begin and afraid that the lump in her throat would betray her anyway.

183

'Is it the boyfriend?' Joyce persisted.

'No – yes – partly,' Laura said, and that said the rest came more easily. Joyce listened impassively, with only the smallest expression of distaste at Barry Moore's threats and the assault on Fergal Mackenzie. When Laura had finished Joyce sat for a moment gazing sightlessly out of the window where ragged dark clouds charged across the sky on a freshening north wind, her face like stone. She sighed.

'Do you love him, your Michael?' she said at length.

'Yes,' Laura said quietly.

'He's leading you a right dance,' her grandmother said, with the merest hint of reproof.

'Yes,' Laura said again.

'Well, there's only one thing you can do then, isn't there?' Joyce said. 'Tell him what you've just told me before this beggar Moore can put his oar in. Then you can publish and be damned.'

'Yes,' Laura said again so softly that Joyce could scarcely hear her. She reached out for her, a gnarled, arthritic and freckled hand taking an identical slim, pale, freckled hand in a fierce grip.

'If he cares as much as you do, he'll understand,' she said. 'And if he doesn't, then you're best off without him.'

'Yes,' Laura said. 'Maybe.'

'So what about this redevelopment then?' Joyce went on, the light of the political fray she loved illuminating her face. 'They want to turn it into another Grassington, do they, with cars queueing up for a space in the car-park every Sunday and antique shops putting the butcher and the baker out of business?'

'It's much bigger than that, and more destructive,' Laura said. 'But surely they won't get planning permission in the national park.'

'Aye, well, in my experience there's some folk will always find a way to get planning permission, if there's enough brass in it,' Joyce said.

'Bribery, you mean?'

'Of one sort and another,' Joyce said. 'There's all sorts of ways of doing it. I thought there was summat odd going on here in Bradfield when that redevelopment company got permission to build on the derelict industrial land on the ring-road. You remember? "Change of use" permission they got, to switch from industry to housing. Makes no sense to me, when what we need is jobs, but there you are.'

'Were Cheetham and Moore involved in that one too?' Laura said, her interest sparked again now.

'Well, they're selling the houses. They don't actually build them. If Barry Moore thinks those plans are important enough to half-kill someone for, I reckon that his negotiations over planning consent are at a sensitive stage. Look for whoever controls the planners up there and see if he leads you back to Barry Moore. That's what I'd do if I had my health and strength,' Joyce said enthusiastically. 'There's always some beggar looking to make a bob or two over the odds. Always was, always will be. You'll see.'

SEVENTEEN

MICHAEL THACKERAY WOULD HAVE BEEN the first to admit that he had too much on his mind that Sunday afternoon. Laura's call had followed quickly on a message from Kevin Mower that Linda Wright's friend Jacquie Coates had asked for a meeting with him. Thackeray had switched off Billie Holiday in mid-lament and agreed to meet his sergeant at police HQ at five o'clock. Laura had rung him minutes later, after she had taken her grandmother home.

'Can you come over? I've got problems,' she had asked baldly, so baldly that he had hesitated fatally over his initial prevarication, seized with a different sense of urgency which tugged him in ways which he could not resist.

'I have to be at work later,' he said quietly. 'Give me half an hour?'

Laura found the wait unbearable. She stood at the window looking down at the tree-lined street below, where a few hardy neighbours were washing their cars, not allowing the biting wind to put them off their Sunday ritual. A couple of children, muffled in ski jackets and scarves, played with a Labrador puppy in a garden a few doors down. It was all so comfortably, domestically normal that Laura wondered if she was imagining the threat under which she felt she had fled Arnedale that morning, the conspiracy of silence in the town, the deeper motive she suspected behind what might have been an ordinary tale of a disturbed burglary gone wrong and a murder which could so easily have been a crime of passion but, she was sure, was not.

'I'm getting paranoid,' she thought. 'I'm catching it from Fergal Mackenzie. He disturbs a common or garden burglary and immediately sees wicked wizards and threatening dragons all around. He's mad. A fey Celt, romantic and melodramatic and mad.' But she knew he wasn't.

Nor, she was simultaneously relieved and alarmed to discover, did Michael Thackeray think she was being paranoid. In fact he took her very seriously indeed as she told him what had happened to Mackenzie, about the plans which had fallen into her possession and her conviction that Rob Tyler was telling the truth when he said he had not killed Faith Lawrence.

'You may be right,' he said with an assurance that did not only rest on what she had told him. 'But what you don't have is any evidence against Moore that would stand up in court. And to get that there'll have to be a proper police investigation.' And one which would fit very neatly with his own inquiries, he thought, with some satisfaction.

'What about Tyler's deal with Moore?' Laura asked.

'Unpleasant, certainly. Immoral for sure. But it's not illegal to persuade someone to sleep with you, even if you do get paid for it. So long as they're willing, and you seem to think she was willing enough.'

Laura recalled Faith's quiet pleasure in her young lover and shuddered at how very willingly she had been duped.

'And the land deals? Buying up land without revealing what you plan to do with it?' she asked, not wanting to dwell on Faith's humiliation.

'Come on, Laura. It happens all the time,' Thackeray said. 'What's more interesting from your point of view is what makes him so sure he'll get planning permission for a massive development like that in the national park. Do you draw up schemes like that without any prospect of success? I wouldn't have thought so.'

'My grandmother suspects there may have been under-the-counter planning deals going on in Bradfield too.' She told him about the housing development which had gone ahead on what had been part of the town's industrial heart.

'I take it you intend to print something about the High Clough plans in the *Observer*?'

'Of course,' Laura said, with a hint of her normal enthusiasm. 'Wild horses wouldn't stop me.'

'Or Barry Moore?' Thackeray said shrewdly. Laura looked away and did not reply.

'I owe it to Fergal,' she said at length.

'Well, it will certainly stir things up in Arnedale,' Thackeray said grimly, by no means unhappy to have Barry Moore stirred up. 'I suppose I'm wasting my time asking you to be very careful? No one knows you've got Mackenzie's documents? Apart from the Butlers?'

She shook her head, though not with perfect confidence.

'I don't see how anyone could know.'

'As for Tyler and the rest of it,' Thackeray said carefully. 'You should tell Les Thorpe what you know.'

Laura shook her head at that, her hair flying wildly around her face like a turbulent sunset.

'I don't trust that man,' she said. 'He tried to warn me off. He's trying to set Rob Tyler up for the murder. Tyler came out of that police station covered in bruises. I hope he does get away . . .'

Thackeray looked at Laura's flushed indignant face and bright eyes and wondered whether the passion for justice he had once had was now quenched to a dangerous degree. It was not that he did not believe that Les Thorpe might be corrupt, but that he suspected that if the temptation were great enough many, if not most, of his colleagues might be.

'What do you mean, get away?'

Laura looked away again, aware that she had said more than she intended.

'Laura!' Thackeray said. 'Is he planning to take off again? If so, you must tell Thorpe. You don't have any choice.'

'I don't believe he killed her,' she said, with an obstinate expression he was becoming only too familiar with.

'That's neither here nor there,' Thackeray said. 'If Thorpe wants to question him again, that's his prerogative.'

'He's in cahoots with Moore,' Laura said recklessly. 'He must be.'

'You don't have any evidence for that, Laura,' Thackeray said. 'And DCI Thorpe's investigating a murder. If you won't call him and tell him what Tyler's threatening to do, then I'll have to.'

It was bound to happen eventually, Laura thought miserably as she took in Thackeray's suddenly implacable expression. They had been on a collision course before and had always drawn back at the last minute, their professional concerns which could so easily take them in opposite directions coming together in the end.

This time it was different. She had no reporter's brief for Rob Tyler, just a fierce conviction that he was about to be the victim of a great injustice. She knew that if he found himself in the dock, facing a jury which would certainly give short shrift to a travelling man, a modern-day heretic for whom public opinion, like the Inquisition, demanded both recantation and punishment without mercy, Faith Lawrence's real killer would walk free.

'And if I end up campaigning to get him out of gaol ten years from now when it becomes obvious he was set up, you'll still be there finding excuses for Chief Inspector Thorpe, I suppose,' she said bitterly.

'You know that's not fair,' Thackeray said. 'I'm not saying you're wrong about Thorpe, just that you're jumping to conclusions on very slender grounds. You've nothing to go on except your own dislike of him and the word of a man who on his own admission is a liar and a cheat. What Tyler did to Faith Lawrence was despicable. I'd have thought you'd be outraged by it.'

'I was. I am,' Laura said unhappily. 'But I still don't think he killed her. It would suit too many people if he was charged. It's too convenient, Michael. It stinks.'

'You still can't cover up for him. If Thorpe's decided to charge him you could find yourself in trouble for aiding and abetting his escape. You can't do that, Laura. I won't let you.'

So this is how it's going to end, Laura thought. I don't need to tell him about my visit to the Sacred Heart. It'll be all over long before Barry Moore decides to carry out that threat.

'If you tell Les Thorpe, I don't think I'll ever forgive you,' she said, knowing she was being irrational and that he would find that hard to forgive.

He sat for a moment, running a hand through his unruly

189

dark hair, his shoulders slumped in an attitude so close to defeat that she wanted to fling her arms round him and promise to do anything he wanted, but that obstinate streak prevented her from moving an inch from her seat. In the end, he sighed and shrugged, his expression resigned, only his eyes showing his disappointment.

'I'll call Thorpe from the office,' he said, his voice level. 'I won't tell him how I know about Tyler's plans. I'll let him think I picked it up in High Clough. You know I have no choice.'

Laura said nothing. She watched silently as he put his coat on and opened the front door.

'Michael, I'm sorry,' she said at last, but it was too late. He had closed the door behind him.

Kevin Mower was already in the office when Thackeray arrived with an expression so Arctic that Mower wracked his brain for sins of commission or omission which might have earned him the chief inspector's disapproval.

'I think we're on to something a whole lot bigger than we thought,' Thackeray said. 'Not just a bit of mortgage fiddling – more likely big money games that could be jeopardised by even the smallest hint of financial irregularities by Cheetham and Moore. Linda Wright's death is just a part of it. I'll talk to Superintendent Longley in the morning. I want to have another go at Sydney Cheetham. In the meantime, you find out from the local council which property company has been buying up land for major housing developments recently – over the last four years, say – and see if there was anything unusual about the planning permission they got, unexpected approvals, permission for change of use, that sort of thing. No news of Jimmy Townsend, I suppose.'

'No, guv. He seems to have disappeared off the face of the earth.'

'Well, let's just hope that he isn't at the bottom of Scarsdale reservoir as well,' Thackeray said. 'It's possible, I suppose, that there were two people in Linda Wright's car when it went into the water, and only one still there when it was pulled out. Ask the emergency services if they can remember whether the passenger door was open, will you. If he was flung out into that icy water he'd likely have drowned very quickly.'

'You want divers up there to look?' Mower asked incredulously.

'Maybe,' Thackeray said. 'But not just yet. You can get on to Manchester police and tell them you'd like to go over there and talk to his mother. And step up the hunt for his car. That can't have disappeared off the face of the earth.'

'Right, guv. And Jacquie Coates? She called, wanting a meeting.'

'Right, you see what she's got to say. And if it's useful, you'd better offer her some protection. We don't want anyone else disappearing – or worse.'

'You think it's that serious?'

'That serious,' Thackeray said.

Mower got up from his desk and slid into his leather jacket.

'Oh, and Sergeant,' Thackeray called as the younger man opened the door.

'Sir?'

'Take a DC with you, for God's sake. I don't want you running into any more temptation.'

Mower closed the door firmly behind him, not quite daring to risk an overt slam of displeasure, leaving a thoughtful Thackeray sitting at his desk with one hand on the telephone.

Was he losing his grip? he wondered. From the very beginning of this case Barry Moore's name had cropped up again and again, and again and again he had dismissed it, afraid that his intense dislike of the boy was prejudicing him against the man. Now he had once more met him face-to-face he had little doubt that Moore the teenaged bully had matured into Moore the adult villain. It only remained to uncover just where that villainy had led.

Reluctantly, he picked up the phone and asked the switchboard to put him through to Arnedale nick. The last task of the day was to betray Rob Tyler's plans to DCI Thorpe, and earn the unforgiving indignation of Laura Ackroyd. There might be something to be said for a less complicated life with a flock of sheep, he thought bitterly, as he waited for Thorpe to respond.

Chief Inspector Thackeray and Superintendent Jack Longley did not look overjoyed to see Sergeant Mower next day when he interrupted their mid-morning conference. Longley, the knot of whose tie dug into his jowls tightly enough to garrotte him, looked at the detective sergeant's open-necked Ralph Lauren shirt with his usual disfavour.

'I get the feeling people are avoiding us, guv.' Mower addressed Thackeray directly, avoiding Longley's frosty stare. 'First Jacquie didn't keep her date with me yesterday. Now it's Sydney Cheetham. You wanted me to bell him to arrange another interview. Well, he's gone. His housekeeper says he's flying to Madeira on holiday with some friends. Won't be back till after Christmas. I thought you'd want to know.'

The two senior officers exchanged a glance less of surprise than satisfaction.

'Right,' Longley said. 'Find out what flight they're on, Sergeant. Who he's going with. Who paid for the tickets. And if there's time, get yourself and a lad with a camera over to the airport and see if you can get some advance holiday snaps of Sydney's little outing. If they've already left, get on to airport security and have a look at the video recordings. They may turn up on them. And if that fails, we'll get on to the Portuguese police and see if we can catch them at the other end.'

'Sir,' Mower said, looking slightly dazed.

'Come on lad, don't stand there gawping,' Longley said impatiently.

'Do you want him stopped, sir, if the flight's not left?'

'No, no, we'll let Sydney have his little holiday. We know where he is if we need him. He's got a villa in Madeira so he won't be hard to track down. And it may be the last holiday he gets for a long while, any road.'

'Sir,' Mower said, looking if anything even more shaken by the turn of events. 'And Jacquie? She's at work. I checked. Do you want her chased up?'

'Ask Val Ridley to have a word. See what's bothering her. And Sergeant,' Thackeray added, as Mower opened the door to leave, 'if you go to Manchester, you could send the pictures back and take the opportunity of that chat with Jimmy Townsend's mother.'

'Right, guv,' Mower said, and closed the door behind him.

'The villa in Madeira,' Longley said thoughtfully. 'He once invited me out there, you know. I said to him, Sydney, you're either a rogue or a fool, and as I'm neither I'll pass on this one.'

Longley turned back to the documents the two men had been studying before Mower interrupted them. 'So there we have it. There's not much doubt our Sydney's been a bad lad, is there?' He ran a stubby finger down a list of names in front of him.

'I wonder which of this little lot are on the flight with him. Six company directors: Sydney's daughter – I went to her bloody wedding years ago – Barry Moore's uncle, Stephen Stokes, the Bradfield manager, and Mrs Alison Freeman, who I can only suppose is the wife of our esteemed council planning officer. And two we can't place. Right?'

'Jonathon West sounds familiar,' Thackeray said.

'Aye, well see what you can dig up on all of them,' Longley said. 'And brief the fraud squad, will you? I want Dales Development Ltd stripped down to its jock-strap. With any luck we'll be able to give Sydney Cheetham a warmer welcome when he gets back than he's had in his sunny island paradise.'

Laura was at her desk early that morning pounding out her story about the High Clough holiday village on Reg Fairchild's ancient typewriter with an energy fuelled by anger and despair. She had driven back from Bradfield the previous night, drunk four vodka and tonics as a foolproof method of ensuring oblivion and fallen into her narrow, chilly bed to shiver alone until sleep swiftly put her out of her misery.

The morning was grey and heavy, with the first flakes of what looked like a serious snowfall already fluttering onto the quiet Monday morning streets outside. It promised a white Christmas, but scarcely a merry one Laura thought as she breakfasted on tea and toast made with stale bread and went straight downstairs, anxious to start work before anyone else had arrived in the office.

Jonathon West was next in. He poked his head around the editor's door without taking his snow-spattered jacket off.

'I just bumped into Detective Sergeant Armstrong,' he said. 'There's been some new development on the Lawrence murder. Do you want me to go down to the nick to see what's going on?'

Laura looked at him for a moment, the feeling of foreboding which had dogged her since the previous evening deepening perceptibly.

'What sort of development?' she asked.

'They've brought that gypsy Tyler in again, by all accounts,' West said. 'They found a gun which appears to be his. Of course he's denying everything but Armstrong's expecting him to be charged. I'll check it out, yah?' The timing of the charge was crucial to the *Observer*. Once it had been laid they could report little but the bare facts of the case.

Laura nodded. She would have liked to have followed up the murder herself but it suited her better this morning to have West out of the office while she completed what he did not yet know would be the lead story. West, she was convinced, had too many connections in Arnedale to be trusted with the information Fergal Mackenzie had almost died for.

'What I don't understand is why that fellow Harding let that lot onto his land in the first place,' West said, obviously curious as to what she was writing but unable to bring himself to appear overtly rude by peering at the page in the typewriter.

'If you ask me, it was asking for trouble. It could take months to get rid of them. My uncle had some trouble with gypsies years ago. In the end, he simply had to take a couple of gamekeepers with guns and dogs to their camp one morning to see them off. I was staying there for the summer. Great sport. Nowadays the beggars seem to have guns themselves. Harding was a bloody fool to have anything to do with them.'

'As I understand it, he needed the money,' Laura said, with little sympathy for Harding's plight. 'Aren't they all going bust, these hill farmers?'

'So Reg keeps saying,' West said loftily. 'Which reminds me, I must call Barry Moore before I get too bogged down. He's coming up to my uncle's place on Boxing Day for the beagling. You don't know what you'll be missing, you know. Old Tom Clayton, the MP for Pennine Dales will be there. And the Lord Lieutenant, of course. You could have made some useful contacts. But it's up to you. I'm sure you know what you're doing. Ciao.'

When he had gone, Laura got up thoughtfully and went into the main office where she took down a volume of *Who's Who*. Lord Radcliffe, she confirmed without much surprise, chaired the National Park Planning Board. She had no doubt that Barry Moore's day out would be much more concerned with his Lordship's thoughts on the desirability of holiday developments in the Dales than on following a pack of excitable dogs across rough country. If he had wangled an invitation to Lord Radcliffe's place, it was not small furry creatures he was after, of that she was absolutely sure. And it explained why he was so desperate to keep news of his scheme appearing too soon.

Laura finished her exposé of Barry Moore's plans for High Clough and carefully collated two copies of the article and two photocopies of the actual plans for the village. She sealed one version of the story in an envelope and addressed it to herself, care of her grandmother in Bradfield.

She had absolutely no doubt that Moore would redouble his threats if he discovered that she had got hold of Fergal Mackenzie's scoop herself and intended to print it. Telling Michael Thackeray about her visit to the Sacred Heart would probably be the least of her worries. She had refused to think about the likely consequences of that ever since he had walked out of her flat the day before. Probing that pain was a distraction she felt she could not afford until she had got the paper out. For the moment she tucked it to the back of her mind, where it nagged like a rotten tooth.

She had promised Thackeray that she would be as careful as she could before the *Observer* came out on Wednesday, but she was determined that if she was not careful enough, there would be an alternative record of what she had written and why. If anything happened to her in the next couple of days, her grandmother would know what to do and could be relied on to do it, she thought. And Moore would hardly envisage a threat from a pensioner in her seventies of whose existence she was sure he would be unaware and whose fighting spirit he could not possibly foresee.

She put on her coat, left Debbie in charge of the office, and walked slowly up Broad Street, crossed the road teeming with traffic and frantic shoppers bundled up against the still persistent snow and posted her letter. She turned down one of the narrow lanes towards the canal, where the *Observer*'s printer occupied premises which looked as though they had been busy soon after Caxton first set type. She pushed open the battered wooden door and went into the clattering oily atmosphere of an unreconstructed print-shop to be greeted by Bert Oldroyd, the foreman, a thin and wizened figure in blue overalls who could have been any age between sixty and eighty.

'Nah then, Miss Ackroyd,' he said, hanging a bundle of galley proofs on a hook inside his tiny glassed-in cubicle of an office and wiping his inky hands on a rag. 'Summat for page two's what I'm looking for reet now, else you'll risk being late to press.'

'I've got you the lead story, Bert,' she said. 'But it's a bit special, this one. Would you do me a favour and set it yourself? Not let anyone see it.'

Oldroyd looked at her shrewdly for a moment and nodded.

'Looks like upsetting folk, does it?'

Laura grinned. She knew that Oldroyd would not be averse to upsetting folk.

'I think it just might,' she said. Oldroyd took the sheaf of copy from her and scanned it quickly, his eyes gleaming behind his thick spectacle lenses as he read.

'You'll give old Reg a relapse with this,' he said appreciatively at last. 'He's been took to hospital, I hear. Not before time, if you ask me.'

'Can you reproduce the plan?' Laura asked, unsure of a technology which was too elderly for her to be familiar with. The foreman looked at the sheet she handed him and nodded.

'Oh, aye,' he said. 'That'll be reet. If you put it across four columns the detail'll come up lovely.'

'And you can let me have the proofs direct? Don't leave them lying about here for anyone to see?'

'Aye, I'll bring them over t'road by hand, love,' Oldroyd promised. 'It's high time someone took on the beggars that think they run this town. Barry Moore'll not hear a word of this till it lands on his breakfast table Wednesday. And I hope he chokes on his bloody Cornflakes, I do that!'

EIGHTEEN

BERT OLDROYD, SWATHED TO THE eyes in an ancient army greatcoat and grey muffler against the Siberian weather, brought Laura her proofs soon after lunch and stood beside her, quivering like a leashed spaniel, in the cramped little office while she read them.

'Fine,' she said when she had finished, sharing his smile of triumph. The old man's watery eyes gleamed with malicious glee.

'There'll likely be demonstrations in t'market-place over that,' he said, the satisfaction bubbling out of him. 'It's time they got their come-uppance, Cheetham and Moore. They've trampled over this town, one way and another, wi' their supermarkets and holiday cottages and I dunno what else, heedless o'what folks really need.'

Together they sketched out the lay-out of the main news page where extra space presented itself now the report on Faith Lawrence's murder had been cut back by the developments at the police station. Once a charge was laid, reporting restrictions applied and only the briefest details could be printed. Tyler was due to appear before the magistrates the next day and Jonathon West had reported back to Laura his conviction that the evidence the police now had would see him remanded to prison.

'Whatever he says he did with the gun, it was lying there in the snow for Ray Harding to find,' West said with the faintly superior smile of a man well vindicated. 'And it had been fired recently, apparently. I knew they were asking for trouble, letting that lot camp up there.'

Laura let it pass, filing the unwelcome news away at the back

198

of her mind, too preoccupied with the immediate problems of bringing the paper out to brood on what she was still convinced was a major injustice about to happen. If she was to help Rob Tyler, she thought, as she was still determined she would, it would have to wait. If he were due in court there was little enough could be done to prevent his remand to prison anyway. Untangling the evidence which had put him there would take time.

She sent Bert back to the print-shop still sworn to secrecy about the High Clough story. With all the copy safely gathered in for the severely restricted Christmas Eve edition, she decided to send Jonathon West and the rest of the staff home to begin their holiday.

'I'll be around until Bert starts printing tomorrow,' she said. 'If anything big breaks I'll give you a call. If not, Happy Christmas.' Jonathon's holiday would be seriously marred by her High Clough exclusive, she thought as she sent him on his way to his uncle's stately pile in the north of the county. It would be only too obvious to the old man, landowner and member of innumerable local committees, why Barry Moore had wangled himself an invitation for the day when half the people who could influence the success of his scheme would be there to follow the beagles. Her own holiday she scarcely dared think about.

After they had gone, she sat in the darkening office without switching the lights on, queen of all she surveyed but feeling no elation at what she had done. There was too much still unresolved, too many threats outstanding, for her to find a chink of light in the encircling gloom. Outside the snow was still falling heavily, with no sign of a break in the louring cloud which seemed to sit above the roof-tops like a heavy weight. She picked up the telephone and called the hospital to check on Fergal Mackenzie's progress.

'I'm very glad you called,' the ward sister said slightly breathlessly and for a heart-stopping moment Laura feared the worst. But it was not Fergal's state of health which concerned the nurse.

'He's asking for you. And as we've not got any sense out of

him about next-of-kin, I thought you'd better come in. Does he have any relations, do you know?'

Laura locked up the office carefully and drove the short distance to the hospital along slushy roads, where the snow was beginning to pile up into dirty heaps in the gutters. She had to confess to the sister in charge of Mackenzie's recovery from his operation that she knew nothing of his family. The nurse raised an eyebrow and pursed her lips and made a note on the forms she was carrying.

'He's from Scotland,' Laura said helplessly, knowing how unsuited Mackenzie was to the ordered, computerised efficiency of the nurse's world where everyone was expected not only to have relatives but be able to summon them up at the stroke of a button. It'll be like America soon, she thought gloomily, where they won't let you over the threshold of casualty without your ID and insurance policies.

'Yes, well,' the nurse said, as if Fergal's northern origins explained his unaccountable lack of appropriate credentials. She led Laura down a short corridor and into a cubicle where a grey-faced Mackenzie lay on a high bed attached to various drips and tubes and monitors. Laura could see from his eyes, the left one free of its dressing now but half-closed by swollen purple bruises and stitches which brushed terrifyingly close to his eyelid, that the sparkle had been almost extinguished. His encounter with death had been closer than either of them wished to acknowledge.

'Princess,' he said faintly in welcome, as she sat down close to the bed and patted his hand with awkward affection.

'Hae ye done it?' he asked in a barely audible whisper as the nurse hovered in the doorway. Laura swallowed hard and nodded.

'I've just passed the page proof,' she said and was rewarded with the faintest of smiles. He reached out cautiously to take her slim hand in his dark hairy one, and she moved closer to the bed, edgily aware of how little she knew about the man and how devastated she would have been if she had lost him. The nurse nodded and left them together, evidently satisfied that Laura was an acceptable stand-in for Mackenzie's elusive kin.

'Grand,' Mackenzie said, brightening a little. 'Now listen, lassie, and we'll sew that bastard up completely if we're canny.'

'Fergal,' Laura said. 'You can't be serious. He almost killed you.'

'Never mind that,' Mackenzie said. 'Have ye got your tape recorder with you?'

She nodded dumbly, checking in her bag to make sure.

'Don't ye see,' Mackenzie said more urgently, though the effort clearly cost him much of his reserves of strength. 'He's not going to give up. The nurse said there'd been a couple of calls asking how I was, if I was conscious and fit to have visitors. You didn't make those, did you?'

'No, I've been busy . . .'

'So who did call? Who wants to see me so desperately? There's only one person, Laura. And he – or his friends – are not going to come bearing get-well cards and bunches of grapes.'

'Let me get the police,' Laura said. 'You need protection.'

'From Moore's mate Inspector Thorpe? You have to be joking, princess.'

For the first time in Arnedale Laura felt the chilly touch of real fear: for Fergus, lying beside her still desperately ill and even more desperately vulnerable, for Rob Tyler, sitting in a cell with little prospect of ever coming out again, and for herself. If Fergal was right, and if the auctioneer was indeed the author of the violence and deceit which had killed Faith and trapped the others, and she had no reason to doubt him, she was the next in line for Barry Moore's attentions. Be careful, Michael Thackeray had warned, but in the coils of a net they could barely see let alone avoid, it was impossible to know how. She reached into her capacious bag and handed Mackenzie the small tape recorder which she always carried.

'The batteries should be okay,' she said. 'What are you going to do?'

'Just keep it by me,' he said, gripping the tiny machine tightly in a hairy paw.

'It's too risky,' she objected, but Mackenzie simply shook

his head and then winced with the effort and she knew that nothing she could say would deter him.

'Visiting time is almost over,' Laura said, glancing at her watch. 'He'll never get in after that, surely. I'll hang about for a while just in case.'

Mackenzie nodded, apparently almost exhausted by their conversation. Laura doubted that he would find the strength to attempt what he was planning. She looked round the small private cubicle but there was not the remotest possibility of finding anywhere in there to hide. She went outside and glanced up and down the empty corridor. There were no lights in the next cubicle, separated from Mackenzie's only by a wood and glass partition. She stepped inside briefly to make sure it was empty and then back to the sick man's bedside.

'I'll be next door, until I get thrown out,' she said and he nodded, that faint gleam still there in his eyes.

'Princess,' he said vaguely. 'Sleeping Beauty? No, no, the other one. With the Beast.' He managed a faint smile and then settled back into his pillows, the tape recorder concealed under the bedclothes, to wait.

It was Moore himself who came, although Laura heard nothing through the partition until he began to speak. She had settled down on the floor of the cubicle, her back to the wooden lower half of the dividing wall, her boots under the bed, wriggling her shoulder-blades inside her thick jacket to find a comfortable position in which to wait. For such a big man Moore had made his entrance with astonishing stealth but his voice carried clearly through the glass and was instantly recognisable.

'You've got something of mine, Mackenzie,' he said flatly. 'I want it back.' Mackenzie's reply was more indistinct but was evidently a prevarication which met with an instant and devastating response.

'I realise threatening you is time-consuming and probably time-wasting as well,' Moore said. 'And time is what I haven't got. I'll give you one minute to think about this. When you first came to Yorkshire you stayed with some friends in Netherdale, the Butlers. Am I right?' Again Mackenzie's reply was inaudible but Laura could imagine the depth of his dismay.

'Three children? Two little lads and a baby? Am I right?' Moore went on inexorably. She remembered those children and felt sick. Moore hardly needed to spell out what he was threatening, but he did anyway.

'Such a pity if anything happened to those kiddies, don't you think? Or their mother?'

'Sod you,' Mackenzie said, finding the strength now almost to shout at his tormentor. 'Sod you.'

'Where are my documents? I want them back, and I want you out of Arnedale,' Moore said. 'That's all.'

'Sod you,' Mackenzie said again, a catch in his voice now, and Laura stiffened, guessing what had to come and feeling the cold tentacles of fear close around her stomach. She had no doubt that she was next in line and that Fergal had run out of ways to protect her. But she was wrong.

'You can't get the papers,' Mackenzie said more faintly. 'No one can get them. Not until after Christmas. I posted them to myself in Edinburgh, to be collected at the main Post Office. With a second-class stamp. There's no way they'll even be there till Hogmanay.'

Laura let out her breath gently and slid down the partition a fraction as relief flooded through her. It was an ingenious story, and one impossible to prove or disprove. Barry Moore would simply have to wait. She would have liked to see the expression on his face as he absorbed what Mackenzie had told him, but all she could hear was an explosive grunt of anger and then a faint cry from Mackenzie which had her scrambling awkwardly to her feet in seconds.

She dashed out of the cubicle to see Moore's burly figure with his familiar bulky sheepskin jacket flying open, hurrying down the still empty corridor. He did not look back. She spun round into Fergal Mackenzie's tiny room and was horrified to discover him clutching several of the tubes which had been attached to his person, with blood spurting from his arm where one of them had been torn free.

'The bell,' Mackenzie said faintly, nodding to a red cord above the bed. Laura gave it a hefty tug.

'He tried to kill me,' Mackenzie said, as she tried to staunch the flow of blood with a towel.

'You're indestructible,' Laura reassured him as two nurses rushed into the room and with exclamations of horror took over her attempts at first aid for their patient. When he was safely hooked up to his drips and tubes again the ward sister took Laura's arm angrily and drew her out of the room.

'What on earth happened?' she asked, and Laura told her, though without naming Mackenzie's assailant.

'You've got to watch him,' Laura said, as angry as the nurse. 'I was only out of the room for a moment and someone got to him.'

'I'll tell our security people,' the sister said grimly. 'What about the police?'

'He doesn't want the police,' Laura said firmly. 'And honestly, I don't think his attacker will be back. But don't take any chances.'

They let her back in to say goodbye and Mackenzie thrust the tiny tape recorder into her hand with a rueful smile.

'We've got him, princess,' he whispered. Laura nodded.

'Yes,' she agreed. 'I think maybe we have.'

She walked back slowly through the almost deserted hospital corridors, from which most of the day's visitors had departed. Her echoing footfalls and the pervasive smell of stale food and disinfectant depressed her. In spite of Mackenzie's jubilation she was not convinced that Barry Moore could be so easily trapped.

On the medical ward, she found Reg Fairchild sitting up in bed, still looking cadaverous and pale, but able to summon up a thin smile when he saw her.

'How are you?' she asked.

'Improving a little,' he said hoarsely. 'The pain's better. I've had plenty of time to think. Cleared my mind and came to some decisions.'

She raised an eyebrow at that and perched herself on the visitor's chair at his bedside waiting for him to continue.

'I've decided to resign,' Fairchild said gruffly. 'There's a nice little job there for you, if you want it. You can put your news on the front page after all.'

Laura smiled faintly.

'Not for me,' she said. 'I don't think Arnedale is where I want to settle down. What brought this on, anyway?'

Fairchild sighed and looked away.

'Oh, a lot of things,' he said. 'But mainly the accident in High Clough and that poor woman's murder. And having the time to think. I suddenly realised that I'd got it wrong. I believed Barry Moore when he said that we could only save the Dales by bringing in new jobs, new development, to keep the young folk here. That you couldn't keep the place in aspic, like the Greens wanted, pushing up the house prices and driving the locals out. But Moore's way doesn't work either, does it? He'll kill the place a damn sight quicker the road he's going. Do you know what his latest plan is? To build a holiday village up at High Clough.'

'So you knew about that?' Laura said, unsurprised.

'Aye, I knew about that,' Fairchild said. 'He told me about it – off the record. All to be launched when he'd got the planners sewn up. Pleased as punch, he was. Do you know what he's proposing to call it, for God's sake?'

Laura shook her head.

'The Heathcliff Experience! Can you believe it? We're thirty miles from Haworth and the Brontës' vicarage. And that's only going to be the first, he reckons. He's going on to build the Wordsworth Experience up in the Lakes, and the Rob Roy Experience in the Highlands. He'll turn the whole country into a bloody theme park – in the name of conservation, he says. Profit, more like! He sees himself as the Billy Butlin of the poetry-reading classes – and a millionaire, too, no doubt. And what'll be left then of the old way of life? I got it all wrong, Laura. I got the best part of my life all wrong.'

Fairchild suddenly seemed reduced to a frail old man, the certainties she had first challenged had drained away with his health, and for the first time she felt sorry for him. He was, she thought, yet another of Barry Moore's victims. The tape recorder in her bag felt as heavy as a guilty conscience.

'So you've had enough?' she said.

'Better to go before I'm pushed,' he said. 'David Ross'll have me out any road, won't he?'

Laura nodded, not able to deny the truth of that. Ross would not need to think twice about the fate of his compromised editor in Arnedale.

'And what about Jonathon West?' she asked. 'He seems to be very thick with Moore too, inviting him up to his uncle's place for Boxing Day . . .'

'Moore's using him like he uses everyone else. Jonathon's a useful line to his uncle and his powerful friends in the national park administration. And Jonathon's willing enough. He'll play along with anyone he thinks can butter his bread a bit thicker,' Fairchild said. 'But he'll not hang about long. He's got his sights set on something more exciting than the *Arnedale Observer*.'

'So what does he get out of Moore? Or has Moore got some hold on him?'

'That I don't know,' Fairchild said, weary now, pulling the bedclothes up to his chin as if to shut out the world. 'Is there anyone Moore hasn't got a grip on, one way or another?'

'Not that I can think of,' Laura said bleakly.

NINETEEN

LAURA HAD SWALLOWED HER PRIDE and rung the police station in Bradfield. She needed help and guessed that only Michael Thackeray could provide it.

'I'm not sure where he is. I've been in Manchester most of the day,' Sergeant Mower said, recognising the note of tension in her voice. 'Is it urgent?'

'Very,' Laura said, not wanting to elaborate but aware that the tape which sat on her desk in front of her was as dangerous as an unexploded bomb. She glanced around the empty office, her nerves strung out like piano wires. 'I can't explain over the phone,' she said.

'I'll locate him for you,' Mower said. 'I'll call you straight back.'

Laura switched the phone through to the upstairs flat, took the stairs two at a time and locked and bolted the door behind her. Outside the snow was falling steadily, the market had packed up early for lack of customers willing to shop in a near blizzard, and in mid-afternoon the light was already fading fast. She slipped out of her business suit and shirt and into jeans, her Arran sweater, thick socks and boots. Driving would be hazardous and she was not taking any chances. Then she sat on the edge of her hard bed waiting for Mower to call.

She was more afraid, she thought, than she had ever been. She told herself firmly that Moore could not possibly know of the existence of the brief cassette recording which, she believed, could finish his career and put him away for a very long time. Nor could he possibly know that she had acquired his plans for High Clough.

And yet she did not convince herself. The man had

tentacles which seemed to extend everywhere in Arnedale. It had taken him less than two weeks to get a grip on her. He might well have eyes and ears in the print-shop where even now the *Observer* was being prepared for press. He might have eyes and ears in the hospital, or have succeeded in reaching Fergal Mackenzie again and forcing the truth out of him. He certainly had eyes and ears at the police station just across the road, so ruling out any possibility of help from that quarter.

On an impulse, she pulled her suitcase out from under the bed and began to pack. She did not think that she would want to sleep in that unrewarding narrow bed again. She jumped when the phone rang again and picked it up quickly, cursing her nervousness.

'He's been called up to High Clough to see his mother,' Detective Sergeant Mower said. 'She's taken a turn for the worse. He said the weather's turning very rough and he might not get back to Bradfield tonight.'

'Oh, damn and blast,' Laura said softly.

'Is there anything I can do, Laura?' Mower asked, worried by the obvious anxiety in her voice. 'Are you in some sort of trouble?'

'Is the weather bad with you?' she asked, prevaricating. It might be easier, she thought, to drive down the valley to Bradfield than up into the hills.

'Terrible,' he said. 'The M62 from Manchester is barely moving. I thought I might not make it back. And there's been an accident on the Arnedale Road, if you're thinking of heading back here. It's blocked just north of Eckersley.'

'I'll see if I can get to him in High Clough,' she said soberly, knowing that the climb up to the village would not be easy in heavy snow. 'Kevin . . .' She hesitated, wondering if paranoia was finally getting the better of her. She shrugged. What the hell, she thought.

'Kevin, are you still pursuing Barry Moore?'

'Too right we are,' Mower said.

'Well, if for any reason I don't get in touch with Michael, you must talk to Fergal Mackenzie, who's in Arnedale Hospital, and to my grandmother. You remember my grandmother?'

'Laura, what's going on?' Mower asked, filled with real alarm now.

'Probably nothing, just an over-fertile imagination on my part. But just in case – you'll remember that?'

'Of course. But are you planning something dodgy up there? Something dangerous?' He had vivid memories of occasions when Laura Ackroyd had taken risks for a story which had brought her to the very edge of disaster. 'Laura! Mike Thackeray will never forgive me if I let you do something silly!'

'Won't he?' she said, with a faint smile, wondering if Mower knew something that she didn't. 'Don't worry,' she said. 'I'm only going up to High Clough to find him. I promise.' And she put the phone down before Mower could make any further objections.

The snow was falling steadily, but presented no real difficulty while Laura headed west on the main road. Gritting lorries had been out in good time and although the roadway gradually narrowed as the sprayed snow piled up on the verges, she was able to keep up a reasonable speed, with hardly any other traffic on the road. But once she had reached the Drover, barely visible on her left through the whirling snow, things got more difficult as she turned onto the steep lane which wound for several miles up the hill to High Clough.

The snow was drifting now in the high wind and twice she slid broadside across the road into deep patches and twice, with wheels spinning, she just managed to extricate herself again. The only comfort was that on this narrow lane she met no other traffic at all. The country folk had very sensibly decided to heed the advice being offered on the local radio to all motorists to stay at home unless their journey was really necessary.

As she struggled on, with the wipers barely able to clear the clinging ice and snow from the windscreen and visibility ahead reduced to little more than a head-lit tunnel of whirling white flakes, she began to wonder if she would make it to the top of the hill. In the old days, she thought, motorists used to have chains to attach to their wheels in weather like this, and she wondered if such things still existed.

Almost despairing of ever reaching the village, she suddenly recognised the stone bridge over the beck, and changed down a gear just in time to take the sharp bend which led into the main street. On her right she could make out the church and the Lawrences' farmhouse before the road swung away to the right. Suddenly and terrifyingly she found herself confronted by the headlights of another car looming through the whirling white curtain of snow. Instinctively she slammed on her brakes, skidded sideways and came to a halt, unscathed, right up against the wall of the Woolpack.

The other car did not stop, and turning awkwardly in her seat, she saw the disappearing tail-lights of a large, dark red saloon – a Jag or a BMW, she guessed – rounding the bend behind her, still in the middle of the road.

'Pig,' she exclaimed in exasperation. Gently, she put the Beetle into reverse and tried to ease it out of the deep drift into which it had plunged, but the wheels spun wildly, the engine whined impotently and it was clear she was finally stuck.

She eased open the driver's door and stepped out into a foot of soft powdery snow, and was generously spattered with more as a heavy lorry ground down the hill past the pub. If she had met that on the bend, she thought grimly, there would have been no chance of getting out of its way. In this weather, on this road, a heavily laden lorry was another accident waiting to happen.

Gingerly she picked her way to the main door of the pub and to her surprise found that the latch lifted at her touch and the bar greeted her with a steamy cloud of beery warmth. The landlord glanced across from a small group of men deep in conversation leaning on his bar and raised an eyebrow.

'Got thisen stranded hast'a?' he asked, without much sympathy. 'We don't do rooms, love.'

'No, no,' Laura said quickly. 'I'm not far from where I want to be. But I've got the car stuck. I wondered if someone could help me push it out?'

The group had turned towards her as one man, broad shouldered and stocky, for the most part, and only mildly curious at her arrival. But with a sense of shock she realised that one of their number was Ray Harding, his blue eyes distinctly unfriendly under the bristling red brows. He had evidently just come in and there was snow still glistening on his padded jacket as he lifted a pint to his lips with the enthusiasm of a man about to take his first draught after a year in Riyadh.

'Tha'rt the reporter woman: the *Observer*, isn't it?' Harding asked, smacking his lips in appreciation of the beer, but still watching Laura with cold concentration. 'Wheerst'a heading now? Tha'll not reach t'quarry, that's for sure, if it's t'bloody gyppos you're after.'

'No, I was trying to get to West Rigg . . .'

'Joe Thackeray's place?' Harding asked and she nodded, not wanting to elaborate.

'What are you driving?' the landlord asked doubtfully.

'A VW Beetle,' Laura answered and was greeted with a roar of laughter from the company.

'Tha'll not meck it up theer in that little beggar in this mucky weather,' someone said.

'If you hang on, I'll teck thee,' Harding said grudgingly, drinking down the remains of his pint. 'I'm on my way back up and I've got t'Range Rover. That'll get us theer. Get thisen a drink. I just want one more.'

Laura ordered herself a vodka and tonic and took it to a table close to the fire which was banked well up the chimney in anticipation of a bitter night. Harding did not hurry and she would do nothing to rush him, watching the pint imperceptibly sliding down the sides of his glass as he took fitful mouthfuls in between a long and rambling conversation about the eviction he planned for the travellers now that Rob Tyler was safely out of the way. Laura swallowed her anger at the thought of women and children put onto the road in the dead of winter. She needed her lift with Ray Harding and could not afford to antagonise him now.

Eventually the outside door swung open again and another snow-covered figure staggered over the threshold and shook himself vigorously like a dog to remove the snow from his donkey jacket.

211

'Jesus bloody wept,' the stranger said and then, obviously recognising Harding, threw up his hands in mock despair.

'I didn't meck it, boss,' he said. 'It were a reet bugger at t'bottom o't'hill. I lost her on t'bend and hit the bridge.'

'Tha what?' Harding said incredulously. 'Not another effing accident? I don't bloody believe it!'

'No one hurt, boss, no one hurt,' the driver said quickly. 'But it hasn't done t'bridge much cop. Back end's gone through t'wall and she's hangin' o'er t'beck wi't'load likely to slide. I reckon it'll teck a crane to shift her.'

'You've smashed the bloody bridge?' the landlord asked.

'You've blocked the road?' Laura said.

'Aye, well, you'll not be getting up and down that hill till t'snow's cleared, any road, will you?' the driver said as if that were some sort of consolation for what had happened.

'It'll be longer than that if we've to wait for a crane to get up and shift thy bloody wagon,' the landlord said angrily. 'We haven't all got Range Rovers up here, you know.' He threw an angry look at Harding, who scowled back unabashed at the devastation his stone-moving was causing the village.

'You can always get over t'top from Netherdale in an emergency,' Harding said complacently, and Laura wondered how a farmer as hard-pressed as he was alleged to be ran a Range Rover at all.

'In this weather?' the landlord muttered.

'Didst'a see a Jag on t'way down?' Harding asked the driver a shade anxiously. 'Dark maroon job? Did he get out before you slammed t'door?'

'I didn't see him, so I guess he must'a done,' the driver said. 'Nowt came down after me. Nowt at all.'

'Well, that's summat to be thankful for,' Harding said. '*He'd* not have been too chuffed to be stuck up here for t'duration, I can tell thee that for nowt.'

'Can you put me up tonight, Ray?' the driver asked. 'I can't sleep in t'cab perched over t'beck like that. I'd likely end up in t'water.'

'No more than you deserve,' Harding said unsympathetically. 'How am I going to get my stone out o't'beck if it slides off t'back of your wagon, I'd like to know? You'd best get on

212

to thi boss and see how soon he can fix to get thee back on t'road.'

'You can stop here if you don't mind sleeping on t'couch in t'lounge bar. We don't do rooms,' the landlord said meaningfully, glancing at Laura.

'Aye, well, d'you still want that lift, lass, or are you going to kip in your Beetle?' Harding asked, downing the last of his pint.

Laura swallowed hard and nodded her assent. She knew that she had little choice. Harding shrugged himself back into his jacket, settled a tweed cap firmly on his head and led the way back out into the car-park where a Range Rover, covered with an inch of fresh snow, was the only vehicle in sight.

'Bloody truck drivers,' Harding said as she climbed in beside him. 'You'd think they'd never seen snow before, the way they carry on. Must 'ave come up from t'bloody south wi't'flaming New Age travellers and chips fried in flaming olive oil!'

'Barry Moore was up to see you on business, was he?' Laura asked, making a wild guess as to who had been driving a Jag so recklessly through the snow. The farmer eased the Range Rover onto the snowy road and began to climb steadily but surely up the hill and out at the top end of the village before he flashed her an uncompromising look.

'Nowt to do wi'you who I talk to,' he said.

'I just wondered if maybe you were selling out like Joe Thackeray,' Laura surmised with a winning smile but got nothing but a grunt in return.

'You heard that Rob Tyler was remanded in custody,' Laura said, changing tack.

'Aye, and I hope they keep the bugger theer for t'rest of his natural life,' Harding said. 'And I'll have t'rest o't'bloody tribe out an'all as soon as this snow shifts, if not sooner.'

'You found the gun, I hear.'

Harding flashed her a look which combined triumph and a certain low cunning.

'Aye, I did. Stands to reason he wouldn't have hidden it in t'camp, doesn't it? Police were wasting their time looking for it theer.'

'So where did you find it, then?' Laura asked.

'Up at t'back o't'quarry, under some bracken. I'd not have seen it at all but t'sun just caught the metal, caught my eye like, and I knew I had him.'

'It wasn't covered with snow by then?' Laura asked guilelessly.

'What?' Harding said, drawing the Range Rover gently to a stop at the gate to West Rigg Farm.

'Oh, nothing,' Laura said quickly, opening the door and jumping down into deep snow which came up to the top of her boots. 'I just thought it would have been hard to spot if he hid it after Faith was killed, after it started snowing, that was all.'

Harding stared hard at her from under his fierce ginger brows, an angry flush on his face, as she closed the door. He slammed the Rover into gear and accelerated recklessly away, spraying her with snow.

Laura turned and looked down the slight slope to where West Rigg's low stone farmhouse huddled under the lee of the moor, the windows faint squares of yellow just visible through the still falling snow, although the flakes were coming down with a more deceptive but no less persistent gentleness now the wind had dropped. She trudged down the path to the front door and knocked. For a long time there was silence within and then the sound of bolts being withdrawn and a key turned and she found herself face to face with Michael Thackeray, who looked totally astonished to see her there.

'I've got something for you,' she said, before he could speak. 'Kevin Mower told me you were up here, and now the bridge is down it looks as if I'm stuck. I didn't want to come here, Michael. Truly I didn't. But in the end I didn't seem to have much choice. I'm up to my neck in trouble.'

'Again?' he said resignedly, as he stood aside to let her into his father's house.

In Bradfield a young estate agent by the name of Jimmy Townsend put his head in his hands and wept.

'It wasn't like that,' he said through his sobs. 'It wasn't like that at all. You've got it all completely wrong.'

Townsend was sitting across an interview room table from Sergeant Kevin Mower and DC Val Ridley, having presented himself at the front desk of the police station an hour before. He had had a phone call from his mother, he said, who had been alarmed at Sergeant Mower's suggestion earlier in the day that he too might be dead.

Somewhat startled by the efficacy of the pressure he had put on Mrs Townsend to persuade her son to give himself up, Mower met with a pale young man in a crumpled suit and far from white shirt who seemed relieved rather than apprehensive at finding himself in police custody.

But if Townsend thought that the police would give him credit for his unexpected resurrection, Mower soon disabused him. He told Townsend brusquely that he was investigating the death in suspicious circumstances of Linda Wright, arrested him, cautioned him and had him banged up in a cell within minutes to await questioning.

Mower's first, instinctive, impression of Townsend had not been favourable. He was a tall, skinny rather than slim young man who looked as though he had not slept well recently, his short brown hair unkempt, dark circles beneath his pale grey eyes which refused to meet Mower's, and a full, slightly sensual mouth which began to tremble as soon as Linda's name was mentioned. Val Ridley glanced at the sergeant curiously as they settled the suspect across the interview room table and she unwrapped two audio-tapes for the recorder. She could see the anger in Mower's eyes and did not entirely understand it. It seemed too personal.

'You knew Linda Wright?' Mower had begun. He made it a statement of fact rather than a question, and Townsend nodded, barely trusting himself to speak.

'Mr Townsend nodded,' Mower said for the benefit of the tape recorder at his side. They were in the same room in which he had taken a statement from Linda herself a couple of weeks previously, and he was very conscious of his reaction then to her almost conventional prettiness, too sweet for his taste normally perhaps, but given an edge by a slightly teasing smile and a definitely interested gleam in her bright blue eyes. 'How well did you know her?' he snapped.

Townsend hesitated, glancing at the inexorably turning recorder and swallowing hard.

'We'd been out a few times,' he said at last, so quietly that Val Ridley, sitting slightly behind Mower, who faced Townsend across the interview room table, had to strain to catch what he said.

'Speak up,' Mower said brusquely. 'How many times had you been out with her? Roughly?'

'Once in Arnedale, when she came up to the branch on a training day. That's when I first met her,' Townsend said. 'And then when I transferred down here, fairly regularly, a couple of times a week, for the last six months or so.'

'Serious then, was it?' Mower persisted. Townsend shrugged, and then, remembering the tape recorder again, struggled to explain.

'I think it was more serious on my part than on hers,' he said.

'Did you sleep with her, Mr Townsend?' Val Ridley asked quietly.

Townsend looked at her for a moment, not able to hide the anguish in his eyes.

'We did,' he said. 'But not that often. She was . . . she played hard to get. She took her time saying yes.'

'She turned you down?' Mower asked brutally, and Townsend blenched.

'At first she did, yes,' he said. 'She said she wasn't for rushing. I think she had her sights set on someone else, quite honestly. I was okay for an odd night out but I don't think she ever regarded us as an item.'

'Right,' Mower said. 'Let's get to the matter in hand. Did you see Linda Wright on that Saturday night? The night she disappeared?'

Townsend swallowed hard and looked around the bleak little interview room as if seeking inspiration.

'We had a date,' he said at last. 'We were going for a pub meal and then on to a disco. But she cried off.'

'Oh, yes, and why was that?' Mower asked sceptically.

'She didn't say. Just that something had cropped up.'

'So you never saw her at all that night?'

Townsend shook his head miserably.

'If I had,' he said, 'she might still be alive.'

'So that's it, is it?' Mower snapped. 'You never saw Linda Wright the night her car went into the reservoir?'

'That's it.'

'What time did she call you to cancel your date?' Val Ridley asked, slightly more gently.

'About seven, I think,' Townsend said. 'I was getting changed.'

'Can anyone vouch for that call? Was anyone else there at the time it came through?'

'No, I used to share a flat but my flatmate left and I've been on my own for a while.' Townsend's misery seemed to grow with every question and each inconclusive answer.

'Can you imagine what Linda was doing up on that moorland road by herself that night? Where she was going, for instance?' Mower pressed him. 'The weather was dreadful.'

'I don't know where she was going but I do know she doesn't like driving on the motorway. You know what the M62's like? It puts the fear of God into me half the time.' He buried his face in his hands for a moment before facing them again, as if steeling himself for what would inevitably come next.

'Well, let me put another version of the facts to you, Mr Townsend,' Mower said. 'What I think is much more likely is that you, or perhaps someone you know, someone you work for probably, got a bit worried about Linda, especially when they discovered that she had been helping us with our inquiries recently. You suddenly got a bit worried about the security of your mortgage scam and decided to make sure that Linda quietly disappeared for a bit. Or even for good. And wanting to watch your back and protect your nice little earner you arranged for Linda and her car to disappear on Saturday night in that reservoir. I've no doubt it would have been a near-perfect crime but for the fact that the reservoir embankment is a bit uneven at that point, a bit bumpy, so the car didn't go straight to the bottom and in daylight a local farmer spotted the boot and back bumper just above the water-line. If it had sunk any deeper we might not have found Linda for years, might we? It was just your

217

bad luck that she turned up so soon. Spoilt a near-perfect murder.'

It was then that Jimmy Townsend threw himself across the interview table in a paroxysm of weeping.

'It wasn't like that, it wasn't like that at all,' he said over and over again. 'You've got it all wrong.' But he would not elaborate further.

TWENTY

THACKERAY HELPED LAURA PULL HER boots off, banged the snow off them and put them close to the kitchen range to dry. They had been out to his car, fighting their way through two-foot drifts, to listen to the tape she had brought him. His father had no cassette recorder in the house and the batteries had gone flat in her portable machine.

She pulled the heavy oak carver up to the range to warm herself and unpinned her hair so that the glistening icy droplets could dry out in the homely warmth of Joe Thackeray's kitchen. Thackeray brushed a hand across the red-gold cloud as it tumbled down her shoulders, but with an ear cocked for the old man, who had resumed his place at Molly's bedside once he had acknowledged Laura's presence with a dour nod which offered neither welcome nor reassurance. Thackeray had introduced her merely as an acquaintance from Bradfield and Joe had made no comment on that before stumping up the stairs again.

Laura reached up and took Thackeray's hand and held it briefly against her damp, flushed face.

'I take it they won't approve of me, your parents?'

Thackeray shrugged.

'They don't approve of me.' The lightness of his tone was clearly strained. 'So no one else stands much of a chance.'

'So what do you think about the tape?' she asked, deciding this was neither the time nor the place to push him.

'If you and Fergal Mackenzie will give evidence I think we've got him on attempted GBH, possibly even attempted murder. That'll do for starters.'

'Great,' she said, with feeling. 'I'm sure he tried to kill

Fergal. Not necessarily the first time, during the burglary, but then, in the hospital. He was like a spoilt child who couldn't get what he wanted so he decided to smash up whatever – or whoever – stood in his way.' She was very aware that she might figure high on Barry Moore's smash list when he realised what she too had done to thwart him.

'He was always like that,' Thackeray said thoughtfully. 'I remember him as a lad at church terrorising all the other altar boys. His speciality was to find out what each one of them had done that Father Rafferty wouldn't approve of, and then threaten to tell if anyone refused to do what he wanted. And if that didn't work, he had a nice line in criminal damage – a bike wheel bent here, a school book mysteriously ripped up there.'

'Did he threaten you?' Laura asked curiously. Thackeray smiled thinly.

'Once or twice,' he said. 'In the end I told him to get lost and do his worst. So he went telling tales to the priest, who cuffed him round the ear and sent him packing. Which was a useful lesson in standing up to blackmail. Mind you, I got my bike bent just the same.'

'He hasn't changed,' Laura said, with a catch in her voice that took Thackeray unawares and pitched him back to a present even more problematic than the past. 'The trouble is I may have more to lose than you had,' Laura said slowly.

Thackeray looked at her sharply, but she would not meet his eyes, staring steadfastly into the flames of the open range instead, her face flushed by the heat now, and the fire lighting up her hair to a burnished copper.

He pulled up a wooden stool and sat down close beside her and took her hand.

'Tell me,' he insisted. She gave him a small, uncertain smile.

'You said don't pry,' she said. 'But I took no notice. I rooted about in the *Observer* files to see what I could find out and then I went up to the Sacred Heart and bumped into your Father Rafferty. Moore found out somehow and threatened to tell you if I didn't tone down what I was writing. And I couldn't do that . . .'

'Laura, Laura,' Thackeray said, his grip tightening. 'Do you really think I imagined for a moment you wouldn't pry?'

'What?' she said, shaken.

'Give me credit for knowing you a little by now,' he said. 'I guessed that if you were in Arnedale for any length of time you'd stumble on someone willing to tell you exactly what happened to Ian, and a whole lot more. You'd find out one way or another.'

'But you said . . .'

'Wishful thinking,' he said, staring into the fire blankly. 'You can't hide from the past. It always catches up with you in the end, like a shadow. And maybe it should, if the future's to have any firm foundation.'

'I'm sorry, Michael,' Laura said, though the words seemed an inadequate approximation to what she really wanted to say.

'So you see, history does repeat itself,' he said, turning the subject deftly away from what he was clearly still deeply reluctant to discuss. 'It's nearly thirty years since I told Barry Moore to get off my back and now here you are doing the same. Mind you, you'll likely get your bike bent.'

She reached out for him impulsively.

'Michael . . .' she began but he put a finger on her lips and glanced meaningfully at the stairs.

'Not now,' he said. 'Not here. Please?'

She swallowed hard and nodded in acquiescence as he moved his stool a prudent distance to the other side of the fire. The spirit of Molly Thackeray seemed to haunt the house although she was still clinging tenaciously to the approximation of life the disease had left her. Laura could see that Thackeray would never relax under this roof, that the house locked the older Thackerays and anyone else who crossed the threshold in the vice of still raw memories from which she was impotent to free them.

'So how are you going to stop the rise and rise of Barry Moore?' she asked.

'With difficulty, until I can get back into Bradfield,' he said. 'Somehow I think calling Les Thorpe and asking him to arrest Moore on my say-so is a pretty forlorn strategy.

This is going to have to go right to the top before it's sorted.'

'And there's Faith's murder,' Laura said. 'I'm sure Ray Harding is lying about finding Rob Tyler's gun. He looked quite startled when I asked him why it hadn't been covered with snow.'

'You never give up, do you? You won't be satisfied until you've got Tyler off?'

'No, I won't,' Laura said flatly. 'Harding could just as easily have killed Faith. We know he's violent, we know he has a shotgun, we know he hated her and her campaign against his lorries, and we know he's thick with Barry Moore. He must be a suspect.'

'Obviously Chief Inspector Thorpe doesn't think so,' Thackeray said thoughtfully. 'Though it would be worth finding out if Tyler's gun had really been dumped in a bog or not. Forensic should be able to settle that one way or the other. There'll be traces of mud no amount of cleaning will get rid of if what Tyler said is true. But whoever is telling the truth about the gun, Harding may still have a cast-iron alibi for the day of the murder.'

He sighed.

'It's all speculation,' he said. 'And Faith Lawrence's murder isn't my case, Laura.'

But Laura was no longer willing to be satisfied with that. She persisted.

'We know now that Chief Inspector Thorpe was wrong about the burglary. He just wasn't willing to believe Moore was involved in the first attack on Fergal Mackenzie.'

'One thing's for sure,' Thackeray said. 'My investigations in Bradfield and his in Arnedale are getting hopelessly entangled. When I get back someone's going to have to decide which of us takes charge of the Barry Moore investigation now we've got evidence against him at both ends. In the meantime I'll call Kevin Mower and see what he's turned up. Are you sure Mackenzie has no idea who sent him those plans?'

'He said not,' Laura said. 'Though I suppose he may just be protecting his source.'

'I wonder,' Thackeray said. He called Mower from the

222

old-fashioned black phone with a wheezing dial which stood on his father's dresser and listened impassively as the sergeant filled him in on Jimmy Townsend's sudden reappearance and his interview with him and other developments in Bradfield. Laura could hear the excitement in Mower's voice from where she sat.

'You've shown the photographs to the super?' Thackeray asked when he got an opportunity to speak.

'It's a development company jolly,' Mower said. 'Mr Longley recognised most of them, including the planning chief.'

'Good,' Thackeray said. 'And Townsend? You're checking out his story?'

'What there is to check, which isn't much. It's all pretty thin,' Mower said quickly.

'Where is he now?' Thackeray asked.

'I left him to stew in the interview room for a bit,' Mower said unfeelingly. 'He seemed to want a good cry.'

'Move away from Linda's death for a bit and ask him about the fraud,' Thackeray said. 'And give him a hint that far bigger fish are about to be arrested. That might encourage him to talk. And see if you can find out whether he had a hand in appropriating some plans Moore has for a holiday village at High Clough. Someone leaked them to the Press and it could just have been him.'

'The Press found you then, did she?' Mower asked airily.

'Concentrate on the job in hand, Sergeant,' Thackeray said. 'Does this lad seem to have been genuinely fond of the girl?'

'Val Ridley thought so,' Mower said sceptically.

'Val's no fool,' Thackeray said sharply. He trusted the judgement of one of his few women detectives. 'Try a different tack,' he advised. 'Ask Townsend if he passed those documents to a man called Fergal Mackenzie. And if so, why. Keep me in touch.'

'Come on then. Let's hear what women's intuition tells you,' Mower said irritably to DC Val Ridley when he put the phone down, seeing the possibility of an arrest for murder slipping away from him.

'There's no need to be patronising, Kevin,' Val Ridley said sharply. 'I just thought his grief seemed genuine, that's all. If it's not, then he's a bloody accomplished actor.'

'Yes, well, the boss seems to think you might be right,' Mower said. 'He wants us to try a different tack.'

When the two officers went back to the interview room Townsend was still sitting at the table where they had left him, his polystyrene teacup picked to sticky shreds between his fingers. His eyes were red-rimmed but his helpless sobbing had stopped and he squared his shoulders when he saw them and met their eyes.

'I want to make a statement,' he said.

'A different statement?' Mower asked. 'The truth this time?'

'The whole truth this time,' Townsend said. 'I don't see why I should carry the can for that bastard.'

'Which bastard would that be?' Mower asked, trying to conceal his excitement as he turned on the tape recorder again. Townsend took a deep breath.

'Barry Moore,' Townsend said. 'It all goes back a long way, about five years, when I first joined Cheetham and Moore as a trainee in Arnedale. My father – he's dead now – had a shop in Broad Street, fancy goods, tourist tat, Brontë biscuits and lemon curd, that sort of thing. Only the tourists stopped coming, what with unemployment and the recession and everything. It was all looking pretty grim, till I persuaded him to take out a mortgage on the property. Seemed obvious really, as a way to see him through the hard times. The property had been in the family since my grandfather's time, commercial premises, living quarters over – you know . . . ?'

He smiled a thin smile.

'Sorry, I sound as though I'm trying to sell it. Just habit.'

'A mortgage, you were saying,' Mower brought him back to the point sharply.

'Well, not one mortgage, two actually,' Townsend said. 'One would have got him by, two would set him up for a while. It seemed simple at the time. The building societies are easy to con. And I had a friend who's a solicitor's clerk who helped.'

'And who recommended this novel approach to re-financing your father's business?' Mower asked.

'Recommended?' Townsend said. 'No one recommended it. I knew it could be done, that's all. But then Mr Moore found out. Had me in and threatened me with the police.'

'He did what?' Mower said incredulously.

'Well, at first he threatened me with the police,' Townsend said. 'But then he changed his tune. Said that if I could get away with the scam for myself, I could get away with it for him. A nice little earner, he said, and at first I didn't know whether he was joking or not. He wasn't.'

'I bet he wasn't,' Mower muttered under his breath. 'So then what?'

'So then I became his chief fixer,' Townsend said. 'I didn't have much choice, did I? He took a cut of all the deals I did.'

'Right, you can fill in the details in a minute,' Mower said. 'First off, how did Linda Wright fit into all this?'

'She didn't at first,' Townsend said, looking as if he were on the verge of tears again. 'But Barry suggested that working in the show houses she was in an ideal position to recommend people who looked as if they needed a bit of extra help with the finance. So I brought her in on it. She didn't object to the extra.'

'You seriously expect us to believe that?' Mower said. 'A pillar of the community like Barry Moore of Cheetham and Moore.'

'I'm not stupid,' Townsend said. 'I took precautions to cover my back. I can give you chapter and verse.'

'So why did it all end in tears?' Mower asked.

'It was Linda, really. I'd fallen for her in a big way and I reckoned the only way for us to get together properly was to get out of Bradfield. So I laid my plans. I got myself a new job in Manchester for the New Year. I wanted Linda to come with me.'

'And she turned you down?' Val Ridley said.

'She said she had bigger fish to fry,' Townsend said bitterly.

'So you drove her up to the moors and pushed her into the reservoir?' Mower challenged him.

'No, no, you don't understand. This all happened a couple of weeks ago. I guessed it was Barry Moore she had hopes of. She'd been very evasive. But I'd suspected for a long time he'd his eye on her. And suddenly she seemed to be washing her hair an awful lot. You know? The old excuse? So I tried to get my own back. I photocopied the plans of his secret development in High Clough. I knew that getting planning permission was going to be a delicate operation and that publicity might scupper the deal. So I sent the whole lot to the new paper in Arnedale.'

'And then you decided to get your own back on Linda as well?' Mower persisted.

'I didn't kill her,' Townsend said, with desperate intensity. 'But Barry Moore rang me that Saturday. He said he wanted to talk to Linda because he thought she'd played a dirty trick on him. I think he thought she'd nicked the plans. He wanted me to drive his car up towards the reservoir and wait for him there. When I objected he threatened to report the mortgage deals to you lot. So I went. I waited for him for about half an hour in the snow, and when he came down the hill on foot I drove him back to Arnedale. That's all, I swear. It wasn't until the next morning I heard on the radio that Linda was dead. I got in my car and drove south. I was scared I might be next.'

'You seriously expect us to believe that just when you are furious with your girlfriend for ditching you and jealous of some other relationship she's having, someone else comes along and half-strangles her and dumps her in a reservoir?' Mower said.

'It's the truth,' Townsend said desperately. 'You can check it out.'

'Oh, we will, Mr Townsend, we will,' Mower said, putting a new tape in the machine. 'And now you can start on the chapter and verse.'

TWENTY-ONE

LAURA STOOD AT THE WINDOW of Molly Thackeray's bedroom watching her husband and son struggling to rescue Joe's ewes from the suffocating embrace of the blizzard. Behind her Molly's shallow, even breathing made a counterpoint to the first tentative chirrups of birds. It was soon after dawn.

Laura had slept, alone, fitfully and chilled to the bone, in the Thackerays' spare bed and had been wide awake long before she had heard Joe's halting tread as he moved around the bedroom next door, murmuring softly to his wife, before he made his way downstairs to the kitchen.

She had dressed quickly and slipped down after him, avoiding the closed kitchen door and going into the parlour where Michael Thackeray had slept alone and, she hoped, just as unhappily, on the sofa. He too was already dressed, in a thick sweater too small for him, his face lined with tiredness. He was pulling back the dusty velour curtains on an icily grey morning, the snow still drifting down slowly onto a world transformed into a billowing ocean of white, with only the very tips of the dry-stone walls indicating where yard and open moorland ended and enclosed fields began.

She had slipped an arm round his waist and stood beside him, shivering in the unheated air of the austere best room.

'I don't think I'm cut out for a farmer's wife,' she said quietly.

'Just as well I don't want to be a farmer then,' he said, returning her embrace.

'That's a very chaste bed your father keeps up there,' she said. 'I was bloody freezing.'

'You've lived all your life in towns,' he said. 'You don't know how bleak it can get up here. Even I've half forgotten.' She turned in towards him and pulled his head down and he met her lips, unresisting at first and then with increasing passion, until the sound of the door opening behind them made them draw quickly apart.

'Tha could wait until thi mother's departed this life, before tha flaunt thi mortal sin,' Joe Thackeray said sourly. 'There's food on t'table.'

His son had not replied, ushering Laura into the kitchen with a hand on her arm and helping her to breakfast at the old oak table where Joe had assembled a frugal meal of toast and butter and jam and a pot of dark, strong tea.

'Wi'luck most o't'ewes will have huddled under t'bottom wall and kept thisen alive theer,' Joe said. 'But we'll have to check t'rest o't'field.'

'Will you sit with my mother while we see what we can do out there?' Thackeray asked, and Laura nodded, expecting Joe Thackeray to object. But the old man merely gave her one of his impassive stares, as cold as charity, she thought, and without a hint of gratitude.

'Aye, that'd be best,' he conceded, and as the men bundled themselves up in an assortment of jackets and scarves and thick socks inside wellington boots, she went slowly upstairs again with her cup of tea to take up her station close to the dying woman, but not, she thought, in any sense with her.

Molly Thackeray, she felt, had already departed that place in everything but body. She lay deathly still, making a mound beneath the bedclothes so small that she might have been a child, her face peaceful and her eyes closed. Her hair had clearly already been carefully brushed for the day and her rosary entwined between her fingers with loving care.

I hope someone loves me enough to care for me to the bitter end like that, Laura thought, as she brushed a hand across the smooth coverlet and turned away to the window, from which she would be able to see the rescue of Joe's flock.

The two men had equipped themselves with long crooks of the traditional kind seldom seen except in such treacherous conditions. Joe let the two dogs out of the barn where they had spent the night and as the men ploughed through drifts up to their thighs in places the dogs leapt and jumped ahead of them, almost hysterical with excitement but well enough trained to remain aware that there was a serious purpose to this unexpected expedition in a foaming sea of snow spray.

There were two fields to search and as Joe had predicted most of the flock had huddled against the lower wall for warmth and were relatively easily cleared out of the soft drifting snow, bleating miserably but alive and well. But the dogs seemed to know there were others and leapt through the virgin drifts excitedly, stopping occasionally to bark and point their muzzles and scrabble with their paws at a particular spot in the snow which to the naked eye looked little different from any other as the wind whipped the soft, dry surface snow about.

But careful probing with the crook more often than not revealed a fleecy back beneath the drift and a frantic dig with the spade Joe had brought, and on Thackeray's behalf, with bare hands, enabled them to pull a luckless Swaledale, black-faced and bleating and weighed down with matted snow, to the surface. The rescued sheep struggled away to join their fellows in the lee of the lower wall of the field as the search went remorselessly on and Thackeray began to feel pain in toes and fingers, less than adequately protected from the cold in borrowed boots and mittens.

'How many more?' he asked breathlessly after four ewes had been sent wallowing down the slope to safety. His father, who barely seemed warmed by the task, cast a practised eye over the rest of the flock and then at the dogs, who were still exploring further up the hill.

'Two or three, mebbe,' the old man said, turning to watch the dogs which had begun to dig like small black and white Furies into a drift which rose to the very top of the field boundary wall. 'Over theer,' he said, and side by side they trudged up to join the dogs. Thackeray could feel the muscles of back and arms protesting at the unaccustomed exercise. This bleakly beautiful country had once been his world, he thought, and he came back to it now as a stranger, the closeness to the hills and the animals which sustained his father in his struggle through winter after bleak winter now dissipated and forgotten.

All three of the missing ewes were where the dogs had found them, huddled against the wall and covered in two feet of snow. Thackeray hauled out the last one with a sigh and watched as it staggered to its feet and scrambled away to join the rest.

'They'll be reet now,' his father said, leaning on his spade and surveying the fields for a last time with a sharp eye. 'They're daft beggars, sheep,' he said with a note of pride. 'We've not had a fall like this for a few years, neether.'

'How soon before the road is cleared?' Thackeray asked, gazing at the Arctic scene which surrounded the farm and which was coming more sharply into view as the falling snow petered out and the clouds lifted a fraction, revealing the rolling white expanse of the farther moors above them.

'Happen Ray Harding'll get down to t'village with t'tractor,' Joe said. 'Tha'll not get thi car out for a while yet, though. In a hurry, aret'a?'

'I need to get back to Bradfield.'

'Aye, well, if t'bridge is down, tha'll have thi work cut out,' the old man said. 'Now let's see if that lass o'yourn can cook bacon, shall we?'

Thackeray opened his mouth to protest at that for all sorts of reasons and then thought better of it. For once his father had let him glimpse, through the carapace of obstinate taciturnity and unyielding rectitude, a glimmer of humanity. It took him totally by surprise.

'Not mine,' he muttered. 'Not now, perhaps not ever.'

'Aye, well, tha must meck t'best o'things,' Joe said. 'Tha knaws thi mother'll not bend but Father Rafferty reckons theer's mebbe more'n one road to heaven.'

They plodded in silence back to the farmyard where Joe waved his son indoors while he began to fork a load of hay from the barn. In severe weather the sheep could not reach their normal pasture of thin grass through the frozen snow and unless they were fed by hand they would starve.

Thackeray took off his boots, knocked the snow off them, and stripped off the layers of outdoor clothes he had put on to help his father and realised that he felt fitter than he had for a long time after his exertions. He met Laura coming down the stairs and to her surprise took her in his arms and kissed her.

'We're instructed to cook breakfast,' he said. 'Since you're evidently a townie, my father doesn't think you know a rasher of bacon from a black-pudding so you've a lot to prove.'

Whether she actually proved anything Laura never knew, because almost as soon as the three of them had finished their meal the telephone rang shrilly. Joe Thackeray picked it up and immediately glanced towards his son.

'Aye, he's still here,' he said. 'It's Len Smith at t' Woolpack. Wants to speak to thee.'

Looking puzzled Thackeray took the receiver and listened to the breathless landlord at the other end for a moment.

'Is the road clear?' he asked at length and, apparently satisfied with the answer, nodded.

'Right, I'll come down. But I don't guarantee that I can do much to help.'

He turned away with a wry smile.

'Len Smith seems to have appointed me sheriff,' he said. 'Faith Lawrence's young son is apparently running around with a shotgun and he wants something done about it.'

'That's the lad spends all his time wi't'hippies,' Joe said. 'Run wild, that 'un has.'

'A shotgun?' Laura said, horrified. 'Where did he get that?'

'It might be well worth asking him,' Thackeray said grimly.

Laura's stomach lurched as a new and unwelcome suspicion asserted itself.

'You don't imagine . . . ?' she began, and then shook her head dismissively. 'No, it's unthinkable,' she said.

'Don't jump to conclusions, Laura, one way or the other,' Thackeray said quietly. 'I'll go and take a look. Len says the road's passable on foot now the tractor's been up and down a couple of times. If we need reinforcements, we can call Arnedale nick from the pub. The village may be technically cut off but if we really need help we'll get it.'

'I'll come with you,' Laura said in a tone which brooked

no argument. Thackeray took in the stubborn set of her jaw and the determination in her eyes and decided it would do no good to protest.

The door of the Lawrence farmhouse stood wide open and the snow had drifted softly across the stone flagged floor, piling up into miniature castles against the legs of the pine table. Thackeray hesitated for a moment on the threshold but Laura had no such inhibitions and went into the kitchen, though with a heightened sense of foreboding because this was the last place she had seen Faith Lawrence alive.

There was no warmth there now, either physical or emotional. The Aga stood cold and forlorn in its alcove, the fire door open and not the faintest spark amongst the grey ash within. The table was littered with dirty dishes and the sink was full of used pans. An open can of baked beans lay on the floor, its contents spilling out in a lumpy orange streak, already hardening at the edges.

The door leading to the rest of the house was closed and for a moment she hesitated. After they had trudged through the snow to the pub the publican had been vague about Tim Lawrence's whereabouts, simply reporting that he had been seen with a gun in his hand about an hour earlier.

Laura glanced at Thackeray, a shade uncertain now.

'If we've come this far we'd better finish it,' Thackeray said quietly, opening the door and going through ahead of her. They found themselves in a narrow hallway with several further doors leading off it. Only one was open and from that they heard a rhythmic snoring.

Cautiously Thackeray stepped over the threshold with Laura close behind him and they entered an old-fashioned sitting-room furnished with what must certainly have been Faith's aunt's original three-piece-suite of drab moquette, a blue Persian rug and equally dark velvet curtains pulled almost completely across the windows to create a deep gloom. The snoring came from the settee where Gerry Lawrence lay flat on his back in complete abandonment, two empty gin bottles on the floor beside him.

Thackeray drew a sharp breath and pulled back the curtains

with more vigour than it really required. Laura glanced at him curiously. His face was set and he left it to her to shake Lawrence's shoulder in a vain attempt to wake him.

Laura gazed at the sleeping man with a combination of fascination and horror. His colour was high and his breathing laboured, and a faint dribble of saliva ran down his chin and had formed a damp patch on his open-necked shirt. He was evidently as oblivious to the bitter cold of the room as he was to their arrival. She shook him again and he gave a faint groan but his eyelids barely flickered.

'He's out for the count,' she said.

'He could sleep for the day,' Thackeray said, his voice full of anger and distaste. He went out into the hall and came back with a couple of coats which he handed to Laura.

'Cover him up,' he said. She tucked the coats around Lawrence and propped his head sideways with a cushion. His mouth hung open slackly and he groaned faintly again but still did not show any real sign of returning to consciousness.

'Come on, let's have a look at the rest of the house,' Thackeray said dismissively. 'He's not going to tell us where the lad is.' Laura drew the heavy curtains again as much to shield Lawrence from the outside world as to protect him from the bright white daylight.

Room by room they worked their way around the house which had evidently been neither tidied up nor cleaned since Faith's death. Dirty plates and glasses cluttered tables and window-sills, silted up ashtrays overflowed, empty bottles stood unregarded on the floor, a pile of letters lay untouched by the front door. And all the time they searched Laura was aware of the emotion Thackeray was attempting, with increasing difficulty, to keep in check.

In the Lawrences' own bedroom, where the double bed lay unmade in a tangle of grubby sheets and blankets, she opened a cupboard and a small torrent of bottles fell with a clatter to the floor.

'Jesus Christ,' Thackeray said startled and sat down abruptly on the bed, his face ashen.

'What is it?' Laura asked gently.

'I never saw so clearly just what I did to Aileen,' he said.

'I was always too drunk. Like that bastard downstairs. I don't suppose he knows, either. You need to see it when you're stone-cold sober to understand.'

'Michael, it was a long time ago,' Laura said, but she felt no confidence that anything she said would reach him when he was as determined to stretch himself upon the rack as this.

'That has very little to do with it,' he said, getting up as abruptly as he had sat down and going quickly out of the room.

The last door they opened led into what was evidently Tim Lawrence's bedroom. Not that he was there, but all the evidence of his presence was: the elaborate stereo, the stacks of discs and tapes, the posters lining every wall, even the faintly stale smell of unwashed laundry from the discarded clothing which littered the floor.

But it was not this evidence of teenage anarchy which caught the eye. On Tim's bed there was a long leather case, which Thackeray seized upon with an exclamation of surprise. He undid the catch to reveal a padded interior upon which nestled a single shotgun beside an empty space clearly moulded for its twin.

'So he has got a gun,' Laura said softly.

'This can't be his,' Thackeray said, looking at the remaining gun, without touching it. 'These are very classy guns indeed.'

'Gerry's, perhaps? A remnant of the good old days when money was no object. Tim claims he hates shooting, anyway.'

'Does he?' Thackeray said drily. 'I wonder why he's running around with a loaded shotgun, then. I can't see any cartridges, so I assume he's got them with him.'

'We've got to find him, Michael,' Laura said, 'before he does someone some harm.'

'Or himself,' Thackeray said.

'Oh, no,' she said, desperately. The implication of that, she thought, was that Tim had killed his mother, and that she did not want to believe.

Tim Lawrence's tracks led in a determinedly straight line from the back door of the farmhouse, across the garden, over a low stone wall and through the deep snow of the fields beyond. There was no telling how long it had been since he set off and for a moment Thackeray hesitated, wondering if it made more sense to go back through the village to see whether there had been any further sightings.

'Where would he get to, going that way?' Laura asked.

'Round the back of the village, up towards the quarry,' Thackeray said, recalling similar expeditions of his own as a boy when he too had wanted to remain out of sight of the adult world.

'And beyond that, to Ray Harding's place? Tim hates Harding. Maybe he's convinced himself Harding killed Faith.'

'I think we'd better follow. It'll take too long to get help,' Thackeray said. 'It's not as if we need our Boy Scouts' tracker's badge.' The clouds had lifted at last and the sun was beginning to break though, turning the snowy slopes behind the village into sheets of glittering gold and throwing the path Tim had made through the snow into sharp relief as far as the eye could see.

They set off in single file in the boy's wake, plodding through powdery snow which came over their boots and clung in a sparkling film to their clothes. In other circumstances it would have been an exhilarating walk, but although the cold air and the exercise brought colour to Laura's cheeks and a sparkle to her eyes, she was driven by a sense of deep foreboding. She had seen the depth of Tim Lawrence's despair on the day Rob Tyler had been arrested. Driven to desperation she was not sure what he might not do.

The path they were following kept below the brow of the hill which offered the village shelter from the worst of the winter winds, but eventually Tim seemed to have broken away and headed directly up the slope towards the skyline.

'Is that smoke?' Laura asked, slightly breathlessly as they began the steep climb upwards. Thackeray eased back for a moment and stared at the dark haze drifting between them and the sun across the clear blue sky.

'If it is, it's coming from the quarry,' he said. 'And it looks too thick to be just a cooking fire.'

They quickened their pace, forcing their way through drifts as they topped the rise, and stopping there to take in the bizarre sight of Tim Lawrence apparently dancing like a dervish some hundred yards away across the snow in front of them, the shotgun still firmly clutched in one hand.

Thackeray laid a warning hand on Laura's arm.

'Take it easy,' he said quietly. 'We don't know whether that gun is loaded.'

Very cautiously they approached the boy who eventually spun in their direction and stopped his manic stamping and arm-waving, standing stock still for a moment looking at them before flinging himself to the ground face down and lying still. He did not move again as they approached and made no attempt to stop Thackeray taking the gun out of his hand and breaking it open to let two used cartridges fall to the ground. Laura let out a long sigh of relief and then took stock, and was horrified by what she saw.

They were on the very edge of the quarry. Just beyond where they stood, the land fell away sharply to a sheer rock face, and below them they could see what was left of the travellers' camp. A huddle of people stood around aimlessly, dogs and children amongst them, watching as the burnt out wrecks of a dozen vehicles and mobile homes, reduced to dark patches in the snow like so many scattered dominoes, sent dying wraiths of smoke into the clear cold air.

Further away, on the other side of the rocky crater, where the track led up to the main road through the village, half a dozen men were marching behind a tractor up the slope, a solid phalanx of evidently self-satisfied citizenry confident enough of the rightness of what they had done to be turning their back in contempt on their victims. Only the stutter of the tractor's engine disturbed the silence: neither complaint nor jubilation rose up from the deep basin below. Even the travellers' dogs were silent.

'Oh, God,' Laura said. 'What have they done?'

Tim Lawrence stirred at their feet at that and Laura knelt and helped him to sit up. He hugged his knees, his head down and his shoulders shaking with emotion.

'The bastards, the bastards,' he said. 'I saw them coming and I couldn't get down there. At least with the gun we might have driven them off.'

236

Thackeray looked down at him dispassionately.

'Did you fire at them from here?' he asked, glancing at the spent cartridges at his feet.

The boy nodded.

'I knew it was pointless, it was much too far away. I thought the noise might scare them.'

'Do you have any more cartridges?' Thackeray asked. Tim reached in the pocket of his camouflage jacket and threw the box into the snow at the chief inspector's feet. Thackeray took out a handkerchief, carefully picked up the spent cartridges and the box, wrapped them up and put them in his pocket.

'You know that if the cartridge that killed your mother has been found there is a possibility that it can be connected to the gun that fired it, don't you?' he said. Tim stared at him with eyes that burned in deep, dark sockets and shook his head.

'I didn't know that,' he said.

'Did you see exactly what happened down there?' Thackeray asked, nodding at the quarry below where people were beginning to pick through the wreckage of their burnt-out homes. 'Did you see clearly enough to recognise anyone involved?'

'Oh, yes,' Tim said. 'That was bloody Ray Harding on the tractor, wasn't it? Leading the way, as usual. You could see the sun catch his ginger hair even from up here. And some of the others I know by sight, even if I don't know their names. Fred Rawdon, and the landlord from the pub, Mr Smith.'

'Who sent us well out of our way to the other end of the village at the crucial time,' Laura said bitterly.

'Where were you running to, Tim?' Thackeray asked, but the boy had evidently had enough questions. He turned away, his face closed and withdrawn, and shook his head mutely.

'Right,' Thackeray said in a tone which brooked no contradiction. 'First we need to call in the cavalry, so we must get to a phone. Then I want to ask you some more questions with your father present, young man.'

'No way,' Tim said wildly and spun on his heel in the snow as if about to make a break for it. But Thackeray took a firm hold on his arm, firm enough to make the boy wince and Laura to open her mouth in a protest which she instantly thought better of as she sensed what Thackeray

237

was thinking and accepted, with appalled horror, that he was probably right.

'Timothy Lawrence,' Thackeray said formally. 'If I have to arrest you, I will, but one way or another you're coming back with me to answer some questions about your mother's death.'

TWENTY-TWO

'FUCK THAT!' THE BOY SAID furiously. 'I thought I'd got rid of it all.' He stood in the kitchen of his mother's house holding an empty bottle of whisky which they had found on the pine table and which had not been there before.

'Stay there,' Thackeray said grimly to Laura and the boy, and they listened as he moved swiftly through the rest of the house.

'He's gone,' Thackeray said when he returned. 'And he's taken the other gun with him.'

'Surely he won't get far, the state he was in,' Laura said.

'He'll be okay for a while if he's had another drink,' Tim Lawrence said knowledgeably and Laura caught Thackeray's bleak nod of assent.

'You took a box of cartridges. Were there any more?' Thackeray asked the boy, who nodded. He led them into the room where his father had been sleeping and opened a cupboard.

'He's taken them,' he said.

'Have you ever felt that your father might be suicidal?' Thackeray asked gently.

Tim shook his head. He sat down on the sofa where his father had been lying, as if his legs would no longer support him. Laura drew back the heavy curtains, letting in the bright white morning light.

'If he'd wanted to shoot himself he'd have done it when my mother died,' he said. 'That's what usually happens, isn't it?'

'You understand that what you tell me can be used in evidence in a court of law?' Thackeray said. The boy's eyes widened but he nodded.

'When did you take the gun-case from your father's room?' Thackeray asked. Tim looked down, refusing to meet the chief inspector's gaze.

'This morning,' he mumbled at last.

'And had you ever borrowed a gun before?'

The boy nodded dumbly, but did not elaborate.

'And what did you intend to do with the gun you took out with you?' Thackeray asked.

Again the boy hesitated.

'Nothing,' he said. 'I was going up to the travellers' camp to see Topaz. I thought the gun might be useful.'

'You weren't planning to use it?'

'Do you mean was I planning to shoot myself? Commit suicide?' Tim asked incredulously. 'You've got to be joking! Though if I'd met Ray Harding I might have been tempted to use it on him.'

'Because you thought he'd killed your mother?' Thackeray asked, aware that the room had gone unnaturally silent now as Laura concentrated on his inexorable questions.

'No,' the boy said, very quietly.

'You didn't think he'd killed your mother?'

'I knew he hadn't,' Tim said.

'How did you know that, Tim?' Thackeray asked.

'I can't tell you that.' The boy looked down again, refusing to meet Thackeray's dispassionate gaze.

'Was it because you killed her yourself?'

The question hung above them all like a thunder-cloud about to split the room apart with a bolt of lightning. But there was no explosion, just a long sigh from the boy who had a single tear beginning to make its way down his pale and grubby cheek.

'No,' he said so quietly that they had to strain to hear him. 'It was because I knew my father had killed her. I saw him come back to the house over the fields that day with the gun in his hand.'

Two hours later Laura stood beside her car, which had been manhandled out of the snow-drift she had left it in and had its nose turned downhill towards the narrow bridge. She felt deflated.

She had sat for a long time with her arm round Tim Lawrence as they waited for the urgent reinforcements that Thackeray had summoned to follow a snow-plough and lifting gear up the hill and fill the village with blue uniforms and flashing lights. Eventually a policewoman had arrived to escort Tim to Arnedale for further questioning. He had turned to Laura impulsively as he went.

'Topaz and the children have nowhere to go,' he said. 'Tell them they can have beds here, at least till Rob gets back. That's what my mother would do. They'll have to let him out now, won't they?'

'Yes, they'll have to let him out,' she had reassured him. He would be, she thought, when he found his way through his adolescent uncertainties and his present grief, his mother's son.

Ray Harding had been the next to depart in police custody, protesting so furiously at his arrest for the part he had played in the attack on the travellers' camp that he had to be handcuffed to a burly officer before he was also led away down the village street through the snow to a waiting police car.

Laura had watched Thackeray as he had taken charge of the operation which would now concentrate on tracking down Gerry Lawrence and his gun. She felt excluded from the dispassionate forces of the law he had called up to restore order to High Clough, and ignored by Thackeray himself as he moved with an impersonal authority amongst uniformed and plain-clothes officers who did his bidding without question.

It was inevitable, she knew, that in these circumstances their jobs should put a gulf between them, but she resented it all the same, and once her car had been extricated from the snow and the lorry hauled inch by inch from its precarious resting place on the bridge, she felt an overwhelming desire to get out of High Clough.

Thackeray's final task had been to arrange for an ambulance to come up to West Rigg to take his mother on what he and Joe knew would be her last journey to the hospital in Arnedale. The old man had gone with her, unspeaking and rigid with emotion he could not express, and Thackeray had watched silently from beside the police car which was to take him down the hill, his face set and his eyes blank.

Laura opened her car door and dropped heavily into the driving seat and rested her head on the steering wheel, overwhelmed by what had happened. She only gradually became conscious that something was very wrong. The smell of whisky should have alerted her but it was not until Gerry Lawrence jabbed his shotgun into her side from his concealed position on the back seat that she understood her danger.

'I want to go to Arnedale,' Lawrence said very slowly and distinctly. 'I want to go to Barry Moore's place in Arnedale. And if you drive very carefully you won't come to any harm. So start the bloody engine now!'

Chief Inspector Thackeray swept into Arnedale police station like an avenging angel. He went straight to Les Thorpe's office and found his erstwhile colleague sitting at his desk with his topcoat on, looking stunned.

'I've just had county on,' Thorpe said with deep reluctance. 'I've to give you every assistance. And your sergeant's on his way over. Says he's got summat important to show you.'

'Good,' Thackeray said shortly. 'Any news of Lawrence and his shotgun?'

'The search teams are still working their way round the village, according to the duty inspector. They've found nowt so far.'

'I can't see how he could have got out of High Clough,' Thackeray said. 'His car was firmly snowed up, and I've put a guard on it.'

'He's never in a fit state to drive,' Thorpe said. 'You must know what his problem is. What stirred him up any road? He's never given any trouble before.'

'As far as I know, no one's wanted to arrest him before,' Thackeray said, ignoring Thorpe's first question. 'But I agree, in these conditions I don't think he'll get far.'

'They want to know at county if they should call out the Armed Response Unit?'

'Not at the moment,' Thackeray said, remembering Thorpe's recent premature call on the élite firearms squad. 'Quite honestly, in spite of what his lad says, I think he's more likely to harm himself than anyone else.'

'So am I permitted to know why you want to arrest him? Or is that a bloody state secret?' Thorpe said, recovering something of his normal belligerence.

'His son says he saw him out with his shotgun on the day his mother was killed,' Thackeray said shortly. 'By the way, I've got Ray Harding down in the cells waiting to be questioned about an arson attack on the travellers' camp. You might like to take the opportunity of asking him again where and when he found Rob Tyler's gun.'

'What do you mean by that?'

'I mean that it seems very likely that Gerry Lawrence shot his wife. And it's not beyond the bounds of possibility that when Harding realises we're going to throw the book at him and his friends over the attack on the travellers, he might want to reconsider his convenient discovery of Tyler's gun. In other words, it looks increasingly likely you've got the wrong man remanded for Faith Lawrence's murder. And the sooner you unscramble that mess the better it'll be for everyone, not least you.'

'Who says we're going to throw the book at Harding?' Thorpe said.

'I do,' Thackeray said. 'And as I understand it from Jack Longley, county will back me all the way. Did you ask forensic to check the gun for mud, to see if Tyler's story of throwing it in a bog stood up?'

Thorpe did not answer and Thackeray shook his head in disgust.

'You're as bad as those yobs in High Clough,' he said. 'You're quite happy to see him go down for it whether he's guilty or not.'

There was a tap on the door and Sergeant Mower came in, muffled in a tartan jacket, his eyes bright with triumph.

'Morning, guv,' he said cheerily to Thackeray, giving Thorpe the merest frosty nod of acknowledgement.

'What are you looking so cheerful about?' Thackeray asked. 'Have you checked out Townsend's story?'

'I've left people working on that, guv,' Mower said unabashed. 'But I thought you'd like to see this first-hand.' He passed the chief inspector an envelope and watched as he took out a shiny black and white photograph. Thackeray stood quite still for a moment as he took in the flash-camera image of Barry Moore and Linda Wright, in evening dress and evidently flushed with drink and excitement and, crucially, with their arms around each other.

'Where did you get this?' Thackeray said, not allowing his satisfaction to change the inflection of his voice by an iota, although Mower was aware of the excitement in his eyes.

'Linda's friend Jacquie, when we finally pinned her down and persuaded her to come clean. It was taken at that new nightclub in Leeds, the Parsonage. She happened to be there herself one night and saw them both. She asked the photographer for a copy of the picture, meaning to give it to Linda, but she never got the chance. It didn't arrive until after Linda was dead. She dropped it in for me this morning. It looks as if Linda thought she'd found someone special, doesn't it?'

Thackeray turned to Chief Inspector Thorpe, who was sitting at his desk in sullen silence.

'Barry Moore still lives out on the Grassington Road, does he?' he asked quietly, dropping the photograph onto the desk in front of Thorpe. 'I need to talk to him about the murder of a young woman he claimed he hardly knew.'

Laura Ackroyd turned the Beetle carefully into the drive of a substantial modern house set well back from the road as it climbed out of the Maze valley towards the hills above Wharfedale. The snow on the curving drive and the extensive lawns was crisp and untouched, the trees still bearing the weight of the heavy snowfall, sparkling now as the sun broke through. Behind her Gerry Lawrence gave a grunt of satisfaction as they saw the maroon Jag parked outside the front door with its boot open.

'Stop here,' he said, nudging her with the muzzle of the shotgun which had nestled against her ribs for the entire journey down from High Clough. 'You can bugger off now. This is between me and that bastard.'

Even as he spoke they saw Moore himself come out of the house with a suit-case and give a puzzled look in the direction of the VW which Laura had brought to a standstill just before the drive widened out to form a turning circle, effectively blocking his exit.

'Don't do anything crazy, Gerry,' Laura said with what she hoped sounded like quiet confidence although the nausea which had threatened to overwhelm her as she had inched along the icy road from High Clough did not diminish as she pulled on the handbrake. 'There's been enough damage done,' she said.

Moore had put down his suit-case on the step leading to the front door and was wading through the snow towards them, squinting against the sun as if to try to see who was in the car. When he recognised Laura his face darkened and his step quickened and he waved his arms around angrily. Laura eased open the driver's door.

'Go back, Mr Moore,' she shouted suddenly. 'Gerry's got a gun!'

For a moment Moore stood paralysed in the snow, his face distorted by anger and indecision. Then, as Gerry Lawrence struggled to extricate himself and his shotgun from the back seat of the Beetle, almost sobbing with frustration, Moore realised his danger and turned and ran back into the house, slamming the front door behind him.

'You silly bitch, you silly bitch,' Lawrence said, standing awkwardly in snow almost up to his knees. Laura could see now for the first time that he was dressed only in the slacks and light sports shirt he had been wearing as he slept off his binge earlier that morning. Within seconds he was shivering uncontrollably in the bitter wind. He held the gun loosely in one hand, the muzzle hanging down at his side and trailing in the snow. Laura got out of the car very slowly, not wanting to provoke him, but aware that if she remained in the driver's seat she was the original sitting target.

'More violence won't help, you know,' she said. 'Let it rest now.'

'It was all his fault,' Lawrence said, turning suddenly towards the house and raising the gun again. Laura stood very still.

'But it can't be mended,' she said. 'Not that way.' She was aware of another car slowly crunching the snow behind her and stopping but did not dare take her eyes off Lawrence in case he turned again and threatened her.

'Come on, Gerry,' she said. 'It's Tim you should be thinking about now.'

'He'd be better off without me. He'd be better off with me dead,' Lawrence said and Laura could see him swing the gun backwards, hunching it awkwardly under his arm, as if to turn it on himself. She was conscious of more activity behind her but did not dare risk even a glance over her shoulder in case she lost Lawrence's attention.

'That's not true, you know,' she said, taking a couple of cautious steps forward towards the now violently shivering figure. 'He tried to protect you, couldn't bring himself to tell anyone that he'd seen you with the gun.'

Lawrence froze at that, standing very still before half-turning towards her, with a beseeching look, tears streaming down his face.

'Really?' he said. 'Did Tim do that?' Laura took the final step towards him then, putting one arm around his shoulders and taking the gun out of his limp hand with the other.

'Really,' she said faintly, as they both turned to face Jonathon West, Chief Inspector Thackeray and Sergeant Mower who had been standing watching, stock still and aghast, in the snow behind them.

'Jonathon?' Laura said stupidly, as the two policemen moved quickly to take hold of Lawrence and the shotgun.

'I came to take Barry to the airport,' West said. 'What the hell's been going on?'

'I think I only know the half of it,' said Laura as she watched Mower handcuff Lawrence and bundle him into the back of

246

the car he and Thackeray had arrived in. Thackeray himself put an arm around her and she found that she too was shivering uncontrollably inside her thick jacket.

'Don't do that too often,' he said, tightening his grip. 'I don't think I can take it.'

'You were bloody quick, I'll give you that,' Barry Moore broke in. He had re-emerged from the house, carrying another suit-case, and with a mac over his arm.

'Quick?' Thackeray asked.

'I dialled 999, said there was a nutter here with a gun. Bloody alkies. They should be locked up for their own safety, I say.'

'Ah, we must have arrived like the demon king, then,' Thackeray said, giving Moore the benefit of a positively wolfish smile. 'I was on my way here already, you see. And you? Where were you on your way to?'

Moore's face darkened and his eyes flicked quickly around the curious group and back to Jonathon West.

'I'm off up to Lord Radcliffe's place for Christmas,' he said. 'Right, Jonathon?' West did not meet his gaze, knowing that he had already offered a different reason for his presence there.

'I came here to ask you to come back to Arnedale police station with me to answer some questions,' Thackeray went on conversationally.

'You what?' Moore said. 'What the hell for?'

'In connection with the death of Linda Wright,' Thackeray said.

'I hardly knew the girl,' Moore said. 'What is this, some sort of joke? Where's Les Thorpe? What are you doing in Arnedale any road? It's not your patch.'

'Les isn't going to be able to protect you any more, Barry,' Thackeray said. 'I'm in charge, and I also want to talk to you about the attempted murder of Fergal Mackenzie. And in connection with a series of mortgage frauds and property deals here and in Bradfield. And I have to warn you that anything you say may be taken down and used in evidence.'

The familiar formula drained the colour from Moore's

cheeks as for the first time he evidently realised the seriousness of his position. For a second he looked about him wildly as if to run, and then he shrugged.

'There's nowt you'd like better than an excuse to give me a good thumping, is there, you self-righteous bastard?' he said to Thackeray. 'My God, you've got a bloody long memory.'

'So have you,' Thackeray said.

'You watch him, lass,' Moore spat at Laura. 'Just think on. He's the one who got away with murder.'

It was late on Christmas Eve and Laura Ackroyd and Michael Thackeray were sipping a final coffee at a corner table, the last late diners in Bradfield's new Thai restaurant. Laura picked up the warm, damp hand-towel and sniffed the rose-water appreciatively before she bent her head and held the cloth to her throbbing head. It had been a scrappy, unsatisfactory sort of meal, a fitting end to a scrappy, unsatisfactory sort of day, during which she had tried half-heartedly to keep up with the frantic police activity in High Clough and in Bradfield.

'You're tired,' he said, watching Laura push strands of copper hair from her eyes with the damp, scented towel.

'Just saddened by the tangled webs we weave,' she said.

'Well, at least your New Age traveller Tyler is off the hook. You won't need to pursue that miscarriage of justice after all.'

'There'll be others,' she said. 'Will they convict Gerry Lawrence of murder?'

'Who knows?' Thackeray said. 'In the state he's in he may not even remember what happened. You can lose whole days of your life when you've been on a binge . . .'

'But he'll get treatment now, surely?'

'The only treatment he'll get is to sit in a cell raving until eventually the gremlins stop leering out of the walls at him,' Thackeray said.

'Poor man,' Laura said softly. She was silent for a moment, hoping Thackeray would share his evident misery with her but he stared determinedly at his coffee cup, until she turned to anger for release.

'It's a pity you can't charge Barry Moore with Faith's murder as well,' she said. 'He was the one to blame.'

'Barry is going away for a very long time,' Thackeray said. 'The fingerprints on Linda Wright's car were his.'

'But why?' Laura said. 'What did she do to deserve that?'

'Oh, I think she was becoming a nuisance. As you know, Barry likes to do the manipulating. Always has. In Linda he met someone who tried to manipulate him. She had ambitions, had young Linda, and thought Barry could fulfil them for her. She made a terrible misjudgement there. She should have stayed in her own league with Jimmy Townsend.'

'And Jonathon West?' she asked. 'Was he up to his neck in it, too?' She had wanted Jonathon taken down a peg or too, but had hardly envisaged his ending up in gaol.

'We've let him go for the moment. He's undoubtedly up to his neck in the fraud, but that's going to take time to pin down. We have to wait for Sydney Cheetham and his friends to come home before we can take that much further. But he did have airline tickets in his pocket for Moore who had evidently been warned his time was up.'

'Warned?'

'Les Thorpe has been suspended pending further investigations. My guess is that he was keeping Moore informed about the progress of my inquiries.'

They fell silent again, both shaken by the present and a past which had unexpectedly engulfed them.

'So much guilt and so many victims,' Thackeray said.

Laura did not think he was simply thinking of this latest case.

'You're beginning to sound as much like a woolly liberal as I do,' she mocked him gently, trying to shake off the gloom which seemed to engulf them both. 'You'll be patting the criminals on the head and sending them for psychotherapy before you know where you are.'

He shook his head and smiled at her with some relief.

'So what about you?' he said. 'Were your bosses pleased with your exclusive planning story?'

'Very pleased,' she said.

'And are you going to be the new editor of the *Arnedale Observer*?'

It was the question she knew he had been wanting to ask all evening but had avoided, evidently afraid of the answer. She smiled and took his hand across the table.

'Better than that,' she said. 'They've offered the job to Fergal Mackenzie.'

'So you're coming back to Bradfield?' The relief in his voice made her smile more broadly, it revealed so much more than he realised.

'I'm coming back to Bradfield, as soon as Fergal's well,' she said. 'And you're coming back to my place to spend the holiday with me.'

For a moment she thought he would refuse. He hesitated and then the tension seemed to drain out of him. He looked at his watch and smiled. It was two minutes past midnight.

'I give in,' he said. 'Happy Christmas, Laura.'